ONE YEAR

ONE YEAR

AUBREY GRACE TOMLINSON

One Year

This book was originally published in paperback in 2016
by Tomlinson Media

First Paperback Edition

To Monica. This one's for you kid.
And to Destiny. Until we meet again, stay strong.

"The way he looked at me that day changed everything.

What I thought was hatred turned out to be something

worth suffering for."

My dearest Olivia,

I hope this letter has reached you, wherever you are. Your sister told me you wanted to keep your location and address secret from your mother and I, and I completely understand. I know things didn't go exactly as you planned and it hurts me as much as it hurts you, and I wish I could be there for you right now. Wherever you are, I wish I was sitting next to you, and doing my job as your father. But I'm not. I don't even know where you are, and it kills me to be in the dark. No father, or mother, wants to ever feel useless when it comes to their child. But I must respect your decisions, and I need to let you go your own way. It's the very least I can do. After everything.

Olivia, sweetheart, I need to tell you something. If you're reading this, and I hope you are, I want you to know that everything your mother has ever done was done with your best interest at heart. You may not be able to see that now, but she does love you. She thought her way was the only way, and maybe someday, when you become a mother and have a little girl of your own, you'll know what it's like to move mountains for your child.

Wherever you are, I hope you're safe and happy. I hope that the pain from the past doesn't haunt you, and I hope you find it in your heart to forgive your mother. And please, please write back. I need to know you're okay.

Love you forever and always,

Dad

My Darling Olivia,

Four years and still nothing. I'm starting to think you're mad at me.

I mean you can't possibly blame me for his choices. Yes, I never approved of that garbage you called a boyfriend, and reading his letter, I now know I was right. Just look at that letter of his, he proved just how right I was all along.

Olivia, you can choose to hate me forever, you can choose to ignore me, but it's never going to change the fact that he left you. He left you darling. Remember that.

So stop this, seriously it's getting old and quite frankly we've all had enough.

Oh, and before I forgot, I saw him a few days ago. Guess the loser never left town. He asked about you, I told him to go screw himself. Wherever you are, and whatever you're doing, I know you're doing a million times better

than he, and we have him to thank for that.

Write me back!

Mom.

CHAPTER ONE

Friday, March 4th 2016

"Auntie Olivia, are you alright?"

I stare up from the crumbled piece of paper to meet Jensen's eyes. He watches over me carefully, his eyes darting back and forth from me to the letter resting in my hands. Here I am, an entire continent away and that woman still manages to ruin my life.

It's been four years since I left gloomy Colorado, and ran off to the gloom that is Cambridge. I thought if I put some distance between my family and I, maybe, just maybe, I could learn to forgive them.

Well, forgive mother, I should say.

After all these years, this is what I get. No apologize or explanation.

I received my mother's letter a whole two days ago, and I finally worked up the nerve to open it and this is how it goes. She still refuses to see any fault in the part she played that led me to England.

Out of the six Universities I applied to, I decided on Cambridge, seeing as it was the only one that was not only out of Colorado, but also out of the country. I had to run, and yeah, I know running from your problems doesn't solve anything.

Well the person who coined that phrase never met Keira Fitzgerald.

I push the letter into my lap and smile. "Of course, I'm alright. Why wouldn't I be?"

Jensen shrugs and bends over to pick up his new action figure. "I don't know; your eyes just look sad."

He sits on the floor next to me and leans against the couch, his head resting near my knee. Just four-years-old and the kid is smarter and more alert than any adult I know.

My fingers brush through his soft, yellow curls as I look off into space. When I first arrived in England, I had no idea what to do. Cambridge wasn't my first choice. It wasn't even my second choice. Leaving the country was never in my ten-year plan.

I had it all mapped out. First, I would move to California, study English Literature and graduate from UCLA. From there, Niall and I planned on taking a few months off to travel around the United States, hoping to hit every single state on our way back to California.

Niall always had a love for photography. He would take millions of snapshots of something simple, like a random frog outside his parents' house and call it art. He loved the small things. We both did.

I shake my head, hoping the thoughts of him fall out from my memory permanently.

He's gone Olivia. He left you with nothing but a letter and a broken heart.

My hand reaches for the letter and crumbles it up more. He left and I never received a reason behind why. Well technically he did, but it was a lie. The things he said in that letter were words direct from mother's mouth, I know it. We were packed, we had our tickets and our apartment. We had it all and he backed out the last minute. That isn't who Niall was. He was a good man. At least I thought he was.

I turn my attention back to Jensen. I suddenly feel the excessive need to stop torturing myself. "Where's your sister munchkin?"

He scoffs. "What she always does; reading."

"And what's wrong with reading?"

Jensen turns to me; his wide blue eyes smile up at me. "There's nothing wrong with reading, it's just, that's all she ever does. When you're here, when you're not here, I just get bored playing all by myself. Mum's always working, dad's always on the road and Lily always has her nose in a book. I have no one to play with. I miss you when you're not here."

Her nose in a book. He's already starting to sound like me.

I reach down and pull Jensen onto the sofa next to me. My arm drape across him as I lean over to kiss the top of his head, his curls tickle my nose. "That's because I'm cool Auntie Olivia."

He laughs, my kiss no doubt tickled him. "I wish you'd live with us. Why can't you live with us? I can share my room with you."

A huge smile spreads across my face. "I do live with you, Jensen, remember? It's only the weekends when I'm not here."

He pulls away from me, his Thor action figure clutched in his fist. "I want you here every day."

"Oh, my Jensen. I would if I could, but you know I have to work at my other job. And when I'm not there, I have school almost every day. I thought I told you this wasn't the only job I have. Although, it is the best."

He looks back up at me, his eyes a bit wider. "Really?"

"Really. Now go tell your sister I said to put her books away for an hour and to play with you. I bought you two those checkers and you've never opened it. Go on."

Picking up his action figures, he stands on the sofa to kiss my cheek and runs upstairs to find his sister. I watch him go. They may not be my kids, but I love them as if they were.

Getting a job as a nanny was easy for me. I was always good with kids, just never cared to have one myself. Well I did, once, but that was a different life. Working for the Atwater's has been a blessing. I couldn't have asked for a better family to be a part of.

I sit back and listen as Jensen asks Lily to play a game of checkers with him. She refuses and tells him they should play with his new action figures instead. I can just sense the smile on his face. My sister and I were once that close, but that changed the day I left home for good. None of it was her fault, I was the one who wanted to run.

I lift mother's letter from my lap and open it once more, rereading the part about Niall. It bothers me. Four years and not once has he looked me up, or tried to get into direct contact with me.

Makes me wonder what's changed his mind.

Well it doesn't matter what he has to say. He had his chance to tell me the truth, but he chose the cowards way out. And I will not dig up a past I happily buried.

"Aunt Olivia, come play with us." says Lily.

If there's one thing that's certain, it's this; my life might not be what I wanted, but I'm sure as hell happy with the way it's turned out.

I stand, tossing the letter behind me, and letting it fall on the floor next to my bag. She managed to go these past two years without writing, or calling me, and when she finally decides to woman up, she tells me my ex came looking for me. The same ex she hated with every little inch of her black soul. If she's writing to me, it's because there something else she wants to tell me, but she's slowly easing her way into it.

Well I for one refuse to buy into her crap. I'm not going back to the woman I first was when I moved all the way over here.

"Coming."

I force my key into the lock, lifting the door up and pushing it a little to left, I thrust my shoulder into the door until it finally bursts open. I walk inside, throwing my things near the coat rack and slam it shut behind me.

"I swear to you I'm getting that fixed. Just waiting for my brother to get up off his lazy arse. Honestly, it's probably much easier if we just call a repair man."

As soon as I walk into the kitchen, I'm greeted by my roommate Jade, and this burnt onion-y smell. Jade is bent over the counter doing her hardest to try and cook us what she calls dinner. I love the girl to death, but cooking will never be something she'll ever excel in.

She looks up, flour pasted to her face and her smile fades. Since our first night as flat mates, Jade has always been good at reading my body language. Even when I used my best form of poker face.

"Uh oh, I know that face. That is the look of utter disappointment. What's happened?"

I slump down in the stool closes to me and hand her the wrinkled up paper without saying a word. She looks at me before taking the letter, semi afraid of what she's about to witness. I stand once again and head over to the stove to try and salvage the disaster Jade refers to as her special dish. The food always turns out so bad, and burnt to a crisp, that I never figured out what it is exactly.

"Jade, where's the pepper, this could really use pepper. And a lot of other things. Like tossing it in the garbage bin."

The paper crumbles up behind me, and I know what's about to come out of her mouth.

"Oh, Olivia. I'm so sorry."

I refuse to meet her sorrowful gaze. "Yeah. Me too."

"Still no apology huh? Please forgive me for saying this, but your mum seems like a real tosser."

I turn to face her and can't help but laugh. "No offense taken. Although I would've used the term bitch."

Jade spits out the bread she's been stuffing in her mouth since I first walked through the door, unable to control her laughter. I join in with her.

I've told Jade everything about my family, while she was interviewing me for the roommate position. She knows so much about them, she's practically family.

"Still, I know how much you've been waiting for her to explain why she did what she did. I know it hurts to get letter after letter and still you wind up with nothing." She hands me the pepper. "Are you going to write her back?"

Staring at the letter in Jade's hands, I think if that would be the smartest thing to do. Writing her would only end badly for the both of us. I'll most definitely never get the answer I want, and she'll only get satisfaction knowing I caved it, believing I miss her.

There's no way I'm giving her that.

CHAPTER TWO

Saturday, July 14th 2012

"Just think about it. Me and you, no parents, no one we know, just the two of us. Together forever."

"Oh, that sounds like something straight out of a Nicholas Sparks novel. Except for all the sad parts."

"It's not a dream anymore, Liv. Just one more week and were free. California here we come."

My eyes open and meet his. The soft grey eyes I fell in love with ten-years-ago. I still remember it to this day, how could I forgot, it was the day I knew I found the one I'd spend eternity with.

We were only eight, I wore my favorite green polka dot dress and those ugly, white shoes that your mom forced you to wear to church every Sunday. It was picture day, so I had to look my prettiest. The entire day I stood near the basketball courts, between the water fountains and drama class, not wanting to get my clothes dirty. At least not until the pictures were taken.

The other kids played so freely, not caring if they stained their outfits or their faces. I used to watch in envy, wishing I could kick off those clunky shoes and run over to be with them, wanting to be a kid and not an adult who should always be on her best behavior. Granted none of those kids had a mother like I did. The smallest drop of ink or paint and she could tell.

And I'd be dead.

I watched them, running back and forth, kicking around a ball. And in an instant one boy fall over, right in a huge mud puddle left from the previous rainy day. The other kids kept running, not one of them stopped to acknowledge him, or help. But I noticed him. There was something about him that I couldn't put my hands on. My mind told me to leave him be, there's no way I could help him without getting myself dirty. But I never was one to follow my thoughts. Or mom's rules.

Picking up my jacket, I went over to the warzone and reached an arm out for him to take. Covered from head to toe in mud, he looked up at me, his grey eyes the only feature standing out from under the ick. He looked at my hand then back at me.

"I don't want to get your dress dirty."

A small smile flashed across my face. "It's okay. I hate this thing anyways. Come on, I'll help you get cleaned up."

He looked at my hand once again and put his in it. The first time I felt his touch, was the first time I ever felt love.

His grey eyes stare down at me now, ten years later and nothing's changed. Ten years later and he's still mine.

"What are you thinking?"

"About the day we met."

He smiles that ever charming smile. "You mean the day I embarrassed myself."

"What do you mean, embarrassed yourself? If you never would've fell in that mud I never would've had to help you up, then there would be no us."

He brushes his hand across my forehead, pushing my loose hair back into its place behind my ear. "We always would've found our way to each other. It was meant to be."

"You sound like a soap opera."

He laughs and leans back, the sun bouncing off his dark hair. "Where do you think I get all the romantic things I say?"

I sit up and turn until were face-to-face. "Please tell me you don't get your lines from a cheesy soap opera?"

"Maybe I do, maybe I don't." He leans in, his body giving off a blazing heat. His lips find my nose, planting a soft, gentle kiss. I lift my head, guiding my lips to his, pulling him in closer. A tingle shoots up my spine, my heart beating faster than it probably should. But I ignore it. Nothing in my life has made much sense until the day I met Niall.

I know they say you can't know real love until you're older and wiser, but what do they know? I think anyone can fall in love, at any age. Age in nothing but a number, it's your maturity that matters.

Pulling away, I wrap my arms around his neck, burying my face in his sweater. Living with my parents has been hell since the day I could first talk. Mom was always criticizing me, raising me to be the perfect girl so I could score the perfect man. According to her, only doctors, lawyers, or anyone in the medical field would do. So imagine her surprise when I fell for Niall- a soon to be Web Developer.

She refused to accept it. Web Developers make good money, but he didn't fall in her chosen group, so he was no good. It didn't matter that I loved him either. 'Love is for the weak, Olivia. Security is what matters.' The woman disgusts me.

"You're thinking about your mom, aren't you?"

I bury my head deeper into his chest. "No."

"Then why are you hiding? You always hide when you think about her."

"I didn't think it was against the law to hide."

"Liv?"

My head rises from Niall's chest, but my eyes don't meet his. He's right about her, but to be fair, I'm usually stressing about the things mom says or does ninety percent of the time. She has this effect on me. I'm never going to do, or be, what she wants, but I can't help but feel hurt. She's been trying to pimp me to the richest man since she found out she was having a girl.

Niall runs his hand through my hair, resting it on the small of my back. "I don't care what your mother thinks of me, and neither should you. I'm not going to be sorry I didn't choose to become some world famous doctor, or some lawyer who spends all his days working at a career I'm not passionate about. I'm happy with the life I've chosen. If she can't accept that, then oh well. I gave up trying to impress that woman years ago. So should you."

I finally women up to meet his eyes. "Do you think I care about your job? Niall, I never cared about that. As long as you weren't planning on working at a McDonald's for the rest of your life, I could care less. The thing that gets to me is why she can't see the pain she's causing. She's supposed to be my mother, Niall. She should just be happy I'm not a drug addicted, pregnant teen, who's dropped out of school at the age of fourteen."

He pulls me in for a hug, holding on tighter than he ever has before. "I know, Liv. We don't always get the life we want. Or the parents we deserve."

"Please stay."

I turn to see my sister, sitting on my now bare bed. I've been packing up the last of my things for the past two hours, obsessing over if I've forgotten anything.

Leaving means freedom for me, but depression for Delphine. My sister and I have always been close. Having the same, horrible mother can create a bond that's hard to break. She isn't just a bad mom to me, she's been terrible towards the both of us and now my little sister has to endure the next six years alone. With her.

My arms reach out to Delphine, inviting her in for a sympathy hug. She runs into them. "I'm sorry sweetie. I am, but I can't do this anymore. The more time I spend here, the more I grow to want to kill her. If I could take you with me, I would stuff you into one of these boxes and not think twice." I can feel my shirt cling to my body and I know there's tears streaming down her face.

I pull her away, forcing her to look at me. "Delphine, love you have to be strong now. I won't be here to protect you from her anymore, so it's up to you. Get a job, join every sport you can get in, or a club that seems mildly interesting to you. Save up every last dime, and hide it away somewhere safe. Remember where my secret stash used to be?" She nods in my chest. "Good, it's yours now, hide everything in there. And when the time comes, get the hell out of here. Come find me, I'll keep you safe from her. That's my job isn't it, to protect my little sister from the big bad wolf?"

The tears pour from her eyes, her pain permanently etched across her face. This is the hardest part for me.

"Delphine, please promise me something. Never, ever let her control your life. Do not let her force you into marrying a man you don't want. Do you understand me?"

She raises her head, the tears coming to a slow, and nods. I pull her back in for a hug, ignoring the wetness on my shirt.

I sit on our old swing set, waiting for Niall and the U-Haul truck to get here. The last time I heard from him was early this morning. He called me, excited that the day has finally come, ready to hop on the plane and leave our old lives behind.

But he hasn't answered his phone since, which worries me a bit. Then again, he was the one who insisted on taking care of everything. Renting the truck, getting the airline tickets. My job was to find our apartment and pack my things. I did both, and now I'm starting to wonder if he's done any. Of course, he has, the man is way too responsible to leave anything to the last minute.

Then where is he?

The back door swings open and my head flies up. My excitement dies down when I see it's dad and not Niall. His glasses are pulled down on the tip of his nose and his hair in disarray, like he's be pulling on it before he came out here.

There's no way he has any good news.

I jump from the swing, the metal poles creaking as I hurry over to him. His hand goes up, telling me to stop where I am. Scared, I do as he says and stop right where I am, then notice he's holding a piece of paper in his hand. Whatever it is, it's causing him grief, which in turn is causing me grief as well.

"Dad, what is that?"

He reaches up to pull his glasses off and rubs his eyes.

"Dad? Dad what's wrong, what is it?"

"I'm sorry baby." He stretches his arm out, passing the paper over to me. But I don't take it. Somehow my heart already knows what it is.

I back away slowly, not wanting to get any closer. Not many things upset my dad like this, so whatever's written on that paper must be bad. And I want no part of it.

"Olivia, honey, you need to read it."

He hasn't answered any calls since this morning. "Niall?"

Dad nods, stretching his arm out further, his eyes glossed over. "Do you want me to read it to you?"

"No! No. I don't want to know what's written on it. I'm not going to read that. I'm not. I can't, I can…" I turn and run, straight out the back gate and down the street. I don't know where I'm going, but I don't stop. I keep running, my feet dragging me far away from this place.

I knew something was wrong. As soon as he didn't answer my first few calls and text messages, I knew there was something wrong.

It was all planned. Everything. Today was supposed to be the day our old lives ended and our new ones began. I was going to forget the past and live out a beautiful future, but that all fell apart before I was given the chance to experience it.

How could he do this to me?

My Dear Olivia,

*I don't know why you insist on blaming me for
everything that's gone wrong in your life. Maybe I haven't
been the best mother I could be, but don't ever for one
second believe I never loved you. Because I do honey,
whether you believe me or not.*

*Everything I've ever done was because I love you. You
can't possibly hold me responsible for what that coward
has done. Not to point the finger here, but you are as much
at fault as he is. You were the one who chose him. You
chose to fall for that man, yet I'm the bad guy here because
I quote, 'ruined your life.' Didn't I tell you a no good man
like him would break your heart and walk away when you
needed him most? I tried to warn you baby. I did what any
mother would do; I protected you as deeply as I could. I*

interfered all those years because I cared about your happiness and your future and I will not apologize for that.

I hope you can get over this little fantasy that I'm some sort of evil witch, hell bent on ruining your life. And even if I were behind this little letter fiasco, am I really the one at fault here? In the end, it was his choice to walk away and that's exactly what he did. No real man would ever walk away from the woman he loves, and if he does, well then he's no man, is he?

So please stop this nonsense and come home. Your sister tells me you've moved to England. Olivia, stop being dramatic and get on a plane straight home. I think you've made your point already, my darling.

Mom

CHAPTER THREE

Thursday, March 10th 2016

"Olivia, honey, wake up. You're going to be late!"

My eyes shoot open, the light from my bedroom temporarily blinds me. I have no clue what's happening.

"Olivia, love, it's time to wake up. You're going to be late for class, you need to get up."

Now I'm awake.

I've totally forgotten. Today is the last day of classes before I go on holiday, and I'm late.

I jump out of my bed at the Atwater's home and scramble around for my bag. I can't be late on the last day. I actually like my English class.

Mr. Atwater searches for my bag with me, no doubt feeling guilty for being late and in turn making me late.

"No wait, I remember, I left it downstairs." I pass by him, running all the way down the stairs and into the sitting room. My bag sits on the sofa, waiting for me. I snatch it up and grab my mobile sitting on the table. "I'll see you when I get back." I scream at no one in particular, and head for the door.

I hear footsteps hurry down the stairs and turn to see Mr. Atwater. "Here, take these. You can't run all the way to class."

He tosses the keys to the spare car and for a second I look down at them, lost. I have my license, it's just I don't drive very often in England, not since the accident of 2014. "Are you sure? I'm not the best driver, you know."

"You'll be fine, just take them."

"Thank you. I'll bring it right back, I promise."

He smiles at me. "Nonsense. The only person who uses that car is you. Keep it, it's yours. The least I can do for making you late."

I smile back at him in return, never imagined in a million years I'd get a car as a random gift. I wave to him as I run out the door, nearly tripping on the last step as I head down the driveway. The door chirps open and I jump inside, throwing my bag to the side, I take off.

I must've fallen asleep waiting for Mr. Atwater to come home. This is great. The last day before break and I'm late. It's a good thing we took our midterm last week, or else this would have been very bad for me.

The Atwater's only live five minutes away from campus, which is a good thing. Speeding down Trinity Lane, I realise how glad I am for choosing a job so close to school. If I was back home at my flat, it would've taken me a good thirty minutes to get here. An hour without a car.

Usually this is a happy time for any student. Five weeks off, no homework or waking up early, holiday in Paris, but not me. Every time life is looking great for me, a family member has to ruin it. I spent all this time hating mom, when I probably should've been hating my father as well. He stood in the background and watched as she her daughter's lives. Any real human would've stepped in and stopped her, but not him. The man always was a coward.

Anytime I have some free time off, I spend it thinking about all the things that have gone wrong in my life, which is why I'm not looking forward to this break. On the other hand, I am going to France with Jade and the other girls, so that should keep my mind busy for the next few weeks.

Hopefully.

I nearly miss my turn and have to swerve, barely missing another car. Sometimes I wish I could be done with my family forever.

My bag is on my arm as I race out of the car and head inside. English Studies: 18th Century and Romantic Studies; why does that class have to be so far away? I head down the halls, speed walking, so Mrs. Lanchester doesn't get me in trouble for running. Again.

It doesn't work. She looks up at me, her eyes narrow as they follow me down the hall. The phone behind her desk rings and when she turns to answer it, I break into a run, almost ripping the door off its hinges as I burst inside the classroom.

The entire class turns and looks at me. I wish I hadn't done that. I hate it when all eyes are on me. I scan the room, and the only available chair is right in front, in the center of the class. Next to the professor's desk. Great.

"Ms. Fitzgerald, you care to join the rest of us, and not make a scene?" I look up and professor Edwards, sits on the corner of his desk, his arms crossed and his eyes looking me down. I rush to the front, refusing to meet his eyes as I take my seat.

Mr. Edwards stares at me, his glare burning a hole through my forehead. The man never did know how to smile.

He stands, his eyes still on me, and walks over to the board. "Now, if there will be no more disruptions, let us continue." I hate this man sometimes.

I keep my head down, my fingers fiddling around with the strap of my bag, and dig around for my notebook. Why did I come? I took my test last week, and all were learning today is what we've already learned throughout the school year. I could've stayed home. It would've saved me the embarrassment if I just stayed asleep.

My mind starts to wander as Mr. Edwards reviews all that he's already taught. I start to doodle, sketching out random drawings as I count down the clock. I've never been good at drawing, but anything's better than listening to this rubbish.

Without thinking, I start to draw a group of mountains. They're decent-ish, but it reminds me of the mountains of Colorado and I stop. I may have hated my life while I lived there, but it was still my home for seventeen years and I miss it. My eyes close, and my thoughts drift, thinking back to the innocent days, when I was still a child.

Our house was near the mountains, so Delphine and I would ride our bikes to the little river that flowed through them. We'd stay out there for hours. I mean who would want to go back to a home like ours?

We were stupid, silly kids. We'd jump into the cold, freezing river, our school clothes still on and wade around. It felt amazing, ignoring the below zero water, to be free without hearing our mom's voice nagging us.

I miss our river. I miss my sister.

"Ms. Fitzgerald!"

My eyes shoot open and Mr. Edwards stands before me. I look around the room, the entire class looking at me. I turn back and face off with him. What did I do?

"Yes?"

"If my lecture is that boring, then maybe you'd should've stayed home."

My mouth goes dry. "What are you talking about? What did I do?"

He scoffs at me. "You fell asleep."

When? "I did? I'm sorry, I don't remember falling asleep."

"Look, the door is always open. If you want to leave, then please go, but do not disrupt my class again!" He walks back over to his desk, talking to the class as if nothing has happened.

Everyone looks at me. Sympathy floods their faces as I sink lower in my seat. Mr. Edwards has always been one cold son of a bitch, but I never thought I would be on the opposite side of one of his outburst.

I look up from my ever moving fingers, sweat moisten my palms. My eyes meet his once again, and although he's talking, his dark gaze never leaves mine. I don't need to read minds to know he's probably thinking of other ways to humiliate me.

My god, what an asshole.

Hey baby,

Long time no see. What's it's been, four years now?
Wow, it's seems like just yesterday I was dropping you off
to your first day of senior year. Do you remember that day?
I do. I don't think I could ever forget it. You were so happy,
so optimistic. You had your entire life planned out. God I
was so proud of you. Still am. I'm just sorry things didn't
go the way you wanted. The only thing I ever wanted for my
daughters was to see them happy and you were. I wish your
mother could've seen that. I wish she would've been more
supportive. Myself as well.

I can't blame you mother. Not for all of it. I'm your
father, I should've been there as well. I should've stopped
her; I should've protected you. If you really want to hate
someone, then please hate me. I sat back and watched as

she slowly pushed you away from us. Hate me, because trust me, I hate myself more then you'll ever know.

I should probably wrap this up, I don't want to take up any more of your precious time. I know you're a busy woman these days. The real reason I'm writing is to tell you we're coming down your way. We've all been itching to take a vacation, or holiday as you say over there, and we thought what better place than Merry Ol' England, where our beautiful daughter resides.

I know I'm asking you for a lot, hell I'm probably asking for the impossible, but it's only because I miss you baby. I miss my little girl, and right now I'd do anything to see your face again.

I hope you can find it in your heart to forgive me. To forgive your mother. I know getting over something like this is going to take some time, so I won't push you. I do hope we can see each other, at least once while we're in England. If not I'll understand, but know that I love you.

Your sister loves you. And your mother, no matter how much she doesn't show it, loves you. You're our daughter and we will always be here for you.

P.S. There's something else you should know. A few days ago, Niall Parker stopped by the house. He came by looking for you, I guess he hoped that you somehow made your way back home. He said there were a few things he wanted to tell you and doing it by phone or writing a letter wasn't enough. I hope you're not angry with me, but I gave him your address. Supposedly, he's flying to England on business and is desperate to see you again. I don't know if he plans on stopping by your place, and if he does, is it a bad thing? I know you Olivia, and I know you've been craving answers since I handed you his letter all those years ago, and you deserve them, so here's your chance. Don't let this opportunity pass you by.

I hope you don't hate me for this. And if you do, I hope you can find it in your heart to forgive me someday.

Love,

Dad

CHAPTER FOUR

Monday, March 14th 2016

"Liv, we are in Paris. The city of hot French men who are open for just about anything, and you're choosing to slump around the hotel all day." Avery, always the loose one, never the wise one.

Instead of starting another two-hour long argument about why I'm boring and reserved, I just shrug at her. "It has nothing to do with that Avery. Since last night's regrettable rendezvous, I'm just not feeling all that well. I think there was something spoiled in my food."

"Or it could just be the food here period. It's not exactly the best. No offense to France." says Emma, the innocent blonde who really has no reason to be friends with people like us.

Jade chimes in, poking her head out from behind the bathroom door. "Look guys, if Liv isn't feeling good, then we can't force her to go with us. If anything, we should stay here, order a movie, and get fat off room services delicious pastries. What do you say?"

Jade gives a me a quick smile, telling me she knows I'm lying and trying to get out of going anywhere. Sly bitch.

My head drops, signaling that I give up. There's no way Jade is going to let me stay in my hotel all day and wallow in my own pain and misery. Perhaps I should thank her. I've been playing this same game four years now, and it's starting to get annoying.

Standing up, I head over to my closet and pull out my favorite little black dress and place it in front of me for all to see. "What do you say we go dancing?"

Avery jumps up and down on the bed, excited that she doesn't have to stay and cheer up a bummer like me. "Let's meet us some suave, sexy, French men."

Jade and Avery walk ahead, leaving me and Emma to bring up the rear. We kick around a crushed up soda can, the silence doing me some good. The club was a bust, hence Avery's fool mood. She thought she was taking us to the best nightclub in all of France, turns out that the best nightclub in all of France, happens to be a gay one. The rest of us had no issue with it, I found it quite fun, but going to a club meant for those who prefer the same sex is not for someone like Avery. Well actually, it kind of is. I just think tonight she would've preferred the company of a man instead of a woman.

It's a good tale to relive for the rest of our days though.

I can see Emma seeking glances at me. There's definitely been something on her mind since we left the hotel. Since we left England actually. Emma has always been the quiet type, but this isn't just silence. This is fear.

"Everything okay Em?"

She jerks her head to me, and plasters on a fake smile. "Yeah, why? Are you okay?"

I let out a little chuckle. "Emma, come on, let it out."

She looks around, as if someone's spying on us, or that what she's about to say is top secret and could get us both killed if she dares utter it out loud. Without hesitation, she moves closer to me, her arm hooking through mine.

"Liv, I haven't told anyone this, mainly because I'm afraid and have no idea how you girls would react, but you've always been the sensible one of us all, so I'm coming to you."

She stops in the middle of her sentence and looks down at her shoes once Jade turns to check on us. I look up to Jade and she nods her head, asking me if I'm okay. I nod back, given her a reassuring smile. When she turns again, I lean down, my lips inches from Emma's ear. "So, does this little secret of yours have something to do with Jade?"

Her face is still down, so I can't see her reaction, but I can see that her cheek is now bright red. I slow my pace, letting Jade and Avery get at least a two-minute head start and pull Emma down a separate alley. Once were out of their line of sight, I force Emma's face up to mine. Her snow white skin burns bright red.

"Emma, what is it? What have you done?"

Her eyes dart back and forth, panic flooding her body. I grab her shoulders and force her up against a wall.

"You have sixteen seconds to tell me what the hell is wrong, or I drag you to Jade and have her muscle it out of you. And who's more intimidating, me or Jade?"

Emma grabs onto me, scared that I meant what I just said. Of course, I wouldn't do that to her. She's the kind of person who cries if both teams don't win during a game of football. "Please don't. She'll never speak to me again."

Now I'm in panic mode. "Em, what's going on? You can trust me, you know that, right?"

She finally caves in. "Of course, I know that, it's just… It's not you Liv, it's me. Deep down I'm frightened, and I don't know how you'll see me after I say what's been bothering me.

"I won't see you any differently, that's a promise. Go on, tell me."

"Promise me something, yeah? Promise me you won't ever tell anyone what I'm about to tell you? Not until I'm ready. I need to hear you say you'll never tell another soul. Promise me?"

I raise my right hand. "I promise, Emma."

"Okay, good. Alright, just try not to judge me, please. Okay, so about a month ago, I ran into Jared. We started talking and went out for a cuppa, when one thing led to another and…"

My mouth drops. Oh my gods. "Emma, Emma honey, please tell me you didn't sleep with him?"

She takes a step back from me, clearly offended by my accusations. "No, I would never, that's just disgusting." She comes closer to me, leaning in so only I can hear her. "You know I wouldn't give my flower to a man without a ring first."

I can't help but laugh at her. "First off, there is no one else here, you don't have to whisper or get so close. Second, please stop calling your virginity 'flower.' It's just creepy." She blushes at me. Like I said before; innocent. "So tell me, if you didn't sleep with him then why are you so nervous?"

"Because."

I wait for her to finish. When she doesn't, I continue. "Because what, Emma?"

Leaning in again, she whispers softly in my ear, making it almost impossible for me to hear her. "Because we're dating."

"What!"

"Olivia, please, keep it down. It's not that big of a deal. Is it?" She is so pure.

"Are you fucking kidding me? Yes, yes it's a big deal, it's a huge deal! You're dating one of your best friend's ex-boyfriends. A man she was with for eight years. A man she was supposed to marry. A man she is still madly, deeply, desperately in love with! Oh my gods Em, what the hell were you thinking?"

She collapses on the ground, her face in her hands. "I know, I know. I'm a complete slag."

I want to berate her some more, but the girl has the mentality of a twelve-year-old preachers' daughter.

Without hesitating, I sit down on the street next to her, my arm pulling her in for a hug. She buries her face in my jacket, ashamed of the stupid mistake she's made. I stroke her hair, while rocking her back and forth. "Listen honey, I didn't mean to snap at you. Really, I didn't, but what would you do if you were in Jade's shoes? What if she started dating a man you were in love with without asking if it was okay with you first? How would you react?" I look off into the distance, unsure if Jade or Avery has noticed us missing. "Em, sometimes in the moment, if something feels good, a hundred percent of the time, it's not. You must think about all the pros and cons before diving head first into certain situations. This, love, is one of those situations. Do you understand what I'm trying to tell you?"

Without lifting her head, she nods along, either agreeing with me, or doing whatever it takes to shut me up.

I hug her tighter, lowering my voice so only she can hear me. "You have to tell her."

"This is boring; can we go?"

How did we ever become friends? "Just because you don't enjoy it, doesn't mean it's boring. Some of us love vintage shopping." I scold Avery.

She scolds back. "I know, it's just, why must you have horrible taste in what's fun and what's not."

I stand, everything in me keeping me from hurling the awful duck lamp Emma was staring at, at her head. I turn from the shelf of classic novels, and face Avery. "Well if you don't like it, then leave!" She takes a step back, insulted, but I don't care. We've been on holiday for three days now, and all she's managed to do was complain and screw every man who smiled at her.

"Fine, I don't want to be in this stupid shop anyway. Come on girls, let's go."

Jade protests. "I'm not going to leave Liv alone in a strange city, at night."

I turn to Jade. "It's alright, I'll be fine. The hotel is less than a mile from here, I can take a taxi. Besides, you would rather be exploring the city then to be stuck looking at old books in a dusty shop. Go. Seriously."

Emma butts in. "Liv, are you sure?"

"Positive. Get out of here, the lot of you." I lean closer to Jade. "I think she needs you more than I do." I nod my head over to Avery and smile.

Jade furrows her brows, looking from Avery and back to me. "Fine, but I'll be ringing every five minutes, so you better keep your mobile close."

"Yes, mum."

Jade wraps her arms around me, planting a kiss on my left cheek before grabbing Emma's arm and dragging her alongside. Emma takes one last glance at me and I smile at her, giving her a thumbs up. Her face turns bright red again, scared to be alone with Jade, without me. Avery gives me a half smile and leads the pack out of the door and into the city lights.

That was easier than I thought. I was done looking twenty minutes ago, I was only waiting for Avery to impatiently suggest leaving, like she always does, and take the girls with her. Leaving me alone to do whatever I want. And right now, that's going back to my room and watching a cheesy movie on the telly.

I plop the books on the counter and smile at the clerk, who hasn't taken his eyes off me since I first walked into his shop. The man is old enough to be my great grandfather. Avoiding eye contact, I fish around inside my bag and hand over my cash. He takes it, but his eyes are still on me. Now I'm really uncomfortable.

"You know what, keep the change."

I don't bother waiting for him to load the books into a bag. Instead I grab them and head for the door. The weight of four hardcover novels pressing down on my arms, but I ignore it. I'd rather suffer through the pain, then be ogled by this old man any longer.

With no hands, I turn, using my butt to open the door, but someone beats me to it. Tripping out the door, I fall right into the arms of my teacher, Mr. Edwards.

As if this trip couldn't get any worse.

I knock back another rum and coke, the last hour on repeat in my brain forever. I came on this trip with high hopes of forgetting my family and the embarrassment I suffered from that last day of class. Now, not only am I burdened with my father's letter, I'm now in the same city as the man I hate as much as my family.

Damn this vacation gets better and better by the day.

"Did you want another ma'am?"

I snap out of my thoughts to see the bartender staring at me. Pretty sure four rum and cokes is enough for one person. Especially someone who doesn't drink. This is what dealing with people turns you into; a lonely drunk.

Pushing the glass away, I shake my head. "No thanks. I shouldn't have had all those."

He smiles at me and grabs my glass. "You got it, ma'am."

I stand, the buzz from those drinks going straight to my head. Yep, this was a mistake.

"Are you going to be okay, ma'am?"

I turn back around, regretting it as the world starts to spin before me. "Um yeah. My room is just on the fourth floor. I should be fine, thanks."

I pick my books up from the stool next to mine, my father's letter tucked loosely into the one on the top, and head for the elevator. The ride up makes me queasy, but I hold it all in. No puking until I'm safely in my room. The ride's short, and before I know it, I'm stepping out and stumbling to my room, good thing it's only four doors away.

This has been one of the worst trips I've ever taken. I thought running away to a different continent would do me some good, while also putting some distance between myself and the past. Well, that plan failed horribly. I guess giving my address to my sister blew up in my face. I supposed I just never thought she'd be the one to betray me. Then again, everyone betrays everyone eventually.

I stop at my door, attempting to catch my breath. During these past three days, I've had nothing but bad luck after bad luck. Well not anymore. I'm not going to let my mother, or father, or anyone, ruin my life anymore. I'm done letting them control me. I'm done being the downer of the group, coming all the way out here to Paris to only sit alone in my hotel room the entire time to bitch and moan about how horrible my life is.

It's been years Olivia, it's time to woman up and move on.

"Excuse me, ma'am, you dropped this."

My eyes open, my head turns in the direction of the voice, and my bad day has just gotten worse.

I really am a bad luck magnet.

Mr. Edwards stops in his tracks, a piece of paper in his hand, and his eyes on me.

Can I go just one day, one day without being shitted on?

He finally breaks the awkward silence; his eyes drop to the drab carpet below us. "Ms. Fitzgerald, I believe you dropped this." His arm reaches out, a folded and wrinkled letter in his hand. Dads letter.

I walk over to him and snatch it out of his hand, without a word. Turning back around, I fish around my bag for my key, ignoring that he's only a few feet from me.

"Olivia, are you alright." I don't think I've ever heard him call me by my first name. I don't like it.

Still refusing to look at him, I pull my key out and unlock the door. "Like you care." The door opens and I step inside, slamming it behind me.

"I wanted to hate him, but I couldn't. Something about

the way he looked at me made the downsides worthwhile."

CHAPTER FIVE

Thursday, March 17th 2016

Well, this trip is ruined.

I stare off into distance, looking on as all the other students who came here on holiday also, enjoy their time, wanting nothing more than to just go home. I haven't seen Mr. Edwards since our last encounter, nor do I plan on seeing him again. At least until this is all over, then I have to go back to school and his class and put up with his bullshit again.

Life couldn't be any sweeter.

Why do I care so much? It's not like he means anything to me, so why am I so bothered by him? I wish I wasn't, I wish I was one of those people who just didn't care, but I do. He's just my teacher. Not a friend, or a relative, or a boyfriend. No, he's just a teacher, one I most likely, hopefully, will never have again. So why do I care so much?

I don't know, but I hate myself for it.

My attention turns back to the fun down by the pool and I smile. Jade, sitting down near the pool surrounded by men, looks up to me. It's nice to see her this way.

She and Jared have been broken up for four years now, but she's still holding onto hope. She thinks with enough time, he'll come to his senses and run back to her. I know that feeling, doesn't mean I'll ever take Niall back. I've grown too much since then.

Each of us tried everything to help her move on, and if I'm being honest, only my way was the smart way. Emma kept telling her they were perfect together. FYI, never tell that to a person who was dumped days before their wedding, it never sits well. Avery thought sex could fix everything. She tried hooking Jade up with one-night-stand after one-night-stand, which only made things worse and Jade gained sixteen pounds. It's been a horrible couple of years for her, which is why I'm glad she's taking an interest in men again. I just hope she's not going down the path that Avery's on.

I wave to Jade, throwing her two thumbs up, letting her know I'm proud of her. She waves me down, pointing at a very tanned man, then winks at me. I smile, but shake my head. Maybe I'm a hypocrite; I tried to help Jade move on, setting her up on dates with worthy men, but me myself, I haven't been with another man since Niall. It's not that I'm not over Niall, I am, I think I am, it's just now because of the whole situation, I have newly developed trust issues with men and motherly figures. Because of those two, I may never love again.

And that's okay, I don't need a man to complete me. Just look at me, four years and I'm still doing fine…ish.

I throw one last wave at Jade and head back inside, and plop down on the bed. I can't hide in my room forever, nor can I just avoid him forever. I'll be back in his class once Easter Holiday is over, and there's no avoiding that. Well there is, but then I'd fail and have to take the class over again. Still, if I'm to enjoy the rest of this trip, then I must avoid him.

"Why California? It's gloomy and hot and a lot of half-dressed woman walk around. Everywhere they go, they're naked. Is that why you want to go, to find someone hotter than me?"

Niall laughs, throwing his head back as the moon reflects off his pearly whites. "First off stop being paranoid, second, the scenery out there is breathtaking. Lastly, I thought about it and the women out there are hot and very tan, but they're more like a one-night stand. You're more marriage marital, so I guess I'll just stick with you. Until you get old and wrinkly anyway."

I sit up, my head yanks around as I meet his eyes. He smiles up at me as I reach over for one of my favorite pillows, beating him over the head with it. Sitting up, he wraps his arms around me, pulling me back down on the bed of his truck, his laugh ringing in my ears. "I hate you Niall."

He plants kiss after kiss after kiss on my cheek, making me smile. "No you don't. Besides, you know I'm kidding. If anything, you're going to be the one fighting off every man who passes you by. And I would happily get beat up to fight for your hand."

I bury my face in his neck, masking my wide smile. I love it when he says things like this. I take in the smell of him, the fresh smell of a recently taken shower and a crisp, clean shirt. I could lay like this forever, my face hidden away in the sweet scent of his skin.

My lips trace from his collar bones, up to his perfectly chiseled jaw. I close my eyes as I take every last bit of him in, refusing to ever let go. "I'm seriously babe, why California?"

He loosens his grip on me, his eyes settle on the moon above us, that beautiful grey lost in the blank night sky. "I want a new view of life, you know. I'm sick of the weather and the people here. I want to be somewhere else, somewhere fast paced and fresh. A place where we don't know anyone. Cali has this air about it that just sucks you in. I spent one weekend there, and knew it was the place I wanted to run away to. With you of course."

I lean back, my eyes tracing his face. I don't want to forget one moment of it. I find myself doing this a lot lately, as if someone were planning on coming to take him from me forever. My fingers trace his jaw, the kind that would break your hand if you ever tried to punch it. He shivers under my touch, but it's the good kind, the longing kind. Before I can do anything else, he grabs onto my hand, his eyes on me. We stare at each other, not saying a word, but we never needed to. Words make up about twenty-four percent of any relationship, it's actions that matter. And Niall has proven time after time how much he loves me.

He leans down to kiss my hand, and I lean into him, my face buried in his messing, dirty blond hair.

"I love you Olivia Fitzgerald, and I always will."

My eyes shoot open, my face concealed in the covers. Of all the memories, I had to relive that one.

I roll over, my head pounding, my face moist. Was I crying in my sleep?

The clock shows that it's one in the morning, maybe I can go out without worrying about running into the jerk. It's a big city, he can't be everywhere. Although, technically, he is sort of staying in the same hotel as me. On the same floor.

A red light flashes from underneath the thin white pillowcase. Throwing the pillow aside, I find my mobile, and look to find over ten missed calls. I can't help but smile. Jade. That girl will make the perfect mother someday.

I press the button, bringing my mobile to life, but Jade's name isn't the one plastered on the screen. Delphine. My heart starts to beat, going a mile a minute. Delphine never calls me. Ever. Not since my first day here in England. Something must be wrong.

My feet are on the floor, and my fingers pressing away. I may be mad at her for giving my parents my address, but she's still my little sister, and I will always protect her against them.

"Liv?"

My mind goes blank. "Delphine?"

"Yeah, it's me. I thought maybe you were ignoring me."

I collapse back on my bed, a smile on my face. "You know I would never do that."

I can hear her laugh, but it sounds weird. Suffocated. "I didn't want to bother you. I know its spring break here, or whatever they call it in Europe, so you're probably partying it up."

A mental picture of Delphine pops in my head, and I find myself smiling like an idiot. I never realised how much I missed her. "Stop. You know I'm not the partying type. The adventures I prefer are usually of the literary nature."

There's a slight silence on her side. "Did you just quote Supernatural?"

I burst out laughing. All these years and things still haven't changed between us. "I miss you Fe. I wish I could've seen you. Just you."

"I know, I'm not mad at you, I just miss my sister too. I haven't seen your face in a very long time. I'm not even sure what you look like anymore."

The guilt starts to eat me alive. I know that's not what she intends, but it doesn't make me feel any better. But the guilt doesn't last very long. I can hear a voice in the back, a voice telling Delphine what to say next. A voice that has haunted me for the first seventeen years of my life. A voice I hate more than the person it belongs to.

"Mom?"

Delphine stutters. "No, just me."

Too late, I'm already pissed. "Mom, is that you?"

"Liv, it's just…"

"Shut up Delphine, I'm not talking to you. Am I on speaker mom? Is dad there too?"

There's another slight pause and pure dead silence on the other line. I can hear a long sigh as a voice finally speaks up. "Olivia honey, don't get mad at your sister. Your mother and I…"

I hang up the phone before he can finish. My eyes close as water starts to cloud them. They've finally done it. They turned my own sister against me.

The freezing water gets my mind off my anger. A little. I used to think Fe was as strong as me. I used to think it was us against them. Now, in only a few short years, she's picked a side. Betraying me like everyone else who's come into my life.

I dip my head under the water, holding my breath, my mind now clear. Too focused on not dying to think about anything else. My father, Niall, and now Delphine. Is there no one that woman won't take from me?

The weight of the water starts to take its toll on me, and I resurface for air. Why can't I just rid all the negative people from my life for good?

"Please tell me you weren't planning on doing anything stupid?"

Wiping the water from my eyes, I turn to see the infamous Mr. Edwards standing before me. He puts his hands in his pockets, his harsh blue eyes on me.

I'm too pissed to try and be nice anymore. I'm done being the sweet one.

I push my hair behind me, clearing the water that's dripping down my face. "What do you want?"

His eyes soften as he takes a seat on the chair closes to me. "I've been looking for you. You're a hard person to find, especially just being two doors down from me."

Two doors down. Well isn't that just lovely. I turn away from him, not wanting to look that man in the eyes ever again.

"Ever stop to think maybe I don't want to see you. Or talk to you."

I can hear him chuckling behind me. "I deserved that one, perhaps I deserve more than that." There's silence behind me and I start to think maybe he finally left, but his shaky breathing tells me otherwise. "Look, Olivia, I wanted to apologize for everything. I was having a, well let's just say it's been one hell of a shitty few months and instead of dealing with it like a grown up, I took my frustrations out on you and I had no right. I'm sorry, truly."

My gut and brain tell me he means it, and I really believe he does, but after everything that's happened, I don't care. This asshole yelled at me for his own selfish reasons and my heart won't let it go.

I look up from the clear blue water to find his eyes looking me over. "I don't know if you mean that, nor do I care. Everyone has shit going on in their everyday lives. Myself included. Acting like a dick to others may make you feel better, but it hurts the feelings of those around you. So maybe next time, when you feel like being an ass, think twice."

His reaction changes, and I'm very pleased. He wasn't expecting me to fight back. Neither was I. To be honest, I have no idea where that came from, but I'm glad I said what I said. He needed to be put in his place, and I've done that. Beautifully.

"Now if you're quite finished, I would love to get back to my swim."

Without another word, he stands up and nods, faking a smiling as he walks back into the hotel and heads straight for the bar.

CHAPTER SIX

Friday, March 18th 2016

"Get up and get dressed, I want to have some fun."

I jump up and down on Jade's bed. She's sleeping, sorry, she's still hungover from the previous night but I jump on her anyway. Her and the rest of the girls have been bothering me non-stop on this trip, and now it's my turn.

"Get out." Avery, who's passed out next to Jade, throws her pillow at me, completely missing and hitting Emma, fast asleep on the sofa behind me.

I plop down on Jade and squeeze her until she opens her eyes. "Come on guys. The one time I want to do something, you guys want to stay in bed all day. It's two in the afternoon, how long do you plan on sleeping?"

Jade buries her face deeper in the pillow. "We were out all night, Liv, we're exhausted. We'll go out tomorrow, yeah?"

Taking the covers from Jade, I throw them on the floor, making my stand. "No, I want to go out tonight. Now get up and put on your make-up. Seriously, the three of you are in desperate need of it." When no one moves, I toss in the big guns. "You can either come out with me, or you can go back to sleep, comfortable in the warmth of your bed. But I warn you, I'll just have to go out all by myself. In a strange city. At night. All alone."

This gets Jade up. "Alright, we're up. You, arse."

Emma raises from her position on the sofa, completely oblivious of her surroundings. I don't think I've ever seen Emma wasted, not her thing. Weird, especially for a person like her. "I'll go, but can we do something simple. Something with no people, or noises, and no lights. And indoors."

"What, no, I want to have fun. I want to live Paris. You can't do that when you're basically in a dark room. Literally what you're explaining, Emma, is a very lonely, dark room." But I cave. "Okay fine, lets compromise. If you guys go out with me, we can just do something simple like shop, or try weirdly, gross cuisines. Or maybe pick up a few men. Maybe even a woman or two."

Avery shoots up. "Give me ten minutes." She jumps out of the bed, half naked and leaves the room, no doubt heading to her room to slut herself up.

I watch her go and turn back to the rest of the room. "So Avery's in. Are the two of you going or not?"

"Why are you suddenly in the mood to have fun?"

I scold at Avery. "You know, I'm not as boring as you may think. I do like going out every once in a while. I'm not a total prude."

"Olivia, out of the four years I've known you, you only agreed to go out to a club with us twice. And each time, may I remind you, you left only forty-two minutes after we arrived."

I turn to Jade, there's no way I did that. She nods at me. Giving me the 'you know you did face'. Okay maybe I did.

"Well whatever. I'm here now, so let's stop talking and get drunk."

Well that was a bust.

The club scene was never my thing. It took me until today to finally realise it. So maybe Avery was right, maybe I'm not the partying type. Perhaps I'm more comfortable around tea and books. There's nothing wrong with that.

I lasted more than an hour this time, but after having a drink spilled on me, and my butt grabbed, I was done. And so was the asshole who touched me. His crooked, bloody nose will teach him to never touch another woman like that again.

Before anyone could notice, I slipped out without a warning. Didn't want to hear all the drunken, idiotic behavior that came with me bailing so early. I sent them a text to tell them I was heading home, so they wouldn't be too worried, but I couldn't stay in that place one second longer.

I stop at a bin to toss in the many numbers that were given to me as the night progressed. Maybe I am a prude, but there is no way I'd ever date anyone I met at a club. In France. And secondly, I haven't exactly been interested in men since Niall. After a break-up like that, you become committed only to yourself and it's better this way.

My feet stop and my brain has to catch up. I've been walking for almost an hour now and only just realised, I have no idea where I'm going. I take a minute to look around me and can see the *Fontaine des Fleuves* just before me. Beautiful. Everything about this country is breathtaking. I wish I could stay here after holiday. Start over. New friends, new school with newer, and nicer teachers. New life. Don't get me wrong I love England, and I love my friends with all my heart. It's just, wherever I go, baggage seems to follow me. And I'm done letting the past consume me.

For the first time in four years, I'm ready to be happy again. I just don't know how to get there.

"Bonjour belle."

Oh great. I look up to see three men hoovering around me. This is so not what I needed. I turn, ready to take off, but one blocks my way.

"Can I help you?"

"Ah, American girl. I love American girls."

"Yeah, that's nice. Too bad we don't feel the same way about you. Now if you'll please excuse me."

The same gross, greasy man jumps in my path. "Why leave so early, the fun is only beginning."

I reach into my bag. "Move, or you will be moved."

Instead of getting out of my way, he smiles. I hope all French men aren't this stupid. Living in a strange city by yourself has taught me a few things; take no shit from no one.

I pull my hand out on my bag, and almost empty my can of mace in his eyes. I point it at his two friends, not backing down. "Run."

A voice speaks up from behind me. "You heard the lady, get the hell out of here."

They pick up their blubbering friend and drag him off. I watch them go before I dare turn around. This is another reason I chose to be alone. Men are pigs.

My eyes still watch after the men, just in case they try something stupid. "Thanks for that, but I'm pretty sure I had it."

"It was the least I can do, after everything."

After everything? I turn to find Mr. Edwards standing over me, his eyes on the men as well.

He doesn't look away. "Are you alright?"

"Fine. What are you doing here? Are you following me?"

A loud laugh comes out of him, like I just said the funniest joke ever.

"Don't flatter yourself, Ms. Fitzgerald, we both just happen to be at the same place, at the same time."

I scold him. "It's not that funny. And I don't believe you. I think you're following me and refuse to admit. It's alright. Apparently, I have that effect on men." I laugh at myself as soon as the words come out of my mouth.

He smiles at me, which is weird. I don't think I've ever seen a smile on this man. I didn't know he was capable of emotions. "Did you need a cab, or…"

"No, I'm not going to let them ruin my night. Besides, I have enough mace to last me the rest of the week. I'll be fine, thanks."

"I don't feel comfortable leaving you alone in the city. Where are your friends?"

I look away, a little ashamed to answer the question. "I might have ditched them back at a club."

He sounds surprised. "You ditched your friends? And I always thought you were the innocent one out of the group."

I turn back to him. "Hey, just because I left them, doesn't mean I'm not the good one. I'm simply the one who doesn't prefer the club scene, that's all."

He looks down at me as if he's trying to read my mind, which makes me a wee bit uncomfortable, but secure at the same time. Without all the yelling, the dirty looks, and the glasses blocking his facial features, he doesn't seem that intimidating. He seems younger, and innocent. Not like the man I wanted to punch just yesterday.

Maybe he's not that bad, at least on this trip he isn't. Which is probably why I'm starting to feel guilty about yelling at him.

I finally speak up. "Look I'm sorry…"

But he interrupts me. "Have you ever heard…?"

I nod to him, gesturing for him to talk first. "Go ahead."

He shakes his head. "No please, you go first."

So I do. "I'm sorry about the other night. It was wrong of me to take my anger and frustration out on you. I had no right. I was pissed off about something else, and decided to yell at you for it. So, I'm sorry."

His eyes meet mine, I never realised how blue and soft they were. "Thanks, although you didn't have to. I deserved it."

"No, you didn't."

He puts his hand up, silencing me. "Yes I did. I've been a real arse to everyone lately, and you were the only one brave enough to put me in my place. Seriously, I'm not mad at you. I have no right to be."

His attention is now at his feet. He seems so tiny and innocent like this. I wonder what's on his mind. Whatever it is, it's killing him inside.

I decide to bring him back to reality. "You were going to ask me something earlier, what was it?"

He's lost in his own thoughts. Probably already forgotten I'm standing right here.

I push his shoulder playfully. "You still there?"

His head jerks up, snapping him out of his little world. "I'm sorry, did you say something?"

"Yeah, I said what is it you were going to ask me?"

"Yeah, yeah. I'm sorry. I was going to ask if you heard of The Hemingway Bar over in Le Louvre."

I nod my head. "Yeah, actually I have. It was on my list of places to visit while I was here. Why do you ask?"

"I was on my way there. You want to join me?"

"I'll take a white wine please."

"I never took you for the drinking type."

I look across me, still shock to see myself sitting at a table, in a bar, with one of my teachers. It's funny how much things can change right before your eyes.

I turn in my seat so that were facing each other.

"If you don't mind me asking, exactly what kind of person do you think I am?"

His eyes smile at me, while his lips stay unmoved. He leans back in his chair and looks me over, a crooked little smile forms in the corner of his mouth. "Your hand is always the first one to shoot up in class, which is what made me like you. You weren't afraid to seem nerdy or come off as a teacher's pet. You're always quiet, even when you answered my questions, which gave off this shy, innocent energy about you. You sit in the back every chance you get, probably because you didn't want to seem like the center of attention. And excluding our last class, you have always been on time, sometimes I've found you in class before myself. You'd sit right down and pull out your books, never looking up to meet my gaze. Always the first to present, or turn in your homework. You never waste time; you just get things done."

Holy shit! I never thought he paid me any attention. I never thought he paid anyone any attention for that matter. He was always so angry, about everything. He rarely called on any of us, even if our hands were up. If no hands went up after he asked his question, he would just move on, not wanting to waste any time on us.

Before I can open my mouth, he says something I never thought would come from his lips. "And your smile. You have one of those classically beautiful smiles that could light up a room. Every time I handed back your work or test, I'd see you stare down at the paper and smile. I never seen someone so happy in school."

I stare at him, not sure what I should say next. Did he just call me beautiful?

"Did you just call me beautiful?" Why did I have to ask that?

He leans back towards the table; his eyes look me dead in mine. "Yeah, why have you never heard that before?"

Well yeah, I heard it before. I just never thought I'd hear it from him. I look away. This is not how I was expecting my day to go.

Thank the gods for the bartender. "Here are your drinks. Bon appétit!"

"Thank you, ma'am." He waits until she's gone before digging into me. "You've become very quiet? Did my last remark make you uncomfortable?"

A little bit. "N... No, it didn't make me..." This is going to be awkward. "No, it didn't bother me, it's just, I always took you as this emotionless ass, and you turn out to be an average British man. Sweet and refined. I wasn't expecting that from someone like you."

"Wow, I call you beautiful, and I get called an arse. You do have a way with words Ms. Fitzgerald."

Perhaps that did come out a bit meaner than I expected. "You know what I mean. I wasn't trying to insult you."

"I know; I'm just hassling you. Ignore me."

What do I do? I wasn't intimated by this man until about ten minutes ago, now I feel like a high school girl with a crush. I have no idea what to say.

So I say nothing.

I keep my focus on my glass and the three drunken idiots to my right. France sure is a free country.

Before I know it, my drink is gone, the only distraction I had from talking. I contemplate whether I should get another glass, but choose against it. I don't want to get tipsy. I'm not the greatest drunk.

"What's on your mind?"

Man I was hoping he'd take my silence for I don't want to talk.

"Nothing, just taking it all in."

I can hear him chuckle under his breath. "You're just horrible when it comes to lying, you know that right?"

That I take offense to. "For your information, I happen to be a professional when it comes to lying."

"So perhaps I'm the only one who can see past your crap."

I give in and look over at him, and he's proud of himself. He manipulated me. I'm not even mad.

"I'll give you one thing, Mr. Edwards; you're good."

"Thanks. It's a gift."

Without looking away from me, he waves the bartender over, ordering us both another round.

CHAPTER SEVEN

Monday, March 21st 2016

I throw myself onto the bed, covering my face with a pillow. I knew I was going to get 'the talk.'

Jade still isn't too happy with my abrupt exit the other night at the club, and she's even more pissed that I came home around five. She even gave me the talk about the birds and the bees. I'm twenty-two years old, and not a virgin.

She's a way better mother then my birth one, but I'm not a child, or an idiot. I sit up, the pillow from my head thrown at her face. Her reaction is priceless.

"You bloody wanker!"

"I'm not a child, Jade I don't need the sex talk."

She throws the pillow back at me, missing by a foot. "I don't care, it is my job to watch out for all my friends, especially you."

"What do you mean, especially me? I'm not in invalid. And shouldn't Avery be at the top of your list. She's the loose one of the group."

"Avery doesn't just take off without telling us. I was worried sick about you."

"Oh you were, were you? I've only gotten two missed calls from you. Both around the time when you finally left the club. You didn't even notice I was gone until you were done partying. And I'm sorry, but where is Avery now?" That shuts her up.

According to Emma, Avery disappeared with not one, but two men that night. She texted this morning, after a whole day of silence to say she's having a ball. So maybe Jade isn't as protective as she thinks she is.

"That's not the point. You're the fickle one who always leaves without telling anyone."

This talk is getting old. "I left you a message before I walked out those doors. And last I checked, I don't have to explain myself to you. I'm the responsible one of the group, and the oldest and I won't be treated like some stupid kid. Now if we're done, then please, show yourself out."

Jade has always had the temper of the group, and once she's angry, she turns into a hulk.

Before she can do anything stupid, she kicks my bag of books over and storms out. I'm going to live to regret that.

I get to my feet, the need for fresh air becomes a life or death situation. The doors to my patio burst open and I lean over the edge. I hate when people treat me like some gullible idiot. No, I don't like to party all that much, and no I don't drink unless I'm trying to forget something, but I'm not stupid. I have lived through more than any of these other girls have and I'm not going to take their shit anymore.

If they don't like the way I do things, tough shit.

"You don't plan on jumping, do you?"

The sound of his voice sends a smile across my face. Never in a million years did I think he'd be the one to make me smile.

I sit on the ledge facing out towards the pool, my legs stretched to the edge, feeling the breeze shoot up my legs. He leans back in his chair, his book resting on his lap, his undivided attention on me.

"Why is it every time I see you, you're in a sour mood?"

"Why is it you always seem to pop up out of nowhere?"

A smile spreads across his face. "Fair enough, but stop changing the subject. What's wrong?"

I shrug, there's too much and so little time on this earth to try and lay it all out. "Just having a bad day."

"Everyday?"

He has me there. "It's not that big of a deal, really. Just forget about it."

I can just sense him rolling his eyes at me. Even he's fed up with my bullshit lies.

"Olivia, I'm not going to drop this until you tell me what's wrong, so you might as well get it over with."

"What's your name?"

That threw him back.

"What?"

"Your name, what is it? You know mine, shouldn't I at least know yours? It's not like we didn't spend a drunken night, morning, together."

He chuckles, the lines on his forehead appear from nowhere. "You don't remember, then?"

"Remember what?"

"Our drunken night? Or morning, I should say? Wow, you really were hammered weren't you? Olivia, you asked me this same question while we were walking back here. How could you have forgotten already?"

I blush, glad he can't see it. "Sorry, I'm not the best of drinkers. I sometimes wake up and have forgotten my name or where I am." I turn to face him, and his face shows pride and concern.

He gives in anyways. "William. William Thomas Edwards. Would you like to know the day I was born too? Perhaps my favourite color?"

"Well, while we're on the subject, why not." I joke with him, hoping I can shift his focus.

He stands, leaving his book on the chair and leaning over the edge. His eyes never leave mine. "Stop changing the subject Olivia. What's wrong?"

Why do I try?

"You don't know when to give up do you?"

"No I don't, now continue."

I turn away, something about his eyes makes me feel safe and guilty at the same time. "Where should I start? There's my friends, who are constant annoying pricks, and then there's the whole family thing, but I am not ready to open that can of worms."

"Then start with your friends."

"So, you're telling me, your mother somehow forced your ex-boyfriend into ending your ten-year relationship?"

I shrug, the warmth from my teacup spreads throughout my body. "I'm not saying I have concrete proof, but yeah, she did it."

"Is that why you came all the way to England, to escape her?"

"To escape all of them. My father was just as bad as her. He just sat there and watched as she slowly ruined my life. I thought I'd be safe leaving my country behind, but that didn't work out as planned. Delphine gave them my address, and I'm extremely positive they have my number now too. I feel like I'm stuck in this same loop, that I just can't seem to escape."

I can hear whooping and hollering coming from below us, and look down to see yet another party before me. And of course, Jade, and Emma are front in center of it all. I will never fit in with them.

"Why aren't you down there?"

"Not my kind of scene. You?"

William laughs, jumping up on his ledge and crossing all the way over to mine, taking large steps so he doesn't fall. "Are you insane, you're going to get yourself killed. Get down from there!"

He jumps down, landing right in front of me. "I didn't know you cared so much."

"I don't. Okay maybe I do, and I would prefer to not see someone die in front of me, so don't do that again."

Sitting down next to me, he smiles. "Cross my heart. And to answer your question, I think I'm a little too old for that scene."

I calm down a bit, still pissed he would do something so reckless. "Bullshit. There's no way you're a day over thirty-four."

"Is that so?"

I lean against the wall, not backing down. I'm know I'm right, and if I'm wrong, then I would love to learn his secrets.

He stares back at me, but gives up. I can be stubborn when I want. "Thirty-one, going on thirty-two."

I smile, pride spreading across my face. Looking back down at the scene before me, I wonder why it isn't my scene. Most people who go through an ordeal like what I've been through dive head first into drinking, drugs, and sex. I did the opposite. I turned to learning, books, and celibacy.

"Olivia?"

I snap out of my thoughts, not realizing he's gotten closer to me. "Yeah?"

"Hearing you tell me about your family has me on your side. I haven't met her, but I'm almost certain your mum is behind everything, she just sounds like a wicked woman."

"You can say bitch. I do, all the time."

He laughs. "But while your mum and dad are guilty, have you ever stopped to think that maybe Niall is just as much at fault here as your parents? Look, I don't want to start anything, it's obvious you still love the guy, but just think about it. It was his handwriting, you said so yourself, but why would he leave you? Why write that letter? Ten-years, and he threw it all away with a note. Did she bribe him? Possibly. Did she blackmail him? Sure. But still, he chose to leave you. He's just as much to blame as they are."

I look away, I don't want him to see the shame in my eyes. He's right. I spent so much time hating my parents that I never stopped to blame Niall. They didn't force him to walk away, he chose to. I hated him. I hated him for years, but I never put any blame on him. He agreed to leave me without giving me a proper goodbye. Even that damn letter of his was a lie. I just know it. I never got to know why, and I spent so much of my time hating my own family, when I should've been hating him as well.

Warmth spreads across my cold, limp body. I look over at William, his hands wrapped around mine, squeezing them tight. My only comfort in this world comes from the teacher I thought hated me. My eyes stay glued on our hands. I can't look him in the eyes, I don't know why. There's something about his eyes. They used to make me nervous, scared of his glare, but now, there's something amazing about them. Something unforgettable.

We sit in silence, he's smart enough to know when I'm not in the mood, but he doesn't leave my side. He stays here, sitting right next to me, his hands locked tight in mine. Since Niall left, I refused to let another man in. Not just in a romantic way either. I never bothered to make any male friends. Couldn't trust them. But in the split of a week, one man managed to break that rule. I promised myself I'd never go down that road, yet here I am, pouring my heart out to a random guy.

William breaks the silence. "I have an amazing idea. It's nothing that can get us arrested or worse, but still a thought. Want to watch crap movies and splurge on junk food?"

I allow my eyes to look up, scanning his expression as he smiles down at me, his lips formed in a crooked smile.

"I really do."

Looking over at the clock, three hours have passed since we started our marathon. Time flies, especially when you're with someone who makes you forget about it. It's nice, not having to turn to sleep or a drink to forget my sorrows. Niall used to give me this.

William sits up, reaching for the remote to find us another movie to watch and I find myself looking him over. In class, he always seemed so menacing. His hair slicked off to the side and out of his face. Glasses that made his eyes seem wrathful, his stance demeaning. But under it all, he looks so young. Stripped of the clothes that make him look years older, with his hair a chaotic mess as he runs his fingers through it, pushing it from his face. His eyes playful, and cheery. Without all the things that makes him scary, he's very attractive.

Did I just call my teacher attractive?

I jerk my glare from him. This is not the time to be crushing on this man.

"Any suggestions?"

Turning back to him, I see him looking at me this time, his eyes wild with wonder. My gods, I've never noticed the crow's feet near his eyes.

"Olivia?"

"What, yeah. I mean no. Wait what?"

He smiles at me, dimples appearing out of nowhere. Now I'm noticing his facial features. "I said do you have any suggestions? What's going on with you?"

"Nothing, sorry. You caught me off guard."

"Thinking about your family again?"

"No, not this time. No sad stuff."

"Good. You mind if we watch something a wee bit happier then? And better."

"I can go for something that doesn't end with the woman finding herself and then a husband all in two hours and forty-six minutes."

He laughs, turning back towards the telly to find something worth watching. I lay back down on the bed, hiding behind him so he can't catch me staring. Never in four years have I thought about or looked at a man in that way. Why is he so different? In such a short amount of time too.

"Mr. Edwards. William, can I ask you a question?"

"Depends. Are you asking Mr. Edwards, or William?"

"Ha-ha, cute. It's sort of personal, so if you rather not go there, just tell me."

He turns to me, reading my expression before answering. "You opened up to me, the least I can do is answer a few of your questions."

I sit up so that our eyes meet. "You're very helpful when it comes to horrible parents and shitty exes. I'm curious on why that is? What's happened to you that made you this, let's say wise?"

His eyes fall, but it's not sadness or pain. More like shame. "Umm it's quite complicated, and long. I wouldn't want to bother you."

Is he trying to change the subject? I bounce up from my spot and crawl over to him, sitting so that are shoulders touch one another. "You wouldn't leave me alone until I spilled my life story, now it's your turn. It's not like either one of us has anything else to do. If we did, we wouldn't be hanging out here all night watching some of the world's worst movies. So come on, don't you trust me? I trusted you."

The corner of his lip twitches up, but the smile fades quickly, making me regret hounding him.

"But if you honestly rather not talk about it, that's fine. Your life is none of my business."

Without trying, I pushed a nerve, but it's still not anger. I start to scoot back, heading to my favorite spot on the left side of the bed, but his hand is on my thigh before I can go anywhere.

"No, it's okay. Stay."

So I do.

"My parents weren't the greatest. I prefer not to talk about them, mainly because I never considered them to be parents. Work came first, I came forth." His hand stays on my thigh, but his grip loosens, his eyes on the floor. "My nanny raised me. I only seen them, maybe, twice a week. Sometimes not even that much. They never did any shady things like your parents, no offense, but they still weren't there for me. Don't get upset, your family sounds like awful individuals, but it also sounds like you were loved in your household. I would've killed for that."

If he wants them, he can have them.

I let my hand slip into his, squeezing it so he can forget the pain of his past. I want to comfort him, but don't know how. How do you comfort someone who just admitted to never being loved? That's a pain not even I experienced.

I need to change the subject, and quick.

"What about your first love, what was she like?"

He shrugs. "Never had one. Growing up not knowing what love felt like made me hard to those feeling. I never had a real relationship. They only lasted for about a month, then I just gave up. Didn't seem worth the effort anymore, you know?"

I've been so used to being the sad, broken one that I never had to give advice to anyone experiencing what I've experienced. Now that I'm on the opposite side, I have no idea how to react.

"I'm so sorry."

"Why? In the short time, we've spent together, you've showed me more emotion then my parents ever did. If anything, besides my Nana, you're the best thing that's happened to me in a very long time."

I don't look away from his face. One talent I've always had was the ability to know when I was being lied to. And by the look on his face, and the hurt in his eyes, I know I was just fed the truth. He trusted me enough to come clean, and that means something to me.

Leaning in, I rest my head on his shoulder, my hand still tight in his. For years, I thought pushing men away because of what Niall did to me, was the smart choice. I was wrong. It took me a few years to finally find someone I could connect with on a deeper level, and I'm happy I was late to English class that day. Who knows, if I was my regular nerdy self he probably wouldn't have notice me and we probably wouldn't be together like we are now. Or maybe we would. None of that matters now, we're both here. Right now, and I'm not going to lie, but I am a little glad he's here.

William lays his head on mine, his hand squeezing a bit tighter, but it doesn't bother me none. I want him to feel like he matters. Within an hour, he helped make me feel that way, and I couldn't be more thankful.

I break the silence, wanting desperately to cheer him up. "You want to watch another crap movie?"

He chuckles under his breath; his Adam's apple moves slightly across my head. "More than anything."

With my free hand, I reach across him for the remote, looking for anything that sounds absolutely and ridiculously corny.

'You're the best thing that's happened to me in a very long time.'

And if I'm being honest- so is he.

CHAPTER EIGHT

Wednesday, March 23rd 2016

"That can't be true. There's no way."

William laughs under his breathe. "What, don't I seem like a dangerous rebel to you?"

"Well yeah, you're as scary as a bunny rabbit."

He rolls his eyes at me, his lips perk up to one side. "I scared you."

I start to open my mouth, but decide against talking. That much we can agree on.

We zigzag through the streets of France, taking in the culture as we go. I'm not much of a tourist, neither of us are. We prefer to walk around and get to know the country and their lifestyle. Everything is so much richer here than it is back in Aspen, Colorado.

It's been almost two days since we spent the night together in my room spilling our guts to one another, and I must say, I think it made us a lot closer. Somewhere amongst the chaos, we fell asleep, William before me, and I stayed exactly in the same spot all night, unmoved. I didn't want to wake him. He's so peaceful in his sleep, talks to himself a lot too. I only got maybe three hours of sleep, was too worried to close my eyes. He tossed and turned all night. I guess me forcing him to open up brought back some horrific memories.

Yesterday we spent most of the morning too lazy to get out of bed, so we just talked and watched a few episodes of some weird French cartoon. Couldn't understand a word of it. The rest of the day was spent by the pool. There were no parties, or partygoer's anywhere near the pool. The best part was not having to wait until the early hours of the morning just to swim.

"I have a question for you."

He snaps out of his thoughts, too lost in his ice cream cone. "Go ahead."

I turn my attention to the ground. I don't want him to see my face once I asked my question. "If you're not married, then why do you wear a wedding band on your finger?"

My curiosity gets the better of me, and I sneak a peek at him. His eyes are on me, a wicked smile across his face. "So, that's what's been bothering you, you thought I was already taken."

I mock him. "Don't flatter yourself Mr. Edwards."

Looking forward, he lets out a breathless laugh. I follow in his footsteps, his laugh contagious.

"Well if you must know, it was my Nana's. Married thirty-eight years. After her husband passed away, she found it hard to look at, so she gave it to me. She told me to make a woman lucky one day." He looks down at it and smiles. The tiny object the only thing amazing about his past. "It was the only thing she had that was valuable to her and she wanted me to have it."

"How old were you when she, you know?"

"How did you know?"

I look away, my ice cream dripping on my hand. "The way you look at it. It reminds you of her. And there's this painful sparkle in your eyes you get anytime you talk about her. A pain that leads me to believe she's gone."

There's a silence between us, but I don't look over to him. I don't like seeing him in pain. "I was sixteen. For weeks I didn't see her, it was like she just disappeared. I thought she left me, found a better job and walked away." He pauses, the shaking in his voice tells me this is the first time he's ever talked about it. He's never told anyone. Not until I came along. "One day after school I got curious and angry, so I went to her home. I wanted some answers. Turns out she was battling breast cancer for more than a year and kept it from me. The last thing I needed was another heartbreak, and she refused to be the reason for my pain. She thought she could do it on her own, be her own support system." He tosses his ice cream in a nearby bin, mine follows. It's more soup then ice cream now.

"She lost the fight and wanted to spend her last few weeks at home. I decided to move in so I could take care of her this time around. My parents never even noticed." The smile fades from his face. "Before she passed she handed me this ring, told me to run as far away from my family as possible and start a life of my own. And that's what I did. Everything was left to me in her will, including the home she, you know, and all the money she saved up from raising me. She took out this hefty life insurance policy on herself, and the money from her husband policy and his retirement left me with more than enough to start on my own. I moved in, officially, about a month after she died. In that house, I could still feel her presence, she never really left me. It felt good, and horrible at the same time. I knew she was there, I just couldn't see her."

He tugs on my hand, pulling me closer to fill the space between us. "Once I graduated high school, I enrolled at Oxford. I had to move on, holding on to her was only killing me. So I left it all behind and started a new life. And when my parents died four years later, I inherited everything from them too. Didn't want it, but I was the only surviving heir."

Why do I keep doing this? First, I started a heart retching conversation two days ago, now this. I sure know how to ruin a day.

I do the one thing I can do. My hand is in his, my head on his shoulder, and my other hand gripping tight on his forearm. His hand tightens around mine, his chin resting on my head. "Thank you, Olivia."

"For what?"

"Everything."

I can feel him plant a kiss on the top of my head. His touch sends a shiver through my body and I smile. "You are very welcome."

We walk in silence down the streets of Nice, with the beach to my left. I turn my head without taking it away from William's shoulder. It's beautiful here. Now this is where I could die happily.

I turn back, my face hidden in his arm. "Your life wasn't as bad as you may think."

He speaks up, his voice cracking under the misery. "Yeah, and what makes you say that?"

"You had her, your Nana. Your parents may have casted you aside, but she didn't, she stayed and raised you. She was as much your mother as your birth one was, perhaps even better. Some people don't get a second chance like that, but you did. And it was worth it in the end, wasn't it?"

I can feel his jaw stretch on the top of my head, a smile no doubt spreading across his face. "It was."

"Good. Then she's the only thing that should matter. You were blessed with a second, and better mother. Remember that the next time you think about those assholes you call birth parents."

His hand leaves mine and his arm wraps around me. This time he plants a longer kiss near my forehead. "I never thought I'd feel anything for another person once she died. I really thought I was done caring about others. I guess that wasn't meant to last, was it?"

I finally look up, his face inches from mine. "Oh yeah, and who would that lucky person be?" I already know the answer.

He plants one last kiss right between my eyebrows. His words muffled. "You."

Hey baby,

We missed you, more than you know. I don't know why I thought you'd show up to the airport. I pictured it, you with arms wide open, that beautiful smile of yours stretched across your face, and one of those oversized signs with our name plastered across it. You were happy to see us, but not as happy as we were to see you, especially after all these years of silence, I thought maybe you'd realise how much you missed us. Guess not.

Well I'm not mad. I have no right to be. In the back of my mind, I knew you wouldn't be there, so I guess I didn't get my hopes up too high. We did get to see a few sights, it's very beautiful out here. Now I know why you chose to move to this place. The people are loving too, definitely different from home.

I should go, your sister is getting impatient. She's been dying to see the Tower of London, apparently it's this huge thing.

Like always,

I love you.

Dad

I'm so, so, so sorry, Livia, please believe me.

I didn't want to betray you. It's just mom told me to call you because she wanted to hear your voice. What was I supposed to do? She's our mother Olivia, I thought I was doing you both a favor. She gets to hear you, and know you're alive and safe. It's not like we hear from you anymore. You don't respond to any of our letters, and you don't answer any calls from us, nor do you come home like most people do when they go off to college. I just missed you. I miss us. I wish you would just come home. I just want us to be sisters again.

Life in Colorado hasn't been the same without you. I tried to do what you did. I tried getting a job. I met new people, I even joined any sport I could think of to keep me out of the house, but it didn't work. It still doesn't fix the fact that I'm left alone with her. Without you.

I know that doesn't justify what I've done, but I wanted to hear your voice too, and I want you to come home. I just want my sister back.

Please don't hate me. I only did what I thought was right. I only did what any sister would do.

I love you.

Delphine

Well aren't we just being childish.

I mean come on Olivia, ditching your parents, now that's a new low even for you. Your father clearly told you we would be in town, I read his letter myself, so please don't bother lying, or try to get yourself out of this. I came all the way down to this cold hell-hole and you couldn't even bother to show up. I just don't understand you sometimes.

Look, if you want to act this way, then fine, but you can't act like a child for the rest of your life. Eventually you're going to have to grow up and when you do, I'll be here waiting for your apology.

If I'm being honest, that pathetic boy wasn't even worth your time. I did you a favor when I sent him away. He was useless and he still is to this day. You'll thank me the day you meet your doctor. Trust me, I always knew what was

right for you.

Mom

CHAPTER NINE

Wednesday, April 27th 2016

"Another very long and boring day. Is it bad to say I didn't miss school all that much?"

Jade and I always got along well because we've always had so much in common. Besides bad ex's and ruthless family members, we also love school a little too much. "Did the nerdiest of us just say she hated school?"

I think I offended her. "I'm the nerdiest? This coming from the girl with the straight A's. If anyone is a nerd here, it's you, Liv."

"Technically one of those A's is an A-, so it's not straight A's so to speak, and shut up."

Jade intertwines her arm in mine, laughing at me. It's not my fault I get good grades. Can't help that I'm a well-liked student, who just happens to take an interest in learning.

Today's Wednesday, the week after classes resumed, and it's shaping up to be one of the greatest weeks of my life. Not only is class over for the day, I don't have to work at all for the remainder of the week, which leaves just my English class for Thursday, and a three-day weekend from Friday on. Life is looking up.

"So, what are we doing today? Sleep, or something productive?"

"Well my lovely friend, I was thinking sleep. And pizza."

Jade stops, yanking me back with her. "Extra cheese?"

I look her dead in the eyes. "I knew we were meant to be."

Jade can't contain her laughter. I'm right though; there is no better human on this earth who can match Jade Beckham.

"Boy am I glad you said that. I was looking forward to stripping out of these clothes, and not leaving the sofa for the remainder of the day. Unless to wee."

Amongst all the noise and people, I can hear Avery's voice and her excessive honking. I'm starting to regret that invite to let her stay over.

We hurry over to her car, Jade letting go of me and pacing to the passenger side. She has a real problem with sitting in the backseat. "Have you completely lost your mind? Stop that you wanker!" I hop into the backseat, laughing at Jade's temper. "What's so funny back there?"

"You, you psycho."

Avery turns towards the both of us. "Look the two of you wanted rides, so I'm giving you rides. Don't like it, then walk."

I butt in, now regretting not taking my car today. "Is that an option?"

She puts the car in drive and tosses her hat at me. "Shut up back there, you twit."

Ignoring her newest insult, I lay back as we take off down Trinity Lane. Avery not once stopping for the innocent people that lurk in front of us. How this woman managed to get her driving licence is something I will spend the rest of my life wondering.

I can see her and Jade sneaking peaks at me from the front mirror and am very tempted to fake sleep until we get home. But neither of these girls has ever believed in minding their own business. "Can we ask you a question back there?"

My eyes are shut now, maybe they'll see that I'm too exhausted to talk and leave it at that. Then again, they're just going to bring this conversation back up later, and I'm not in the mood to fake sleep or sick for the rest of my life.

Sitting back up, I look from Avery to Jade. "We?"

Jade turns in her seat, sliding back and forth as Avery jerks around a corner. "Yeah, Liv, we have a few questions we've been dying to ask, and now that we have you alone, and in a dangerous car that will likely kill one of us, what better time to ask."

I scold Jade. "We live together. You could've asked your questions anytime."

She looks at me, then back at Avery. "Well were asking now, so stop changing the subject." Jade turns a little more until we're facing off, clenching onto her seatbelt as Avery makes a sharp left turn. "What was going on with you during holiday? I know we had this fight already, and I stormed out, but my curiosity won't let this go. You started off bitchy and I can understand why, you just received that letter from your father right before the trip, but for the next few days, you started ditching us and going your own way. I left it alone because, for the first time since we met, you smiled the realest smile ever. I don't know what happened that made you happy that last week of our trip, but whatever it was, I am grateful. It wasn't until you went to Disneyland that killed me. You know I always wanted to go, and you went without me. That is so not the best friend's code."

Avery cuts in. "Okay, I think you're going a bit off topic there, Jade. Look Olivia, we're only curious onto what happened back there? Did you meet a guy? OMG, you met a guy, didn't you?"

I shake my head. There is no way I'm telling them about William. "No Avery, there was no guy. I was looking for this vintage shop and got lost, and somehow ended up in front of Disneyland. I never got to go in the states, so I took advantage. And I'm sorry Jade, but you guys were hours away and I didn't want to wait all day for you to make your way over to me, so I went alone. And seriously, this is what's bothering you? It's been like five weeks since I went to Disneyland, why didn't you say anything before?"

That's a lie, but I don't think they're ready for the truth.

Hell, I don't think I'm ready for the truth.

Jade turns back around, arms crossed, refusing to let go

of her anger towards me. "Because I was mad, didn't you

notice I was giving you the silent treatment?"

I think back to these last few weeks. "No, not really.

Didn't you talk to me our first night back home. You did,

we watched a few movies together."

She scoffs, but I can see her facial expression in the

mirror. She's thinking back to the first week and now

remembers she did talk to me. Jade's face turns dark red,

now more pissed than ever. Avery ignores Jades emotions

and continues with her suspicious about me. The girl won't

let up. She knows when someone has a new man in their

lives. She's like some weird bloodhound who can sniff the

scent of man on you.

I wait for Jade to unlock the door, yearning for the moment when I'll be in my room and away from these two. "Look, all we're saying is, if there's something wrong, you can always come to us. Well come to me, not her. Avery isn't very helpful in these situations."

Avery pushes her way past us, plopping down on the sofa and making herself comfortable. "I can be helpful; you lads just don't want my help.

"Avery, you went off about Olivia and a fake man for the past half hour. You're not helpful, you're horny."

I shut the door behind me, throwing my bag on the old, shabby chair in the corner. Why Jade hangs onto that old, disgusting thing, I have no idea. Without saying a word, I head for my room, walking slow and low while trying to not grab some unwanted attention.

I'm not as slick as I thought. Jade has me in her sights before I can make it past the sitting room. "Where are you going, I thought we were going to have a Who marathon? You, me, Avery, and a whole lot of Matt Smith."

I stop in my tracks. There's no way I'm staying out here with these two "I just remembered I have an essay that's due tomorrow. My teacher actually gave us homework over the break, I totally forgot to do it." I pause to read Jade's expression. Lying has always been one of my strong suits, but lying to Jade is an impossible task. "It's only meant to be four-to-six pages. I won't be long. Promise. But don't start without me. If you do, I'll never forgive you."

I turn back around, already heading for my room. The longer I stay, the easier it's going to be for her to read my mind. As soon as I pass the threshold, I shut the door, locking it behind me. Enough of that one-sided conversation.

For some reason, deep down, I feel guilt. I don't like lying, especially not to Jade. Avery, well I lie to her on a daily basis. But it's not just Jade. I don't like lying to

Emma, or anyone for that matter. I see it as unnecessary, and wrong. Why lie, when you can tell the truth? My falling out with Niall and my family helped me to develop this logic. But how do you tell your best friend you spent your vacation with one of your teachers. And not just any teacher, but the one who embarrassed you in front of the whole class. A teacher, who by the way is extremely attractive. Oh yeah, and a teacher, who is in fact, a teacher. How do I tell her this? How do you tell anyone this?

Avery would understand, but Jade, well, let's just say I'll never hear the end of it.

I strip my clothes away, getting comfortable before climbing into bed. There's just no way I'm going back out there. I hop on the bed and lay back, my feet dangling over the sides as I look up to the ceiling, counting the tiles, and staring at the spider webs. Pretty much doing anything I can to get my mind off him.

It used to be Niall. I would think about him, and what he's up to now. But not anymore, I haven't thought about him much these past few weeks. All I can think about is William. His personality, his warmth, his smile, those eyes. And his hand in mine. The comfort I felt when he stood beside me. The pleasure I felt when he laid next to me.

No, brain, stop. You can't do this. I can't have feelings for him, or for anyone.

But why can't I stop thinking about him?

I reach over for one of the bears on my bed and hold on tight to him. I need to get William out of my thoughts. My eyes close, my mind drifts. Think about anything else but him, anything else, anything else. It doesn't work, I can't stop thinking about that smile.

My eyes shoot open, and fall on the Donald Duck bear in my arms. No wonder I can't get him off my mind, I'm cuddling the gift he got me. I couldn't tell Jade the whole truth about Disneyland, because if I did, I would have to mention William. We spent almost the entire day there and he bought me a few things. The Donald and Goofy bears on my bed are just the biggest, and hardest to ignore. No wonder he's always on my mind, a piece of him lives with me.

I haven't heard from him since we parted ways on our trip. We left before he did, he decided to spend the entire Easter Holiday in France and I can't blame him. If I could afford it, so would I. Still, it's been weeks, and when he cancelled last week's class, I couldn't stop thinking about him. I wish I could, but I can't.

Man, I miss the days when I had feelings for no one. I want to go back to the old Olivia.

I bury the bears under the covers and throw myself back down. There's no way this is going to end well.

"I told you forever, didn't I?"

CHAPTER TEN

Sunday, May 15th 2016

"I'm watching you Jensen, I swear."

I watch while blond curl after blonde curl bounces up and down, as Jensen attempts to do cartwheels. I must admit; he's a million times better than he once was. Every attempt he's made in the past ended up with him tumbling to the ground as soon as he reached down to touch it.

Today the book store has been closed for what, I don't know or care. It's an amazing job to have, working around books all day long, allowed to take one book a week to keep. But working along with someone who has an obvious crush on me is a bother. Being at home with the nosy flat mate is no better, so when the Atwater's called, I almost jumped out of my seat, happy to take the job. I also was in desperate need for a distraction.

William hasn't been in class for the past four weeks. This past week he called in only minutes before class, giving us the day off since no other teacher was on call. I spent the whole day, wondering if his absences from class maybe has something to do with me.

The two of us separated on good terms. I left Paris before him and everything seemed fine, he even offered to drop me off at the airport. I thought about it, but how would that look in front of the girls, so I said no. Which is why I don't understand why he would avoid me now. Maybe I'm not the only one who feels awkward about our new friendship. Or maybe it was just a vacation thing and now that it's over, we'll go back to being complete strangers.

I hate to say what I'm about to say next, but I regret ever getting involved with William. It seemed like a good idea at first. We clicked almost instantly, which made things so easy for us. Both had horrible beginnings, crappy excuse of families and same taste in almost everything. But somewhere down the road, I started to think about him in a different way. A lot. And now here we are. With him calling in sick to evade me, and I still can't get him off my mind.

Throwing the bears in the back of my closet didn't do much to help either.

The school year is almost over, and there's no way I'll ever take another class with him, so all I have to do is get through these last few weeks and I'll be done with him for good.

But the thing is, I don't want to be done with him.

Frustrated, I throw myself back on the grass. How can I be done with him when he's the only one who can make me forget about everything? When I'm with him, I don't find myself thinking about anything else but the moment. In those two weeks together, he made life worth living again, and now there's this. Now he can't even be in the same room as me.

That's just what I needed- someone to make me feel good about myself, then leave me.

Something hits my leg, I look up to see a ball and Lily standing over it. "Can you play with me Aunt Olivia?"

I sit up, her smile making me forget everything I was just thinking about. "Of course, I'll play with you."

"Come on you two, we should be getting home before it gets too dark."

I fold up our picnic blanket and place it in the basket. Lily helps Jensen up. He's managed to get both legs in the air, before falling face first into the dirt. That I would definitely call an accomplishment.

The two run to me, both covered in dirt and mud, their entire day stained on their skin and clothes. I grab each of their hands and head towards the car. The sky grows darker, giving me indication that the day is over and tomorrow I return to school. Don't get me wrong, I have no problem with school, I just hope I don't run into a certain someone while I'm there. That's if he even shows up.

Jensen tugs on my hand, pointing off to his left. "Can we feed the ducks Auntie Olivia, please?" His eyes beg.

"You know it's time to go Jensen, but I promise you we'll come back tomorrow. You have my word."

He gives me a small smile, but disappointment clouds his eyes. If I didn't hate driving at night, I would stay longer, but it's a long way home and like I said- I hate driving at night.

I pull Jensen alongside me hand, but something off in the distance catches my eye, making me stop to stare. There's a man sitting down on a bench near the ducks. I can't make out who he is, his beanie and coat blocking off most of his face, but one thing about him stands out. His ring, the gold wedding band glows as he tosses another piece of bread out in front of him. The ring around his finger tells me everything I need to know.

William.

My gut, heart, and mind is telling me to keep walking. He obviously didn't want to see me, if he did, he would've showed up to school Thursday. But some stupid part of me is dragging my feet over to the bench. The old Olivia from before the Paris trip would've kept walking, but this new Olivia, no. The idiot walks right up to a situation she doesn't want to be bothered with.

I let go of the kid's hands and take the picnic basket out of Lily's hand. I reach in and pull out scrapes of bread from our leftover sandwiches and hand them over. "We only stay for a few more minutes, deal?"

They jump up and down from excitement. "Thank you Aunt Olivia." Lily grabs her brothers hand and runs over to the ducks, standing only a few feet away as they toss tiny clumps of bread at them.

The man stops feeding them when he sees the kids run up, his head turning slightly as he smiles at them. His blue eyes peek from under his beanie. But they're not happy. His lips smile, but there's tears in his eyes, making it harder not to approach him.

William reaches his hand out towards the kids. "Here, I think they're getting sick of me." He hands over his bread and Lily takes it, smiling and thanking him before breaking it in half and sharing it with Jensen.

My eyes bounce from William to the kids. I really should just go. "William?"

He turns around, his eyes landing on me as he gives me a weak smile. Yep this was a stupid idea. "Olivia, hey. What are you doing here?"

The next words struggle to exit my mouth. "Umm, those two kids are mine. I mean, they're the one I take care of. The ones I told you about. We just wanted to feed the ducks before we left for home."

He nods, turning back towards the ducks and not saying another word. This is my cue. "Well we should be going, it's getting dark and I have class tomorrow, so…"

I take a step forward, ready to grab the kids and run to the car and away from all this awkwardness, but a hand stops me. I look down to see William's hand in mine, gripping onto it as if he'll never hold it again.

My eyes trace his arm and land on him. He's still looking down, but he refuses to let me go. "Stay with me? Please?"

I step back, not sure what to say to him. I spent the last four weeks thinking he had his fun with me and was now done with our whole relationship. But with my hand turning red and growing numb, I think I might have jumped the gun. I never stopped to think that maybe something was wrong with him, that maybe he was sick. Gods I feel selfish.

He finally looks up, the pain in his eyes becomes unbearable and in a quick second, I'm on the bench next to him. My arms wrap around his neck, pulling him in closer. Seeing him like this kills me. He leans in, his face buried in my neck, and his arms wrapped around me tight.

Something's been bothering him all this time and all I could think of was hating him. Now I kind of hate myself.

"Auntie Olivia?"

I look over and see Lily and Jensen staring back at me, confusion written all over their faces. "Feed the ducks sweeties, we'll leave in a little, okay?"

They nod at me, turning back to their ducks. How can I go now, with him like this? I can't just leave him.

I pull him in closer, my face resting on the top of his head. I reach one hand up, pulling off his annoying beanie and run my fingers through his hair. There's no way I'm leaving him.

Usually on Sundays, the kids and I head over to my flat to help me pack my things before going back home to the Atwater's residence. I found it easier to live with them on the weekdays since Lily only goes to school for four hours and Jensen is still not enrolled. Plus, their parents work all day.

But not today.

I told Lily and Jensen I'd come over tomorrow, that tonight I had something personal to take care of. It sucks seeing the disappointment on their faces, but what else was I supposed to do? I love those kids as if they were my own, but I can't walk away from William, not after today. Before we left the park, I promised him I'd come over to his place after I dropped the kids off at home to talk. I intend to keep my promise.

The door is unlocked when I finally make it. He's more trustworthy then I.

It feels weird, being in his home, there's something unnatural, yet comforting about this whole situation. But it's a little too late for changes. I'm already in his living room.

His home is so bare. No pictures on the walls, or anywhere else in the room. Simple furniture spread out in the sitting room, a boring neutral color. This is definitely the home of a man.

"William?"

There's no answer.

I head for the stairs. "William, it's Olivia? Are you up here?"

Still no answer. I know he's here, he texted me the address and told me he was home. Why else would his door be unlocked?

Only one room upstairs has the door open, and a light peeks through. I push it open, a bed, dresser and ottoman the only things in the room. His bedroom. As bare as the rest of the house.

Another door slams. "William?" I walk into his room, the bathroom door now shut, but I can see the light coming through from under the door. "William, are you alright?"

"Yeah, no I'm fine. Sorry, I didn't know you were here."

"I called out from downstairs. You didn't hear me?"

"No, just got out of the shower. I'll be out in a minute."

I can hear rattling from the other side of the door, but can't make out what the sound is. Pill bottles? "I'll wait downstairs for you."

The bathroom door swings open. "No it's okay. Stay." He steps out of the bathroom, steam escapes from behind him, filling the bedroom. His hair still dripping wet and I find it hard to pull my eyes from him. My gaze strays from his hair down to his naked chest. I never thought about what he looked like without his clothes on, but it's hard to not wonder now. I thought he was attractive fully clothed, but now that I have this new image in my head, I have no idea what to do with it.

"Olivia?"

I snap back into reality, my eyes looking at anything but him.

"Yeah?"

"Are you alright?"

"Yeah, no, fine, just great. Not staring at anything."

I can hear him laughing at me. "I'll go put a shirt on then."

Damn it. I knew I wasn't being inconspicuous. "Yeah you do that, if you want."

He takes one last look at me, a wicked smile on his face. Stop flirting Olivia. William walks past me and the heat from his body transfers over to mine and I'm finding it hard not to grab him and throw him on the bed right now.

William fumbles around in a drawer behind me, while I force myself to look on straight. But it's harder than I thought, and I catch myself sneaking glimpses at him. He has his back to me, as he pulls a black t-shirt from the dresser. A small, but noticeable scar lies near his right hip. I open my mouth to ask how he got it, but remembered I'm not supposed to be looking at him.

He pulls the shirt over his head, turning back towards me as he struggles to get it pass his wet hair. I jerk back around, acting as though nothing happened.

"You know you'd make a terrible actor."

Eyes forward idiot. "Excuse me?"

"I know you were looking at me and I don't care if you see me. I have nothing to hide."

Might as well get this over with. I look behind me, William's on his bed now, tugging at his sweatpants as they ride up his legs. He peeks at me through the wet hair

159

hanging in front of his eyes, his smirk will be the death of me.

"What are you smiling about?"

"Olivia, I saw your awful attempt to turn around quickly. You're not as fast as you may think."

I give in. "Okay fine, I'm human, we look. Is that such a crime?"

His lips not the only thing smiling, as his eyes do that thing that makes me get lost in them. "Of course not." He pats the space next to him, inviting me to sit.

I smile back at him. "You may not believe this about me, but I'm not the kind of woman who jumps into bed with any man."

This time he laughs at me. "Says the woman who fell asleep with me in her hotel room in Paris. Four times."

"Okay, that was different and you know it. Those four times we were talking and you fell asleep. Was I supposed to move you?"

"Well this time around we're friends. Closer. And besides, it's not like that. I'm only asking you to sit, nothing else. Unless you'd rather stand the entire time, as I pour my heart out to you." He scoots back a little, reaching for a watch near the pillows. "And if I'm remembering correctly, you were the one who fell asleep the first night."

I think back to that first night, with me plastered off my ass. "Okay, that first time doesn't count, I was drunk. And friends, really?"

He looks back up at me. "You honestly think I'd ask for the other thing? What kind of a person do you take me for, Olivia?"

I shrug. He smiles, but it fades. His eyes doing that thing they did earlier in the park. I really hope he's not playing me?

I sit near the foot of the bed, keeping my distance. "Sorry, I didn't mean to accuse you of anything, it's just. You know what, never mind, it doesn't matter anymore.

So, are you going to tell me what's going on with you or am I going to have to force it out of you?"

Staring down at his hands, he refuses to look me in the eyes. He opens and closes his fist repeatedly, pain scatters on his face every time he opens it.

"William, hey, look at me. Enough, okay. Why were you crying, what's going on with you? And why weren't you in class at all these past few weeks?"

Still avoiding my glare, he looks around the room at nothing in particular. "I've been sick, still am actually. And as for the crying, it was nothing, just letting off some steam."

"You're lying to me."

He's hands shake and I don't think he has control over them anymore. I can feel this terrible shoot through my body as I move closer to him. "No I'm not. All…"

"Look at me. William, look at me."

With hesitation, he finally looks at me. "What aren't you telling me?"

He tries to throw me off with a smile. "Nothing, like I said, just not feeling well and it's starting to get to me. That's all, really."

"No one breaks down in tears, at a park, because they have a stomach ache, or whatever it is you have, so tell me the truth. What's the matter with you? No more lies."

I have him beat and he knows it, but doesn't say another word. Whatever's wrong with him, he's not telling.

Maybe I should be more sensitive, but I'm not. I hop off the bed and walk towards the door. "I left my kids to stay with you. My job, William, and you can't bother to tell me what's going on. I went out of my way and came all the way down here to make sure you were okay, and all you've done is lie to me."

I pick up my bag from behind the bedroom door, and turn back towards him. "If this was all some sick joke to get me down here so that I'd sleep with you, then I swear..."

He jumps off the bed, as pissed as I am right now. "Is that what you think? That the crying in the park, and asking you to stay with me was me trying to have sex with you? Is that your opinion on me?"

"What else am I supposed to believe? You won't talk to me, you won't tell me what's wrong, but yet here we are, hanging out in your bedroom."

"I didn't invite you over to my home Olivia, you offered to come be with me, remember? You did, not me. And how the hell could I have set this all up? I didn't know you were going to be at the park today. It was lucks chance, just like all our other meetings."

I should've read the signs; I should've known this was going to be one huge mistake. I shove William out of my way and open the door wider to storm out, and head down the stairs.

"Olivia, Olivia wait, please?"

His footsteps follow behind, running down the stairs as I speed walk to the front door. I need to get the hell out of here, before I regret everything we've done together.

"Olivia, please. Don't go, please. I'm begging you. I meant it, none of this was an evil set-up, I just wanted you here with me. Just like in Paris. I…" I can hear the desperation in his voice, but I won't look him in the eyes. For some reason, they're my only weakness and every time I look into them, I fall for his shit.

"Would you please just look at me? I'll tell you everything, just please look at me!"

"Why, so you can lie to my face again?"

"None of that was a lie, Olivia. What kind of sick pervert do you take me for?"

My hands on the knob. "I don't trust you, therefore I can't be around you. Goodbye William."

I turn the knob, and walk out the door slamming it shut behind me.

CHAPTER ELEVEN

Thursday, June 9th 2016

I find it hard not to fall asleep in this class now.

Looking down at my watch, only fifteen more minutes before I escape this hell. I look back up at the bore who drones on about the importance of periods. Periods. This man has talked about punctuation marks for the entire class, and I find myself slowly dying inside.

It's been almost a month since I last saw William, also a month since he quit his job and disappeared. I try not to think too much about him, but I fail each time. Especially when I remember we're all stuck with this new professor, while our old one quit out of nowhere.

I heard he officially quit the day after we had our big fight, which leaves me thinking I had some fault behind him leaving. But I don't care. Like an idiot, I started to trust him, and our whole time together he was using me. Everything was probably a lie. His parents, his Nana. All of it.

Damn I feel like a dumbass.

I told Jade I had to go straight to work so she wouldn't ask question after question on why I've been so gloomy lately. After a while you get sick of people questioning you and just need a break.

Today the Atwater's are visiting family in the countryside and don't know when they'll be back. Not only do I not have to work, but they also asked me if I could house sit, giving me the privacy I deserve.

I throw a quick wave at Jade who climbs into Avery's car and I climb into mine. A hand stops my door from closing.

Emma.

"Hey, you, what's up? You look like…"

"Can we talk, please?"

Well she's acting weird. Has been these past few days. "Sure, hop in. I'll give you a ride."

She runs over to the passenger side and climbs in, her face giving her away. "Emma honey, what's wrong?"

"Can we talk somewhere more private?"

I look around, and besides about two dozen kids scattered around the parking lot, there's no one around. But fighting with Emma is pointless. She doesn't give in too easily.

I sit across from a nervous and shaky Emma. She stirs her tea for the millionth time, still not drinking one drop of it. Her head darts back and forth, looking around for someone who's not there.

My hand grabs hers. "Emma, what the hell is wrong with you?"

She drops her spoon in her tea and breaks down in tears. This I was expecting. I rise from my seat and push it over to her, sitting closer so she can whisper in my ear, which is something she loves to do. I lean in closer, resting my head on hers.

"I'm pregnant."

My head snaps up, my eyes on her. "What, how, when, from who?" As soon as the words leave my mouth, I know. I've been so wrapped up in my own drama with William that I forgot about her little confession in Paris. "Jared?"

She nods, bursting into tears. The entire shop turns to us. This is not what I would call privacy. I smile at them, letting them know we're fine and pull Emma closer, so only she can hear my words. "How, I thought you were saving yourself?"

Her words are hard to understand with all the tears and muttering. "I was, it just happened. Olivia, I'm so sorry."

I stand her up, and walk outside, away from all the prying eyes. We sit in an empty set of seats, no one around to hear her dirty laundry.

"I'm not the one you should be apologising to Emma, what about Jade? Did you even talk to her like I told you to?"

She shakes her head. I should've known she wouldn't. I let her go, trying to think of some way to make this all better, but nothing comes to mind. Emma really fucked up this time.

I sit back down, forcing her to look me in the eyes. "Now listen to me, and listen good. You're going to go over to my place, and have a nice long chat with Jade. Well maybe not nice, but still, you two need to sort this out, or at least get the truth out there. Do you understand me?"

She shakes her head again, scared shitless out of her mind. And not just about talking, or betraying Jade. She's afraid to have this baby. My gods, I've been so distracted by this situation, I didn't even bother to stop and ask her how she's feeling.

I put a smile on for her, even if it's fake. "Em, baby listen. I know you're scared. Of having this baby, of losing Jade, but listen to me. No matter what, you won't be alone in this, okay, I won't leave you. No matter what happens, I'll always be here for you. I won't abandon you."

She jumps out of her seat, her arms flying around me as she rests in my lap. That I wasn't expecting.

"I'm such an idiot, Olivia, what am I going to do?"

"You'll do what you have to. That's all you can." She sit's up, her hands resting on her stomach. "Does he know Emma?"

"Yeah, I told him two weeks ago."

Wait. "You've been pregnant for more than a week now and I'm barely finding out? What the hell, Emma?"

She finally climbs out of my lap. "I was afraid, I thought you'd judge me. I thought you'd stop talking to me. All three of you."

"Did Jared? Stop talking to you?"

"No, he actually seems happy. I don't know if it's for my sake or if it's real, but he already has plans made out for us."

"Plans?"

She smiles, her teeth glowing. "He's asked me to move in with him. We even started discussing names."

It's hard for me to not get pissed. "You've been planning your life out with this man, yet you still refuse to tell Jade what you've done. Goddamn it Emma, what the hell is wrong with you?"

Her expression changes, the tears on their way back. "You're mad at me?"

"Yes, of course I'm pissed. Em, you can't go on doing this. What are you going to do when you get bigger and bigger and Jade asks you who's the father? Are you planning on lying until one of you dies? You can't keep this in, and if you do, then I'll tell her everything."

Her face falls in her hands. She knows I'm right, she just refuses to admit it.

"I'll give you until the rest of this week, but if Jade still doesn't know by Monday, then I tell her myself. Deal?"

"Okay."

"No Emma stop. You're not a kid, but you are having one and you need to woman the hell up. Stop acting so innocent and do what grownups do. You need to admit to your screw-ups and face the consequences. Do you understand me?"

She looks up, tears still clouding her eyes. "I understand."

I nod along. I don't want to get involved, but I'm starting to think I have no other choice. I can slowly feel our friendships' coming to an abrupt end.

I reach over to the napkin holder and slide it her way. "You're a mess. Clean yourself up."

She forces a smile, grabbing a napkin and heading inside to fix her face. I turn and watch her go. It's always the innocent ones that surprise you the most. Granted I wasn't expecting her to get pregnant after only dating the man for what, two months?

For all I know, I could be wrong. She could've been dating him longer and lied to me about it. She kept her pregnancy to herself for two weeks, what else is she hiding?

"Olivia?"

I look up at the man standing in the doorway of the shop, a cup in his hand and a beanie covering his face. He looks like hell. Bags under his eyes, the color has long faded from his face, but underneath that beanie and the dark circles, I can still see him.

"William?"

CHAPTER TWELVE

Thursday, June 9th 2016

"You look like shit."

He smiles down at his cup, but even that seems fake and weak. And painful. "Thanks."

"I mean it William. What the hell happened to you?"

"I told you I wasn't feeling well."

"I thought maybe you meant stomach pains, not whatever the hell this is. What's wrong with you exactly?"

He looks up, his eyes all but gone behind the circles. "Nothing serious, just some bug going around. It might be the flu."

"Or the black plague."

That makes him laugh. From the look of him, I don't think he's laughed since we last spoke.

After I took Emma to Jared's, I met up with William in the park. Planted near the ducks, his favorite spot. I don't know if this is some flu, or something worse, but whatever it is, I hope it goes away, and soon. I hate seeing him this way.

"How have you been?"

"I'm not the one who looks like I'm about to die William."

"Yeah, well, I'm sick of talking about myself. Please, just humour me."

I look him up and down. This can't just be a flu. "I'm fine William, really."

He looks back over at the ducks, tossing them a piece of bread to fight over. "Good, I'm glad you're okay." He hesitates, scared to say what he's about to say. "I've missed you Olivia. A lot."

Here comes the guilt. Here I was, again, thinking everything was about me, while he wasted away at home. Alone.

God Olivia, get your head out of your ass for six minutes.

"I never thought I'd see you again. Watching you walk away from me that day…" He trails off, his mind reliving our last moment together. "That's when I realised that I've lost you."

He plays around with his cup of tea, turning it around and around in his hands. I knew there was something between us, but I never stopped to think that maybe while I was developing feelings for him, he was developing the same feelings for me.

"Why did you quit your job William?"

He chuckles. "Not because of you, if that's what you're wondering."

"Answer the question William."

He finally looks over at me, guilt spreading through my body. "I'm done teaching Liv. This isn't what I wanted, not forever anyways. I don't want to spend the rest of my life teaching English to a bunch of people who don't listen to me half the time."

"I listened."

"One person, Olivia?"

This time I look away. "Sometimes one's better than nothing."

He turns back to his ducks, throwing another piece of bread into the group. "I know."

Change the subject Livia. "Okay, I give in. If you don't want to teach anymore, then what do you want?"

He pauses, sneaking a glance at me, before looking back at his cup. "Honestly?"

"Honestly?"

He sits up straight, making a face that tells me even moving hurts him. I reach over to him, forcing him to stop before he makes things worse. In a quick instant, he grabs

my hand, his frozen touch against my warmth feels weird.

It's been so long since I've touched any part of him. I look

down at our hands, wrapping his one cold hand into both of

mine and pulling him closer to me. Through the pain and

sadness, his eyes manage to smile.

I love it when they do that.

He grips my hands tighter. "You."

"What?"

"All I want is you."

Watching him sleep brings me joy. In his sleep, he

seems so peaceful, so full of life. I wish that would spill

into his everyday life. Maybe he doesn't know it himself,

but there is something wrong with him, and I won't let this

go until we find out what it is.

As soon as I got him home and in bed, he drifted off to

sleep. It's good, seems like he needed it. Badly. He made

me promise I'd stay, at least until he woke up. I don't think he likes being alone.

Another thing we have in common.

Without waking him, I rise from my position on the bed next to him, moving slowly and carefully. The last thing he needs is to be bothered. I tiptoe out of the room and head downstairs, not sure what I hope to find. This isn't a normal home. If I didn't know the owner, I would think this was a newly furnished home, ready to be put on the market. No pictures, or lamps. The furniture all boring and neutral colored with no pillows or throws to decorate them. No rugs, or a dining table, but there is one sad little barstool in the corner near the counter. I can see he doesn't have much company over. I thought maybe, there would at least be a picture or two of himself with his Nana, but nothing. Perhaps he still hasn't truly moved on.

It feels wrong, walking around his house, snooping, trying to find anything that gives me a glimpse into who he is. He told me about his early life and his parents, but I still feel like there's so much more he's keeping from me, and I can't help but feel angry about that. I told him everything and still we seem like strangers. Maybe he doesn't trust me after all. Or maybe I'm just jumping to conclusion again. No, from here on out, I plan on giving him the benefit of the doubt before accusing him of anything else.

Seriously, all that's done for me so far is make me look like a fool. Twice.

Before I can take a seat on the sofa, I hear a loud thud come from upstairs. "William? William, are you alright?"

When he doesn't answer, I run up the stairs, pushing the door open, I see him lying on the floor, struggling to get back up.

"Oh my god, what the hell happened? Are you alright?"

He rolls over on his side, the same pain in his eyes. "Yeah, fine. Fun fact about me, I tend to move a lot in my sleep. It's not the first time I've fallen out of bed."

"That would've been nice to know about you before you let me put you to sleep."

"You can't stop me from rolling out of bed Olivia."

"No, but we could've put pillows down to break your fall. You know, less pain."

He stops to think about that, embarrassed that he hasn't thought of that before. "That's not a bad idea, actually."

I shake my head, helping him back onto the bed. "Are you sure you're alright?"

"I'm fine Olivia, really. A little disappointed, that's all."

"Disappointed? In what?"

He smiles at me; the William I know hidden somewhere behind his new sickly appearance.

"You. You said you'd be here when I woke up. You weren't."

It's hard not to mirror his smile. "Wow, how old are you again?"

"Hey, I'm not the one making promises I don't keep."

184

"Back in bed, now. Go on, move it."

He obeys, climbing back under the covers. "I'm not sleepy anymore."

"Do as I say and lay down. Now."

Without hesitation, he lays back down, but doesn't close his eyes. He stares up at the ceiling, somewhat looking a little better, but still a far away from normal.

I climb over him, laying in the empty spot to his left. His hand reaches out to me, grabbing mine and pulling me closer to him. I slide over until my head rest on his shoulder. His arms wrap around me, holding onto me tighter than ever. My face inches away from his chin, taking in every detail of his face.

Even sick and pale, he still manages to look irresistible. Other than his eyes and his dimples, I never noticed his other features, but lying here with him, I can't help myself. He has that perfect, classic British face. The ones with the stunning cheekbones and strong jawlines. The kind that could kill you with one head-butt. And his lips, his extremely, kissable, bite-able lips.

Why have I not noticed this about him before.

"Olivia?"

I come out of my daydream and notice I've been staring at him the entire time. No way I'm getting out of this without lying.

"What are you thinking about?"

Maybe I should stop beating around the bush. It's been years since I've been with anyone, and being in this bed right now, lying beside him feels so right. And I'm desperate not to let go.

"Honestly? I've kind of been wondering what your lips taste like since that first night in my hotel."

This throws him off guard. He's usually the open, playful one, the one who doesn't care what anyone thinks. I'm more reserved, especially when it comes to men. After

Niall, I stopped talking to men, so I guess I kind of gotten a little awkward around them.

But not William. He brings the old Olivia out of me. The happy Olivia.

His smile widens, pleased with my openness. "There's only one way to find out."

Wanting the old, boring Olivia to die, I make the first move, climbing on top of him and pressing my lips against his. While the rest of his body may be freezing cold, his lips aren't, and they taste exactly how I thought they would.

It's been a long time since I've kissed anyone, and the wait has been worth it. I used to think choosing a life alone was the smartest move I could make, but lying here with William, I realise that was the stupidest decision anyone could ever make. Yes, I was protecting my heart, but from what? Just because one stupid man broke my heart, doesn't mean they all will. Then again, waiting was a smart move. Of all the men I've met since I left home, not one of them did for me what William can. He made me feel wanted, and safe, and special with just one look in his eyes. It was worth the wait.

He's worth the wait.

I pull away from him. "Wait, William, stop."

He doesn't let me go. "What is it? What's wrong?"

I grab onto his hands, still planted in my hair and pull them off me, sitting up on his chest. "You're sick, that's what's wrong. The last thing we both need is two sick people who have no idea what their sickness is."

He lays back down, frustrated, but still smiling. "Alright, fine. But if I'm being honest, I'm feeling quite better."

Feeling like a little girl again, I can't stop myself from smiling. What started out as a casual conversation, turned into an unusual friendship and that somehow blossomed into an incredible relationship.

I lean over, my hands rustle through his hair, as I plant a soft kiss on his forehead, his hands find their way to my hips. I don't know where we go from here, or how serious it is for either one of us, but there is one thing I know for a fact.

This is one relationship I know I'll never forget.

CHAPTER THIRTEEN

Saturday, June 18th 2016

"See you Saturday, Liam."

I skip down the steps of the bookstore, happy that my shift is over, but annoyed I'm going home.

Ever since I told Jade about William, it's been non-stop questioning day after day. Gushing over men and talking about them isn't me. I always had better things to do and sitting around drinking wine, and talking about the size of a man's penis, doesn't fall on the list.

Going home last Saturday was like an ambush. She was waiting for me with Avery and Emma at the ready, their questions pouring out as soon as I opened the door. Avery, being the nosy person that she is, looked into a William

Edwards at school, hoping maybe I met him in a class or something. Let me just say, they were shocked to discover he was no student, but a teacher.

When I walked in my flat, they were passing her mobile around, smiles smeared all over their faces. Avery found a picture of him at school, and took a picture, eager to show the rest of the girls. They giggled like a batch of five-year-old's. I wonder if this is what women do in real life?

There was no avoiding their questions, and trying to sneak away from them and hide in my bedroom didn't work either. They pounded on my door until I finally caved in. It was easier to just answer their stupid questions, even though I didn't want to. Maybe it's me, but I believe that any relationship should be between two people. Not a woman and a group of her sex starved friends. Once the questions got too personal, I kicked them out and forced myself to fall asleep. There are some things best kept private.

I head for my car, thinking maybe I should just stay at the Atwater's. They told me they didn't care if I lived with them full-time, they preferred it. I'm more than a nanny to those kids, more like the older sister they cling to. At least at their house I can get some sleep, no one's going to bother me with an endless list of who I'm sleeping with.

Before I can get out my mobile to reach them, giving them a heads-up to say I'm staying another night, I look up to see a few dozen roses on my windshield.

Please tell me I don't have some creepy admirer.

I reach over for the small card peeking out from the top and flip it over. It reads 'Turn around.'

I do as the card says, which probably isn't the smartest idea, but my fear soon passes. William sits on the bench a foot away from where I parked, very pleased with himself.

"Well, well. And here I thought you disappeared on me. Again."

He stands up, the smile still glued on his stupid face, and pulls me in for a bear hug. I want to stay angry, but I can't, not with him. I don't know how he does it. "I can explain everything."

I push him away, trying to stand my ground, but the push was so weak and playful, he winds up laughing at me.

"It's not funny, you ass. Where the hell have you been? I was calling you all week."

His arms wrap around me again, this time holding on tighter so I can't push him off. But this time I don't try. I missed him more than he's missed me.

He talks through a face full of my hair. "I went home to Northumberland. Stayed the entire week. This… flu took a turn for the worst and I felt horrible, so I went straight to the hospital." He stops talking, his lips finding their way down to my neck. This is why I can't stay mad at him. One little kiss from him, and I forget how to breath.

It's not bad though, I see it as more of an honor to be able to kiss these lips every day. "And you don't have to worry, I had a nurse with me the entire time. I took my medicine and now I feel like a brilliant."

I pull away, my face telling him everything he needs to know.

"It was a male nurse Liv, I swear. You think I'd be stupid enough to be alone with another woman?"

"It's hard to imagine you being faithful when you leave for a week, don't tell your girlfriend where you are, ignore all her calls and just pop back up whenever you feel like it. So, yeah, sorry if I feel a little… you know."

"Xavier Clark and Sebastian Holmes."

"Who are they?"

"My doctor for the past six years and the nurse he sent to look in on me. Would you like me to give you the name and address to the hospital too? Perhaps their home addresses?"

I give him a crooked smile. "Are you making fun of me?"

He mimics my smile. "A little." I turn towards my car, making him think I'm ready to leave. "Okay, okay, you win. I'm sorry I didn't call you. I'm sorry I ignored your calls, but it wasn't on purpose. I was drugged for most of the week. Honestly, I don't remember one thing. Would you look at me, please? I'm sorry. There's no way I would ever cut you off, or ignore you. I thought me going away was for the best, I didn't want to get you sick. And I knew if I would've stayed, you'd would've took care of me and I didn't want you missing your last week of school."

I turn away from him, taking what feels like hundreds of flowers, and putting them in the backseat of my car.

"Olivia…"

I cut him off before he can finish his plea. "I'm hungry. You want to get something to eat?"

"You've lived in England for four years now and you're telling me you still haven't tried plum pudding?"

I laugh at my admission. "It's not that big of a deal babe. It's just food."

"Do you have any idea how insulted I am right now?"

Moving in closer to him, I wrap my arm around his hip.

"What, it was hard for me to go years of eating American food and then move all the way across the world and discover new foods I've never heard of. I think you're making a big deal out of this, I tried it tonight and it wasn't that bad."

"Wasn't that bad? Wow, you have no heart, do you?"

I can't contain my laughter. I had no idea he'd get so upset over one little European dessert. It's cute to see him so upset. "Next you're going to tell me you've never tried mincemeat pie."

This would be a great time to change the subject. "So where too next?"

His eyes find their way down to me, doing that thing I love. "Anywhere you want to go love. It's your date. I'm just here to hold your hand and call you beautiful."

I tip my head backwards; my eyes rest on his lips. "Well in that case, I think we should walk around all of Europe." I stand on my toes, my lips brush against his chin. He leans down, making it easier for me to reach his lips.

I pull only slightly away, our lips still touching. I have a better idea. "Or we could just go back to your place. It is getting rather late."

He laughs, which sends a strong, overwhelming vibration throughout my body. "I was hoping you'd say that."

"I swear it was just a horrible, horrible flu. I'm better now, can't we just move past it?"

I wish I could, but apparently, I can't. "I know. It's just, I don't understand why you didn't tell me before you left.

What would you do if it was me who was sick, and I disappeared for a week to recover and failed to tell you? Go on, I'm curious."

He turns away from me, doing his best to hide his guilt. "Okay, alright. You're right, I would be slightly upset if you went away for a week and didn't tell me. But I would forgive you, because that's what you do when you care about someone."

"William, not even you believe that."

"No, I don't, it's call lying Olivia. Yeah, I'd be rather angry with you, but I would forgive you. Especially after finding out you were okay."

Gods, I hate him and his perfectness sometimes. "Yeah, yeah, I know. I'm not mad at you, not anymore. I'm just a little disappointed, that's all. Just ignore me."

"I could never ignore you. I love you too much."

My heart stops. My whole body stops, including my brain. Neither one of us have ever said that word before.

Not to each other. I haven't heard those words since my last day with Niall. Something about hearing them again, and coming from William's mouth. I can't control myself.

"What did you just say?"

"The ignore you part, or the love you part?"

I stammer. "The love part."

He gives me his sly grin. "Are you shocked?"

"Little bit, yeah."

He takes my hands in his, pulling me closer to him. "Well it's true, I love you Olivia. Maybe it's too soon for you, but not for me. Truth is, I've known since Paris, I just wasn't sure. The whole, never loved anyone before part, confused me in the beginning. I didn't know if it was love, or if I was just really horny."

I don't know whether to laugh or cry. Maybe a bit of both? I knew we had something deeper, and I credit our time spent in Paris to getting us to where we are now, but never did I ever think he would utter those words. And so soon.

Is it soon? I think it is? Is it?

"Well, say something."

"Um."

"That doesn't count as a word Olivia. Hey, you don't have to be awkward about this, it's just my feelings. It's not like I'm expecting you to love me back."

But I do. "I love you too."

"What?"

I can't believe my own words. But they are true, and the world is starting to get scary again.

"I love you too. I wasn't sure what it was then, but this past week, not hearing anything from you, scared me. I couldn't stop thinking about you, or where you were. I couldn't get you off my mind, every thought was about you, because I love you. I just needed to hear you say it first."

Everything in this moment feels so right. I love him, and that's one of the scariest feelings one can feel. But it sure feels damn good to feel it again.

William moves to the edge of the bed, his hands on my waist as he pulls me towards him, trapping me between his legs as we wrap our arms around each other. His lips on my chin.

"I love you too Olivia Fitzgerald."

CHAPTER FOURTEEN

Tuesday, July 16th 2016

"You know you don't have to go. There's this new thing that people have been doing, and this is just a rumor I've heard of, but it's called faking sick so you don't have to go to work. It's apparently supposed to be the new 'fad.'"

I lean in, aiming for his forehead but getting his lips instead. "First of all, please never do the air quotations ever again. Seriously, or I will be forced to leave you. And for your information, there's also this thing called, 'I need a job, because money doesn't grow on trees, and I have to pay my half of the rent.' Oh, almost forgot, there's also this thing called, 'paying for Uni.' We weren't all left with money to live off."

He jerks back, pulling his lips away from mine. "Wow, low blow Liv."

I pull back, propping up on my elbow as I take in the sight of William. I love seeing him like this, messy haired with an unkempt beard. He looks so human, so ordinary. So unusual from his normal look of perfection.

He looks on, his eyes resting on his Hamlet poster in the corner of the bedroom, anything to keep his eyes from mine. Even under his scruffy look, I can still see his perfect jawline, clenching and unclenching, like there's something on his mind.

Looking past him, my eyes fall on the clock. 1:14pm. I let out a long, annoyed sigh, wanting nothing more than to stay in bed for the rest of the day, or year, with William, but I know I can't. Not while work awaits me.

I sit up, and look out through the only window in the bedroom. The window with the mediocre view. If I squint hard enough, I can see Big Ben off in the distance. It may be far away, but it's still better than the shitty view of the flats across from mine. My view proudly displays my overweight neighbour, the one who prefers walking around naked in front of his windows.

"I didn't mean it, you know." I turn back towards William. "I wasn't trying to insult you, or call you a rich brat. It's just not many people are like you babe, some of us weren't given a comfy little rainy day nest egg to live off. Us unfortunate ones, need to work to live comfortably. Like myself, who has to watch two lovely children and work at a bookstore, where I'm pretty sure the owner and my co-worker have massive crushes on me."

I can hear his uneven breaths. He's either clearly upset that I'm leaving, or maybe it's the money I now regret mentioning.

Since the day we've made things official, we've been inseparable. I spend most of my days and nights with William. I've used his advice a few times to get out of work, choosing to stay with him instead of going to either of my jobs, but eventually they're going to catch on and the last thing I need is to be jobless.

We've been together for about four months as friends, and been dating for more than one. I guess we found ourselves drawn to each other, and not just in a passionate, constantly having sex way. No, there is much more beneath the surface. Much more than I, or William have ever felt.

Laying back on my side, I sneak a few glances up to William, who's eyes have yet to meet mine.

I reach over, my fingers lost in his hair. "Well say something then."

He closes his eyes, concentrating on something hidden away in his mind. Something hidden away from me. Something that's best to keep buried deep.

"What is it you want me to say? Do you want me to tell you I'm pissed that you literally just called me a spoiled brat? Or maybe you want me to apologise for keeping you from your lovely jobs, particularly the one where you have two men constantly ogling you? Or maybe you want me to admit that I hate it when you're not here? Because I do. I can't clarify how much it pains me to see you leave. Or to have to wait for you to finally come home. Or the fact that I…"

He stops midway through his sentence, ashamed that he let my words get him so angry, but still holding his ground.

Remorse fills my throat. "Is that really how you feel?"

He lets out a long, deep breath. "Does it matter?"

I tug on his hair, but he doesn't push me away. "Kind of does."

His eyes finally open, but still they reject to notice me. "You should get going, you don't want to be late."

"Are you going to be okay?" I question, my hair still dripping wet from the shower, the steam heating up the bedroom, making it hard to see. "Because you don't seem

206

like you're going to be okay, and I don't want to leave things like this."

William turns from me, lying flat on the bed, his face buried in the pillows. "I'll be fine. Have fun at work, yeah? I'll see you Friday night." His voice barely recognizable.

"Can you at least look at me?" He refuses, not budging an inch.

I walk over to his side of the bed, bending over as my hands find his waist, and my lips rest on his back. "I love you William, no matter how pissed off you may be right now." I whisper into his back. Straighten up, I pick up my bags, one handbag and one duffel, choosing to spend the rest of the week at the Atwater's.

He whispers softly enough for me to hear it, even though there's still some irritation in his voice. "I love you more."

I turn around, his face still hiding from me, but I can't help smiling nevertheless. Even when we're angry at one another, we still manage to stow our feelings long enough to reassure each other that we are still very much in love.

Looking from my duffel, and back at William, I drop it on the floor, kicking it back into the closet. "I'll be home around nine." One foot is already out the door when my mobile rings.

Expecting it to be the Atwater's, I pull it from my back pocket, and am a bit surprised to see it's Avery on the other side.

"Avery? Is everything alright?" I don't think I've ever gotten a call from her. We have never been that good of friends. The only reason we hang around each other is because of Jade and Emma.

"Liv, you have to get home. Right now. It's an emergency!"

I was never one to take Avery very serious. Especially since she's known as the loose one and the practical joker. "Why, what's going on?"

"Believe me, it's easier if we do this in person, just hurry."

"Avery, tell me what's wrong right now. If this is another one of your jokes, then I don't have the time. I need to get to work."

Something in the background drops and shatters. Maybe this is much more serious than I thought. "Olivia, please, for the first time since we've met, I'm telling the truth. It's Jade, something bad has happened and I need you down here to calm her down. Please, liv."

Jade would never help Avery with a joke, she hates them more than I do, especially when she's always the victim.

"I'm on my way."

I hang up the phone and stare at it as if it could give me all the answers I want.

"Babe, what's wrong?" I turn to see William sitting up on the bed, concern spreading across his face.

"I don't know. That was Avery, she said somethings wrong with Jade and to please hurry."

"Alright, let's go."

"Wait, what? No, you don't have to do that. It's probably just some girl issues. I'll just pop over there real quick before heading to work."

"From the look on your face, I can tell it's more than 'girl issues', so I'm coming. We can fight about this in the car, but it's not going to stop me."

I stare him down, eager to get him back into bed and head home, but William isn't one of those people you can win against.

The only thing I hate about him.

"What did they say?"

"They told me to take my time. Today is only date night, and it's fine if they're a little late to the restaurant. Mrs. Atwater has always told me to handle my personal affairs before doing anything else. British people. Always so polite and noble."

William reaches over to my side of the car, taking my hand in his. "You say that like it's a bad thing."

I pull his hand up to my lips, kissing it softly. "It's not a bad thing. It's just different from what I'm used to."

"Whatever you say, lo…" Something cuts him off, his attention on whatever's in front of him. "Olivia, love, is that the bear I got you?" Following his gaze, my eyes widen when I see Avery on the street, picking up what looks like all my belongings.

Something in me stirs. I'm pissed, but I don't know why I'm pissed. "Pull the car over."

"Olivia there's no…"

"Just pull the damn car over!"

He looks me over before stopping the car in the middle of the street, cars behind us honk as I climb out. A million angry thoughts race through my head as I run up to Avery.

"What the hell is this? Why is all my stuff laying out here on the streets?"

Avery gets to her feet. Most of my belongings still stuffed in her arms. "Jade knows Liv. About Emma. About Jared. About you. Emma told her over the phone a few hours ago. After throwing the phone across the room, she started to lash out and threw all your things in the streets." She pauses, staring at something behind me before finishing. "I think you should get up there, before your whole bed is throw out the window."

William walks up from behind me, his hand on the small of my back. "Go on love, I'll get the rest of your things."

The door to the flat is wide open, a split going down the middle, I expect, from the lamp that lays between my legs.

"Jade, what in the hell are you doing? Are you mad? You can't just throw people's stuff out on the street, especially when this happens to be my flat as much as it is yours."

She doesn't budge. Instead she turns towards the pictures of herself, me, and the rest of the girls, and tears them off the wall. I want to be mad at her, but a piece of me can't. Her heart is broken, and I don't think there's anything I can do to mend it.

That doesn't mean I'm going to let her continue to destroy my property. "Jade don't ignore me, that's just being childish. Turn around and talk to me."

She moves on to another wall, this time only pictures of her and me remain.

"Goddamn it Jade, what is it you want me to say? Do you want me to apologise for not telling you about Emma and Jared? It wasn't my place. If anything, the truth needed to come directly from her, not me."

I know I should be a little more sensitive, but she did just throw everything I owned in the streets, so… "Listen, I get that you're mad, but if I were in your shoes, I think I'd be angrier with the person directly responsible for screwing your ex." That did not come out right. "Sorry, just, try to see my role in this. Your anger shouldn't be towards me. As much as I love Emma, she was the one who made the mistake. She was the one who made that choice, not me. None of this is my fault, I was the one who made her confess the truth to you. I was the one who told her the whole situation wasn't okay. I thought I was protecting the both of you, and I'm sorry, but I don't feel bad for not telling you. This is between you, Emma, and Jared and I won't get sucked into this."

"You won't get sucked into this?" Jade turns, blood on her hands and tears in her eyes. "You secured your role in this the day, the very first day you chose to protect Emma over me. I was supposed to be your best friend Olivia, not her, me, and you lied to me. You kept this from me. A secret you knew would destroy me. I would never, ever have done anything like that to hurt you. Never." She takes the picture resting in her hands and rips it down the middle. "You sat here, laughing and living with me, all the while you were keeping things from me. How do you expect me to feel?"

"I did what I thought was right, and I'm sorry that you can't see that. But none of this changes the fact that this is my flat too. My name is on it along with yours, and you have no right to throw my things out."

Tossing the ripped pieces aside, she takes a step forward but stops suddenly. "I won't live with someone I don't trust."

I take a step forward, but unlike her I don't stop. "That still doesn't give you the right to touch my stuff Jade!"

"Olivia?"

William stands in the doorway; his eyes bounce around the room. "We should go. You don't want to be late."

My eyes meet Jade's, the tears still pouring down her face. We met four years ago in a café, both of us looking for a flat mate, neither having much luck. Four cups of earl grey, and a plate full of biscuits brought us together. We were sisters, perhaps more than that, but as they say- nothing last forever.

I turn back to William and he nods, he sneaks one last look around the flat before reaching his hand out for me to take ahold of.

I take it and without turning around I speak my last words. "Goodbye Jade."

Olivia,

I can't believe I'm doing this, after all this time, I come to you with a letter of all things. Trust me, this isn't the way I wanted things to go, I would rather do this face-to-face, and a huge part of me hopes we still can, but it's been a very long time, and I know we're not the same people we were and I would totally understand if you blew me off.

God it's been so long Liv. I find myself reliving the past so often, wondering what you've been up to. Whatever you're doing I know it's huge. You were always the thinker and doer. The type of person who went after what they wanted and never let anyone stand in their way. I always did love that about you. Your passion and commitment is what made me the person I am today. Your energy would flow out from your veins and latch onto those nearest you. I miss you Liv. Each and every fucking day.

217

There's so much I want to know, like are you still in school? What about your major? You haven't changed that have you? I know I'm going to be there soon, but how's England? Is it as cold as people say it is? I know I probably shouldn't even ask you this question, but do you ever think of me? No scratch that, I have no right to ask you a question like that. But know that I miss you, and think about you every day. If I'm being honest, you occupy about 99.8% of my thoughts. I always wonder what you're doing. If you're safe and secure. Are you happy? Because that's all I ever wanted for you. Even if I wasn't the one spending the rest of my life with you, I still want you to be happy. I want you to feel loved and wanted, since I failed in that region.

I am sorry Liv. The last thing I ever wanted to do was hurt you.

I don't know if your dad, or maybe Delphine told you, but I'm coming down your way, because we both know

218

your mom would never, ever tell you. Four years and

nothing about that woman has changed.

I don't know if you keep in contact with any of your

family, but I ran into your mother a few months ago. And of

course, she was her usual devil self. I knew I wasn't going

to get anything out of her, so I went to talk to Delphine.

When I went over to your house, a piece of me hoped

maybe you found your way back. Your mother answered the

door and as soon as she saw my face, oh you should've

seen it Liv. If looks could kill, I would've burst into flames.

She still hates me, no shock there right.

Anyways, off the topic of evil parents, I have some

business to take care of in England for the next couple of

weeks and I would love to see you. If that's alright with

you.

It's been too long and I don't think I can go another

year without hearing your voice, or seeing your face. I

know I made mistakes in the past and I've been a total

asshole, but I'm ready to fix it. I'm dying to fix it, Olivia.

What I did can never be forgiven, and you would be an

idiot if you forgave me, but please, please just give me a

chance. All I need is just a few minutes of your time to

explain the shit I've done. All I'm asking for is a second

chance, I know I don't deserve it, but I'm begging you.

Please. Let me make this right.

P.S. I miss you Olivia Fitzgerald.

Thinking of you,

"There are all kinds of love in this world but never the

same love twice."

F. Scott Fitzgerald.

CHAPTER FIFTEEN

Sunday, July 31st 2016

Niall Parker

Suite 208

*I thought it would be too hard to see you face-to-face, so
please forgive me for writing you this letter instead.*

*Where do I even begin? It's not every day someone's ex
writes to them out of the blue, begging to meet up,
especially considering the way we ended things.*

*For years, I imagined the things I would say to you. I
imagined the way I'd react to seeing your face again. In
every scenario, it ended with me breaking your nose, or
kicking you so hard in the nuts, you wouldn't be able to*

walk for a week. But I couldn't. No matter how much shit

you put me through, I could never hurt you. Maybe the old

Olivia from back home, but not the Olivia from England.

To answer your questions- yes, I'm doing great. Yes, I'm

still in school, and no I haven't changed my major. And

yes, I very much DO love England. (Quite cold here

though!) There is so much more I wanted to say, things I

wanted to get off my chest, things that were eating me alive,

but not anymore. I've grown and feel no need to lash out,

or attempt to hurt (or kill) you.

I know you wanted to meet up in person so that you

could explain yourself, but the truth is, I don't need for you

to explain anything to me. You did what you did, only you

(and my mother) know why, and I think it's best to keep it

that way. Hearing the truth would only bring up old

feelings of pain and abandonment, and I can't go through

that again. We can't go back to that day, nor should we.

We're different people now, and I'm content with my new

life, and couldn't be happier. Some of the best things that could ever happen to me has happened here in Europe and I love it. So please, don't tell me the real reason why you left, it will only hurt to relive. And it would only make me hate you all over again.

You should know- I've met someone. His name is William, and he's... Niall, he's one of the greatest things to happen to me. I can't explain it, nor do you probably want to hear it, but I love him, and I couldn't imagine a life without him.

For what It's worth, you will always have a place in my heart. You were my first love and my first kiss. You were my best friend, and I'll never forget you. But eventually, we all move on in our lives. It hurts to start off as strangers, become friends, then to fall madly in love with each other, only to wind up becoming strangers again.

I really do hope you're well, and happy. I wish we could meet, or speak in person, but I'm still not yet ready for that.

Not just yet

P.S. I do miss you Niall. I always will.

Olivia

It took me five days to make up my mind. I thought writing a farewell letter was easier than having an awkward, in person conversation with a man I once loved.

I exit the Corinthia Hotel of London, the same hotel Niall told me he would be staying at on my voicemail. I ignored that call on purpose.

I left the letter with the main desk, asking them to send it up to him as soon as they could. I just want to get this over with. I want the chapter of Niall and I, the same one that's been repeating on a loop, to come to its close. It's been too long and its simply time to move on.

'It's better this way.' I've been telling myself that since I first clicked the pen. Maybe it sounds like I'm not moving on, maybe it sounds like I'm being childish, but we ended with a letter. Perhaps it's time to end everything for good with another letter. That and I'm still not entirely ready for a reunion between the two of us. I don't know if I'll ever be ready.

After my fight with Jade, and my storming down the stairs of my old flat, I found my mail in one of the boxes Avery shoved in the back of William's car for me. Niall's letter was at the very bottom, half crumpled, half ripped. It took me a while to finally look at any of my mail. Losing one of my closet friends sent me into a deep depression. Well, more like an angry depression.

I could possibly be wrong about this, but I still feel no guilt for not getting involved in other's problems. I preferred sitting back and letting them handle their own issues. I have my own family and ex-boyfriend drama to deal with. And half the time I don't want to deal with that.

I stroll down the sidewalk, taking my time on getting back home. I wanted to be done with the letter. I spent so much time and energy on what I should say and how I should say it, that it created a rift between William and I. Exactly how do you tell your current boyfriend that you're writing a very deep letter to your ex-boyfriend without causing a rupture in your relationship. The last thing I want is to lose William, and I absolutely refuse to let Niall be the one who destroyed another relationship for me. I must tell him.

I'm going to tell him; I'm just struggling to come up with how I should explain to him why I've been quiet and sketchy for the past few days. Also, why I ran off so suddenly two hours ago. He doesn't know about my letter or Niall's.

I don't think us moving in together was the right thing to do either. It'll just complicate things move then they already are. He wanted me around more, and now he has me permanently. Clever bastard.

My idea was to stay with the Atwater's permanently, after the whole Jade incident, it's what they wanted from the very beginning, but I chose not to. My second job was much closer to my old flat. That and I didn't have a car then either, and as much as I loved riding the tube, it was just a hassle. But when William recommended, sorry, commanded I move in with him, there was no fighting. Half my stuff was unpacked when I came home from work. I thought it would be tricky, the two of us living together, after only being together for a month's time, but somehow we've made it work. But keeping a secret like this from him will only end in another fight. A fight neither one of us wants. Coming clean is the only option here. If only I could find a perfect way to do that.

"William, babe, I have dinner. It's your favorite. You know, from that little Italian place around the corner."

There's a silence, which is unusual from a person like him. "Babe, are you up there?"

I place the bags of food on the dining table, and shrug off my coat, throwing it aside. I take a quick peek, waiting for him to come down the stairs.

When I see nothing, my mind starts to wander.

"William? William, are you home?"

Still no answer.

"William, can you hear me? I said I brought dinner? Babe?"

It could be me, seeing as I tend to jump to conclusions so quickly, but every time I walk through the front door, William's down the stairs in an instant to greet me. He could be in the shower, or he could be out, which is very unlikely since his car is parked right out front.

I pace up the stairs, he has to be home. Besides myself, I don't think he has any friends or anyone else for that matter. He never talks much about that part of his life.

Before I can reach the door, something beneath my shoe makes a tiny little crunching sound, kind of like the sound you make when you step on a piece of paper. Taking a step back, I bend over to see this small, white, circular wrapper just underneath me. Another one lies right before me, leading into the bedroom.

"William?"

The door squeaks open, the room littered with the same wrappers. The pale blue lamp on Williams side of the bed knocked over, a million pieces scattered across the floor. Panic starts to flood my body, so many thoughts sprinting through my mind.

"William, where are you?"

The bed is in disarray, more of those wrappers lie near the bathroom door. My fear arises as soon as I spot his keys on the ottoman resting at the foot of the bed. Since William has no family, or friends, or hobbies now that I come to think of it, he tends to stay home. A lot. Not one for social gatherings I guess. Which can mean only one thing.

I run back down the stairs and snatch up my bag. Heading back up the steps, I reach into my bag and pull out my mobile, but before I can call anyone I see that there are ten missed calls. Eight from William, two from another number I don't recognize. How could I possibly miss ten calls and not notice anything? Was I that wrapped up with Niall that I could be this careless?

Picking the phone back up, I call William first, ignoring the number I don't know, but he doesn't answer. Even on call number fourteen, he still doesn't pick-up, which only makes my worst fear grow deeper.

I take a chance and dial the other number back, praying that they answer, and hoping that it has something to do with William.

"St. Thomas' Hospital, how may I redirect you?"

Hospital? That can't be good.

"Yes, I've received two missed calls from this number, but I think you might have called me by mistake."

"What was your name, ma'am?"

"Olivia. Olivia Fitzgerald."

"One moment, ma'am."

Without even trying, this day just somehow got worse. One moment I'm finishing and sending off one of the hardest letters I've ever had to write, and now this. A random call from a hospital, a messy scene in our bedroom, and now a missing William.

"Ms. Fitzgerald?"

"Yes, yes, I'm still here."

"You were called because you were listed as an emergency contact for a, Mr. William Edwards. Do you know this man?"

"Um, yes, he's my boyfriend. Did something happen to him?"

"I think it's best if you come down and talk to his doctor yourself. I don't think I should be the one to talk to you about his condition."

"Condition? What condition?"

"I'm sorry ma'am, but you should get down here. I don't have the answers for you."

I sit in the chair opposite his bed, my entire body curled up in a fetal position. The same position I've been in for six hours. I can't see it myself, but I know my face is soiled under rivers of tears, and my mind, for the first time in my lifetime, is completely blank.

My heart must've stopped a thousand times since I've entered this room. The bland white walls start to cave in, making it harder and harder to breath. I find myself gasping for air, hyperventilating as the world around me gets darker and darker. I close my eyes, sending my brain to a happy place, but all my happy places start to crumble.

I want to hate him, I want to claw his heart out, but no matter how angry I am, or how much pain and disgust I feel right now, I can't leave him. Not after everything. Even though I have every right to stand up and walk out of his life forever, there's no way I could do that.

He broke my heart without even trying.

"Ms. Fitzgerald?"

Dr. Clark steps into the room, his fake smile only makes me sicker. "How are we feeling?"

I look away, I'm in no mood for sympathy.

He looks away from me and over to William, fast asleep in bed. "It might be a while before he comes to. You outta go home, get some sleep, take a shower. We'll call you as soon as he's conscious."

"Thank you, but I'd rather it be my face he sees when he wakes up."

"Are you sure?"

"Very. Now if you don't mind, I'd like to be alone. Just us."

Dr. Clark nods his head, the sorrow he feels for both William and I is hard to hide under those black, heavy eyes.

I rest my eyes once again on William. My mind still blank with no tears left to cry. I was ready for my new life to begin. A new, beautiful, everlasting one with only the two of us. Holidays in the country, walks throughout London that could satisfy us both. I pictured that life well, the memory of it carved into my brain, replaying over again as if it's now nothing but a long gone faded memory. I found everything I ever wanted, or needed, in him and now even that must come to an end.

CHAPTER SIXTEEN

Tuesday, August 2nd 2016

"Finding someone you love and who loves you back is a wonderful, wonderful feeling. But finding a true soul mate is an even better feeling. A soul mate is someone who understands you like no other, loves you like no other, will be there for you forever, no matter what. They say that nothing lasts forever, but I am a firm believer in the fact that for some, love lives on even after we're gone."

Cecelia Ahern

I thought about running. Picking up my feet and disappearing into the night. Who would blame me? Who could? Maybe it's selfish for me to think this way, but with these last two days, nothing I can ever do, will be as selfish as what he has done to me.

I tried to hate him. Pick up the heaviest weapon and shatter every bone in his body. Make him feel the pain I feel now. But he does feel the pain. Throughout his entire body, I know he feels a pain that torments him day and night. A pain that will only fade with death.

But how can I stay when it was all a lie?

He hasn't awoken. The doctor says it will take some time, but he'll pull through this. He has before. It gives me little hope, the feeling that any day now, he'll open his eyes, and my smiling face will be there to greet him. Then again, I'm not entirely certain it will be a smile he's met with. I could force it, but William could see through my

237

lies. Even in his drug induced state, he'll see the real pain behind the smile.

It's been an endless cycle of nurse after nurse, checking up on him as well as myself. They look at me as if I'm some wounded animal who, given too much space, will explode, leaving a trail of misery, remorse, and blood she'll never recover from.

I understand their intention. They're doing what any normal human being with a heart would do, but after all that has happened in such a short time, all I need at this exact moment, is peace, quiet, and a whole lot of alcohol.

It all feels like one, sick dream. Like someone out there is playing a cruel, excessive prank. One nightmare I'd give an arm and a leg to end right now. I want it to be a dream. Dreams can't hurt. You feel no pain in a dream. No real pain. Nothing physical that could tear you apart from the inside, threatening your very existence. No, dreams can't hurt you. They're just random images that pop into your head. Sometimes meaning nothing, and sometimes meaning everything. But you move on. Once you wake up, your dream is in the past, already forgotten by the time you open your eyes and realise you're safe. The hallucination is over, and you're off, living your life in the real world.

Even in sleep, he manages to look perfect. With the tubes and machinery encircling him, he's still William. The William I hated for a short period. The William, who out of nowhere, succeeded in stealing my heart.

The William I pictured an infinity with.

You just know. People always wonder how you know you're in love. You just know. There is no certain time frame, nor is there a handbook to help you better understand your own emotions. You just know. I think it's hard to explain for everyone. You try to find the right words to clarify, accurately, how you feel about someone. But you can't. That doesn't mean you don't love the person, no, it simply means you love them so much, that no words can ever illuminate how much they mean to you.

Only actions can prove your love. And this is my action. No matter how confused, or angry, or sick, or just plain pissed off I get, there is no way I can ever, in this lifetime or the next, walk away from the only person who has ever mattered to me.

His soul and mine are now entangled. From the moment I let him buy me a drink, I knew. I knew he would be my forever.

My body aches. Every single piece of me hurts. Not just from the physical pain of sitting in this same chair for days, curled up in the same fetal position, waiting for the second he wakes up. No, I can feel it inside as well. The precise moment when you can literally feel the pain in your chest from seeing or hearing something that breaks your heart. It isn't a normal pain either. I'm not physically hurt in the way of having to use medicine, or anything else that can rid a temporary pain. It's the sense of knowing your heart is slowly being ripped apart from the inside, and nothing on the earth can fix it. Besides death.

There is not one thing in this entire world that will ever repair me.

"How are you Ms. Fitzgerald?"

Sebastian, William's paid nurse, has asked me this same question at least two hundred times. And each time I choose to ignore. He means well, but I'm not exactly equipped to answer a question like that. How is one supposed to feel after learning a horrible truth? Depressed, mad, scared, lonely, disappointed. Empty.

"Well everything looks fine; he should wake up any minute now. Just try and get some sleep. Staying awake like this isn't healthy for you, nor him. He would want you to be okay as well."

Sebastian heads for the door, but I'm not ready to let him leave.

"How would you know? How could anyone know? You stand there and tell me he wants me to be safe and in good health, but how? If he truly cares about me, then he never would've pulled me into this bullshit. You don't do that to people you care about. You don't lie and keep explosive secrets from them. You don't. No one with a heart would do this to another person. He doesn't love me. He wanted to hurt me, and he did an excellent job at that."

"I know you're in pain, but…"

"Oh, you have no idea."

Sebastian turns to William, watching over him carefully, as if to read his mind. "He was trying to protect you. Maybe it was the wrong path to take, but in his own way, he thought shielding you from the truth was the right thing to do. He loves you Ms. Fitzgerald. No matter how angry you may be right now, I know you know it. You just can't see it now."

He turns back around, his glare lingering on me before opening the door.

"Was he here? The second week of June, the week he disappeared. Was he here at the hospital? Or was he really at his family's home?"

Sabastian stops, but he keeps his body facing the door. "No, we weren't. We were at his family's home, out in Northumberland. William hates hospital, spent the last few years in and out of them on a regular basis. He wanted to stay out of a room like this, but was too scared to go home to London and explain to you why he couldn't walk, or keep his eyes open. He thought it best to heal up somewhere else. He didn't want you to see him like that." He pauses and looks over to William. "Like this."

"What if he died while he was there? Did he ever stop to think that if he died out there, or in here without telling me…? How would I have gotten the truth? How would I ever have known?"

"I'm sorry Ms. Fitzgerald."

I stop talking. There's nothing left to argue over. There is no fight left in me.

It was as if the world was over. Not one person, or car, or even an animal flooded the streets. It was just him and I. Side by side, walking, not having to say one word to each other. Silence was the best between us. Being in each other's presences was enough.

We walked for what seemed like hours. Looking at every building we passed on the way. But to where? Did we even have a destination? Maybe not, but who needs one. His hand was in mine, the warmth from his body flowed into mine. This is our forever. Our hands fit right, as if they were made for each other. I can feel his touch, and it fulfills me.

This is our forever.

My body starts to shake, from what, I haven't a clue, but it doesn't stop. It's like I'm gently being rocked back and forth, like I'm doing an endless dance.

"Olivia?"

I hear a voice call out my name, but I see no one around me. I see nothing, just darkness. It's blank, a void, nothing but blackness and emptiness.

"Livia?"

It's hoarse and almost hard to hear, but not impossible. I could recognize that voice anywhere.

My eyes shoot open, pulling me from a dream I hoped would never end. The dark from outside spills inside the four walls that secure us. My eyes try to adjust, blinking rapidly as I come to my senses. Only the pale, dim light from the single bulb above us ignites the room. It's not much, but even with the shortages of light, his eyes glow brighter than the sun.

"Morning."

Not one tear Liv.

"William?"

"Yeah, love, it's me."

I had it all planned. I knew exactly what I was going to say when his eyes first opened. I wanted to let loose. Rant and rave about every little thing that's been eating away at me these last two days. But looking at him, awake and smiling, reminds me why I fell for him in the first place.

That thing he does with his eyes; now I remember why I fell in love with him.

My eyes flood before I can get the words out. "You're okay. They said you'd wake up, but I didn't believe them, and here you are. You're back."

He finds a way to smile, even after all that's happened. "Of course I'm okay. I've been through worse."

"Have you? See I wouldn't know, what with you keeping secrets from me." Please don't say anything you'll regret. "William how could you do this to me? All this time, you knew and you said nothing." Stop before it's too late. "How could you keep this from me?"

His smile fades, seeing the pain on my face crushes him. He was so happy to see me sitting here, waiting for him to come back to me. I don't think he stopped to consider what the truth would do to me.

"Liv..."

I stand, my feet ready to run for the door. "Just answer this one question, please. Were you ever going to tell me?" His silence gives me his answer, but I'm too hardheaded to shut up. "Were you?"

His eyes close, racking his brain for the right answer "I didn't know how. I was never planning on telling anyone. It was my problem, why burden anyone else with it. You weren't part of the plan, Olivia. Meeting you, falling in love with you, none of that was supposed to happen. I was going to retire during Easter Holiday, leave the city behind and retire to my family's home. Then you came along. You did something to me that no one else has ever done. I managed to fall for you without trying. It wasn't meant to happen like this. I don't regret... I don't regret you and I, not for one bit. All I truly regret is ruining your life."

I collapse back in my chair, my face hidden in my hands. I don't want to fall, or break in front of him, he has his own issues and worrying about me and my feelings is not what I want. But it hurts, and I just want it to stop.

"How was I supposed to tell you? How was I supposed to tell the only woman I've ever loved that I'm dying? How do you tell someone that?"

My head shakes. I have no idea. "You could've confessed, when we first met in Paris. You could've came clean then. It would've been easier. We were only strangers then."

"No. No we weren't." His eyes open, splashes of red engulf around the blue. "I knew you were the one that first night in Paris."

I turn, my body running for the door. I didn't want this; my plan wasn't to abandon him. No matter how bad things have gotten, I still love this man with every little piece of me. I saw the future. William and I were together, our own little life, away from the city, away from people. Just him and I, married, maybe a kid or two. I still haven't made up my mind about that topic yet. We had a future, and in the blink of an eye my… our future was ripped away.

I'll hate myself for the rest of my life, and he'll hate me for the remainder of his, but staying isn't an option for me, not anymore. I can't hang around and wait for his time to come to an end. I won't wait around to watch as he slowly breathes his last breath.

CHAPTER SEVENTEEN

Monday, August 8th 2016

"Why were we never closer? One would think, after all these years, we would've developed some closer connection."

I look away from my muffin, not one bite taken off it, but there are dozens of pieces picked and crumpled next to it. My eyes meet Avery's. I sit across from her, in her tiny little flat just a few miles away from Cambridge. I've only been here once before and I feel as awkward now as I did then.

She's right, we never were close, mostly because I never cared for her lifestyle. I don't judge, but I also don't support. And secretly, she hated me for being 'perfect' while she was 'damaged.' Her words, not mine.

"Probably because I was a saint, while you were the devil." I throw a forced smile at her. Those were the words she said to Jade after knowing me for only two weeks.

She smiles back, but it's just as fake as mine. "Jade told you, eh?"

"She didn't have to, I lived in that flat too, remember? Thin walls."

"You were there when I said that?"

I raise my cup to my lips, my tea as cold as the English winter. "Heard every word."

She looks away, her lips moving without one word coming out. There's something else on her mind then our failed friendship.

"I'm sorry Olivia. For everything. I don't hate you, I never did, it was just jealously, plain and simple." Her eyes drift to the window, tiny little drops of rain beat up against the glass. "I wish we could've been closer. Been better friends then excellent enemies. Guess that's all my fault, eh?"

"Why does it sound like you're saying goodbye?"

She lifts her head, a hint of tears in her eyes. Avery's never been the crying type, or the type to show any emotions, besides anger and annoyance.

Another fake smile spreads across her face. "Not goodbye, just making amends I guess."

"And why are you making amends? You going off to prison or something?"

She forces a laugh, but it doesn't last. Her fingers nervously play with the tablecloth; her lips still in motion.

"Avery, why am I really here? Don't get me wrong, it's nice to see this side of you, all depressed and whatnot, but it's not okay seeing tears in your eyes. Whatever it is, you can trust me. I may have lost the respect and friendship of one, but if there's one thing I'm good at, it's keeping secrets. Go on. No judgement."

Her hands squeeze shut, knocking over her cup and plate, her tea spilling all over the floor. I jump, the sudden shift and sound of glass shattering startles me. I look over at Avery, then back down at the cup. She seems like she may need a minute, so I busy myself while I wait. Reaching over for the towel nearest me, my attention on cleaning up the broken glass and mini puddles of tea, but her hand latches onto mine. I meet Avery's eyes, now bloodshot, her face soaking wet. Her grip gets tighter, cutting off any circulation in my entire left arm, both our hands as red as her eyes. I let go of the towel, my free hand grabs onto hers, hoping to loosen her hold on me.

I look her over and can't help but feel a bit of guilt. I don't need to know what's wrong with her, the only thing that comes to mind is how much of a horrible friend I am. Once I met William, I became so impatient, so eager to build a new life. A life where I could finally be happy, a life where I finally met someone worth living for, that I didn't stop to realise my old one was falling apart.

Emma became pregnant by one of her ex best friends, ex fiancé. Jade feels betrayed by every one of us. I fell in love with a man dying from cancer, and now there's Avery. I don't know what's wrong with her, but the rate the rest of us are going, I know it can't be good.

"Have you ever heard something so awful, that the words alone could kill you?"

More than she knows.

"That nothing on this earth, not one thing can ever fix it? That your life has been ruined, and the only one to blame is yourself?" Her eyes open, turning to me. "I fucked up Olivia. I fucked really bad, and have absolutely no idea on what I'm supposed to do next."

I lean in, my arms ready to wrap around her, but she pushes me away, jumping from her seat and flying across the room.

"Don't touch me. Don't get close. I don't want to cock up your life too."

I stand, staying where I am. She doesn't want me near her, I won't disobey. "Avery what's going on with you? What's so wrong that I can't touch you?"

She collapses, her body curled up in a ball in the corner of the room. Her cries become louder and louder, but I do what she says and keep away.

"Was it a man? A woman? Did someone hurt you?"

Her cries grow even louder, and I can't ignore them any longer. My feet move, slowly stepping to her position, but her hand stops me. She keeps it out in front of her, telling me to stay where I am. So I do. I pull the chair over a few inches in front of Avery and sit. My eyes stay trained on her; afraid she might do something stupid if I look away.

I can't stand sitting here and being totally useless. "Avery whatever it is, you can tell me. You and I may not have been the best of friends in the past, but that doesn't mean I never gave a damn about you. The reason I was so distance from you was because I cared so much about what you were doing with your life. I hated standing by and watching you ruin it. Yes, you're a grown adult, and we're all allowed to make our own choices, which is why I never said anything to you. And no matter what I said, or did, I knew you weren't going to change who you were. Not for me. The only way to get you to change was for me to let you live your own life. Make your own mistakes and learn from them. Maybe I should've showed you more emotions and concern, but there's no going back right, so what's the point? We can't go back in time and fix our errors, even if it's what we want the most. If only we could travel back in time."

I trail off, I'm no longer talking about Avery. I close my eyes tight, tying to stop myself from breaking down, or thinking about him. Avery needs me right now, I can't bring my own drama into this, not now.

"I wish we could have second chances, you know. Go back to the day we made our mistakes and change them. Because I would, if I had the chance, I'd walk away before I ever fell." My eyes open, Avery looks up at me, her face screams pain. "We all have our blunders Avery. What's yours?"

She turns her attention back to the dingy carpet, pulling it up from the seams. "I went to the hospital a few days ago. I haven't felt right in weeks, but I thought maybe it was just a girl thing. Turns out it wasn't a girl thing; it was an AIDS thing."

My eyes grow wider. No. "Avery, what are you saying?"

Her lips curl up into a crooked smile. Happy to finally get this burden off her chest. "I'm HIV positive Olivia. Like that shocks you, eh?"

I stand from my chair, my chest empty. "Oh my gods. Avery, I am so sorry. How could this…" I stop, no point in asking that question. "Who else knows? Who have you told?"

"Only you. Jade's disappeared and Emma's starting a life of her own. Besides, you were the only person who never judged. Whenever the rest of us needed to talk, our first choice was always you. You've always had a way with people Liv. I was just told I have AIDS, and sitting here talking to you makes me feel a whole lot better about myself. I don't know how you do it." Neither do I. "I didn't want to burden you, or anyone else with my problems, but I really needed someone to talk to. And I thought since your life was going so well, my confession wouldn't be that big of a deal. I mean it is my problem after all."

My feelings shift. Gods, she doesn't know how wrong she is. My life was going well. For the first time in years, my life was finally looking positive, I could finally start to picture a future for myself, and it looked amazing. And in just one day, it all was snatched away from me. My picture-perfect ending is coming to a close quicker then I wanted it to, and coming to terms with it hasn't been that easy either.

Now it's my turn to break down. "William has stage IV stomach cancer, and he has less than a year to live."

The words are out so quick I have no time to reel them back in. I haven't talked to anyone about this, not even William. I didn't know what to say, or feel. It's not every day you find out the one you love is about to die.

I don't look up; I can't meet her eyes. I didn't want this day to be about me, I was hoping if I hung out with someone like Avery, I would forget him. But I can't. How could I ever forget a person like William?

"I'm sorry, this isn't about me, it's about you. I wasn't planning on bringing my issues to the surface, I was hoping on burying them down deep. Guess that didn't work out the way I wanted it to."

"Olivia, my gods, I'm so sorry. Why didn't you tell me?"

"Because when you called, you said you needed to talk. Today was supposed to be about you and whatever it was you had to get off your chest, not about William and I. I'm sorry, let's get back to the matter at hand. What..."

"What, Olivia, no. Yeah fine, my life is screwed up, but I was the one who left it in shambles. Me. No one else. It was my choice to go around, sleeping with anyone who smiled at me. But William, his cancer wasn't his choice. He was burdened with this and now he's..." She stands, keeping her distance, she places her hand on my knee. "Olivia, you both deserved so much better. I'm so, so, so sorry. From the bottom of my heart."

HIV or not, I wrap my arms around her. I never realised how much I needed a hug. I never realised how alone I felt this past week without William, or Jade, or anyone to comfort me.

William. I've been such a selfish bitch. I thought I had every right to be pissed at him, and he's the one who's dying. I left him in that hospital room, alone, when he needed me the most. I ran. I walked away from a man who loves me. He loved me so much, he kept the truth from me, to prevent me from breaking, and look where we are.

I'm breaking down in someone else arms, when it should be him breaking down in my arms.

I pull away from Avery, my eyes shut as I try to hate myself less. I open them to find her staring at me, concern and pain written all over her face. "I'm sorry Avery. For everything, please believe me. We may not have been great friends, but don't ever think for one second I never cared about you. I only wanted the best for you, for all of us.

William and I aren't the only ones who deserve a better life. We all do. Including you."

My key turns in the lock, almost breaking a piece off as I force it inside. The door slams behind me, and I toss my things to the side as my feet run for the stairs. I try to catch my breath, but can't. I ran from Avery's flat to my car, then from my car to William's house. Our house.

The door to the bedroom flies open, and William jumps up, his hair pointing up in different direction, as his eyes try to adjust to what's happening. The room is a mess. The sheets thrown around, no doubt he's been tossing and turning all week. His clothes thrown on the floor, and an entire medicine cabinet on his bedside table.

In one stride, I'm by his side, his hand in mine as I pull it up to my lips. "William, honey I'm so sorry. I was so mad at you, that I never stopped to see your side in this."

His eyes blink open once more, then fall on me. "Olivia?"

"No, just let me talk. Please." I pick up his other hand and hold them closer to my heart. "I love you. It may not seem like it, what with me walking out on you, but I do. I've always loved you, that's why I ran. I didn't want to live without you, so somewhere in the back of my stupid mind I thought if I walked away early on, then it wouldn't hurt as much. But it did. The only thing I could think about this past week was you and how much I missed you." My eyes close, the pain from my admission kicks in. "We both know how this ends, but that doesn't mean we have to live separate lives from here on out. I know your time is coming to an end, and it's killing me just thinking about it, but I plan on being here every day, until that day comes. And even after you're gone, I'll still be here, every day, until the day comes that we can finally meet again."

He looks away from me, but I can feel the tears as they drop from his eyes and onto my hands. His lips find my hands, kissing away the tears, his breathing shaky and unstable.

"I didn't think you'd come back."

I let his hands go, mine finding his face. I force him to look at me, his eyes back to the perfect blue I remember. "Neither did I."

I pull him in closer, my lips on his, as his hands find my waist. His tongue parts my lips, forcing its way into my mouth as he tosses me on the bed, my body buried underneath his.

His kiss is rougher then it usually is, as he takes my hands and pins them above my head. His mouth making its way down to my neck, then my chest. I reach down, pulling my shirt away from my body and over my head, tossing it to the side, and out of the way. His mouth pressed up against my stomach, his kisses send a white-hot ping of excitement throughout the rest of my body, dragging me

down into an abyss I'll never climb out of.

CHAPTER EIGHTEEN: *WILLIAM*

Friday, March 18th 2016

'Create a bucket list. It will be good for you. It will help get your mind off the pain.' What a load of bullshit.

I throw the crumbled piece of paper across the room, just missing the bin, regretting ever bothering making such a stupid list. Only ten lines on that paper were written on, and not one of those things mattered to me. I could die right now and wouldn't care if I jumped out of a plane.

How does someone make a list of things they want to do before they die, when they only have months left? I'd rather just die alone, in bed, without any doctors or nurses telling me what to do, or how to feel. What the hell do they know anyway? Having cancer and treating cancer are two different things.

Here I go again, lashing out at no one. This is what got me in trouble the last time.

I close my eyes and let myself fall backwards on the bed, landing on my notepad which I toss to the side. At least I can say I completed one task on my list. Well technically it's not on my list. It was on Nana's list.

She was so in love with the whole idea of Paris. The lights, the food, the people. To her it was a place to escape the rest of the world. A place where one could always find happiness no matter what sort of rotten mood they were in. Which is why I to came here. Maybe something about this city can help me forget everything else.

If she were here today… she'd probably smack me. She used to tell me good things and bad things were always going to happen in life, but we did have a choice, we could let them break us or we could rebuild our lives with the broken pieces. She was right. No matter how much I cry or yell, I'm still going to die and no amount of begging is going to fix that. I need to accept it, but that's easier said than done.

I wish she was here today; I could really use one of her hugs right about now.

My eyes blink open, and I use my sleeve to remove the tears from them. No more crying; it won't change my fate. And it won't bring her back.

Before I left England, I went to visit Nana and I made her a promise. I told her I wasn't going to let my cancer kill me before I'm dead. I told her I was going to complete our bucket list. The world screwed us both over in the end, but I'm not going to let it keep me down. I still have a little under a year and I plan on doing something with it.

I get to my feet and reach for my coat. I still have another three weeks here. I'm done spending it in bed crying.

Walking over to the balcony, I grab the handle to close it, but wind up walking outside instead, hoping on the impossible. I turn towards Olivia's balcony; the doors open but no one's there. I can hear music coming from inside, a voice. Her voice. She's singing along.

I find myself smiling and I don't understand why. There's something about her that I just can't put my finger on.

Instead of waiting around, I step back inside and close the door behind me. Even if she was out there, what would I say to her? She made things quite clear the other day, and I'm positive she hasn't changed her mind, so maybe it's best to leave things as is.

"I'll just take the check please." I hold my hand over my mouth, doing my best to keep the food I just ate inside. This is one regret I never plan on reliving.

One of the things on Nana's list was to try the 'nastiest' foods while in France. Why did *Rouille de seiche* have to be on the list? I've never been a fan of seafood, so when I found out *Rouille de seiche* was squid, I almost talked myself out of eating it, but then I remembered I'm doing this for her. But seriously Nana, squid?

"Here you go sir, I hope you enjoyed your meal." I didn't, but I was raised to be polite.

"I did, thank you, but I must be going." I drop a few Euros on the table and head off, never to come back to this place, or any places that serve food like this again.

I take off walking, it's easier to see more of the city if you're on your own two feet instead of a cab. Better for me to be alone anyway. I've never cared for big crowds, or people. I zig-zag through the streets of Paris, taking my time as I take the city in. I've been here twice before, but they don't count. I was only nine months. then three-years-old when I came, and can't remember a thing.

The Eiffel Tower, a few thrift shops, and one restaurant, just about everything on Nana's list of things to do in France has been complete. She was a very simple person, even if she wasn't fortunate to see the sights I've seen, to be able to say she stepped foot in France would've been an accomplishment. But life couldn't give her that. It seems life hates us both.

My eyes close tightly, pushing away tears and anger. I'm not going back down that road. I'm not going to let cancer consume me. For her. I promised that I'd live as cheerfully as I possibly could until we were to reunite in a year, and I don't plan on breaking a promise. Not to her. Besides, there's only one sight left to see, then I can go back to my hotel and cry myself to sleep if I must.

The sun starts to fade as I turn a corner, my last destination only a mile ahead. Number four on her list: throw a coin in the Fontaine des Fleuves, and make one impossible wish. I know what my impossible wish would be, which is why I won't make a wish, I've never been a big believer in the impossible.

"Why are you such a strange child William?"

I look up to see her leaning against the counter, peeling a bowl of potatoes. "You think I'm strange Nana?"

She smiles, her eyes now rest on me. "I do, but a good strange. You're a lovely boy, it's just, you have so much at your fingertips, so much that you could take advantage of if you wanted, but you don't. You rather stay home all day and help the help clean around the house. Why is that?"

"Well first things first; you're not the help, you're family. And secondly, I have everything I need in this room, why should I walk away from it?"

"You are sometimes too proper, even for me. Where'd you learn that from?"

I bite into an apple. "From my mum, of course." I smile up at her. "Mum."

She puts the knife down, and mirrors my smile. "You're too good for this world William, it doesn't deserve you. Neither do I."

"Yeah, well I'm not going to let you go, so get used to me." I pass my apple over, offering her a bite. She reaches for it, her hand shaky as she takes it from me, taking a bite then tossing it back over to me. I barely catch it, she's quicker then I remember.

"Can I ask you something, sweetheart?"

"Always."

"Why have you never had a girlfriend? You're a very attractive young man, yet you come home every day, at the exact same time. You do your school work and then you spend the rest of the day cleaning with me. Why?"

I let out a loud laugh. "Are you insulted because I don't care to date?"

She mocks my laugh. "No. I just think if you gave it a chance, you could find an amazing girl. But never mind me, I'm just a mum venting, that's all."

I shallow hard, thinking about the topic myself. I never told her, but I just always assumed she knew. The apple rolls from my hand and lands into the sink. This gets her attention. She pulls it out, and holds it up giving me a look that usually sent me to my room. "I don't think I'm capable of loving anyone. In that way. I've tried, I have, but they all seem to go the same way: It's good for the first few months, then I lose interest. Every time I try to make it work, I feel like I'm forcing it."

I trail off, the next sentence burns in the back of my throat, but there's truth to every last word. "I don't want to end up like my parents."

My head drops, and my fingers move nervously, but a set of hands are there to stop them. My eyes drift to her hands, the veins from years of working have turned them light purple and pop out every time she clutches them. Her hand moves back and forth across mine, trying to bring me some comfort, but the years haven't been good to her. Her hands are rough, but I don't mind, her touch is enough to bring me out of any mood.

"Look at me love." I do as she says. "No matter what happens, there is no way in hell you will ever become them. There's too much heart inside you, you're too human and that's what makes you better than them. You care more than they ever will, and I know someday soon, you yourself will come to see that and the right woman will stumble into your life and you'll never ever feel like this again. When that day comes, mark my words William, you will never feel like you're alone. Ever again, my son."

"Move, or you will be moved."

I look up, I'm much closer to the fountain then I thought. My eyes fall on a woman surrounded by three men, her hand in her bag and from the look of her stance, she's not backing down. I pick up the pace, one thing I learned from Nana was to always help those who needed it. No matter who they are.

But I'm too late. She pulls a tiny can out of her bag, and sprays it in the leaders face and he goes down, his cries loud enough to be heard from the other side of France. I come to a slow when I get a glimpse of the woman. Her back is facing me, but I'd remember it anywhere. Every day in class, as she's the last one to leave, gathering all her things, neatly, before walking out of the door. A few days ago, as she walked away from me after falling in my arms.

Olivia.

Her hand is still planted in front of her, her body still unmoved. "Run"

I come up behind her, but keep my distance. I don't want to accidently get sprayed by mace, and seeing as things have been tense between us, I'm not exactly sure she'll go easy on me. "You heard the lady, get the hell out of here."

The other two frightened men pick up their perverted friend and drag him off into the night, the three of them both ashamed and humiliated, and I can't stop the edges of my lips from turning up. I always did like her. She's been one of those picture-perfect students since the first day of class, and seeing her out here today, handling a bunch of idiots, reminds me why I liked her so much.

She keeps her eyes in front, watching just in case.

"Thanks for that, but I'm pretty sure I had it."

"I'm not drunk. Honest."

"So it's normal for you to randomly giggle at nothing."

She looks away from me, her smile so wide it reaches her ears. "Maybe I'm just in a fun mood. Sorry that some of us lack the same charisma."

I laugh, my hands flying up every time it looks like she's about to fall over. "I know how to have fun, thank you very much. But there is a difference between fun and drunk, and you are clearly drunk."

Her hand flies up, stumbling forward, but catching herself on my arm. "Okay, maybe I am a little drunk, but I'm still very aware of my surroundings. Like I can clearly tell that's a garbage bin right there."

I pull her in so only she can hear my voice. "Olivia, you just called a little old lady a garbage bin!"

Her free hand flies over her mouth as she turns around to take another glance at the lady. She turns back to me, her face only inches from mine and we both break into a laugh.

Her head rests on my shoulder, as she starts to calm down, her hands grip tight around my arm, fighting to keep herself from stumbling over. "I think we should get back, before you pass out and I have to carry you all the way."

She chuckles softly, as her hand slides up my arm. "Not yet. I didn't come all the way out here to only get wasted and then sent home by one of my teachers. I want to have fun. I want to do something spontaneous. I want to do something illegal."

"Now I really think it's time for us to get back."

Her hands slip from my arm, leaving it cold and alone. I yank my hand out, grabbing onto hers as she takes a few steps away from me. She takes my hand again, holding on tight. "Have you ever wanted to do something impulsive. Something stupid, but never regret it. Something where one day, when you're old and grey, you'll look back and smile, thanking yourself for taking that chance." She pulls back towards me and props up on her toes, her breath warm and sweet against my skin. She looks me dead on, specs of grey encircle around her enchanting brown eyes. "Let's take that chance."

"Don't look up my skirt, I'll know."

My head faces the concrete, my hands heaved above my head as I help her over the gate. "I'm not looking up your skirt, to busy trying to not get caught." Her feet leave my hands and I jerk my head up, but she's gone.

"Olivia?"

After seconds of silence, she answers. "Climb over."

I hesitate, looking around as I hop onto the lowest iron bar, flipping myself over and landing on my feet, colliding into Olivia. I open my mouth to apologise, but she's already forgotten about it. Taking me by the hand, she runs off, I follow, my feet going in rhythm with hers. She leads me down a path that finds us in the heart of *Jardin des Plantes;* the botanical gardens of Paris, France.

Her hand still in mine, she leads me to the arch of roses just above our heads. Her hand slips out of mine and I feel myself reaching out to grab onto it, forcing it back, but I pull away. My mind starts to race, my thoughts on nothing but her. I could blame it on the alcohol, I have been for the past two hours, but I'm not drunk. I'm not even buzzed. Alcohol seems to have no effect on me these days, but if I'm not drunk, then why do I feel myself gravitating towards her. And not just in a 'let's rebel together' sort of way, more like 'I never want to be apart from you' sort of way.

We made up, which is good. I didn't want to leave the world with any anger still in my heart, or another's. But this feeling, it's different and not like one I felt before.

"Mr. Edwards? Come on then, I'm not going to jail by myself." Her hand reaches out, a bright-eyed look on her face. I don't know if she is drunk, or if this may just be her personality, but I like it, and I don't want this night to end.

Ever.

Through the darkness, my hand finds hers and with one last are you sure look, I nod at her and she takes off. Half jogging into the gardens, letting me go once more so she can spin around, her hands slightly touching the flowers that surround her. I find it mesmerizing, the way she moves. She takes her time with each spin, slowly rotating so the drinks from earlier don't find their way back up. Her eyes are closed, but you don't need to see them when the smile plastered on her face gives her joy away. A laugh escapes her lips, echoing all around the gardens and I can't even find it in myself to care if we're caught or not. It will all be worth it.

After a few more spins, she collapses on the ground, and my feet move, running to her side without thinking, but she lets out a sigh, telling me she's okay.

"Olivia?"

Her eyes open, the light from the moon bounces off her face, and for the first time I can see the true beauty of it. I told her she was beautiful earlier, but seeing her face, fresh and glowing by moonlight makes her a billion times more beautiful than I thought.

She smiles, patting the grass beside her. I obey, taking

the empty space next to her and stretch out my legs, my

head looking up at the night sky. There's movement on my

lap, looking back down I see Olivia resting her head on my

thigh, her fingers intertwined and her legs crossed at the

knee. Her eyes are closed again, but I hear her humming,

the corners of her lips move slightly, but never fully come

up. When she opens her eyes again, the moon reflects off

them both, and this time I won't look away. She's so

peaceful like this, so human. I'm so used to the girl who

had her hand up first, or who always had her head buried in

a book, but to see this side of her makes me pleased for

snapping at her that day. Who knows what would've

happened if I never said a word to her. Would I have paid

any attention to her when she fell into my arms, or would

she have given me a second look back at the hotel? I don't

know where life would've taken us if I wasn't an arse that

day, and I rather not think on it. I'm here right now with

her, and for the first time since Nana, I finally found someone who can still make me smile. And knowing that smile is for her, gives me a new outlook on life.

"Mr. Edwards?"

"Ms. Fitzgerald?"

There's a slight silence before she answers me, her head turning on its side so were facing each other. "Do you think we'll get in trouble if we pick a flower?"

CHAPTER NINETEEN

Friday, August 26th 2016

I look down at my feet, my shoes now covered in mud and grass. Sometimes I hate this English rain.

There's a pull on my hand and I look up to see William, his eyes closed and his mind somewhere else. He doesn't come here often; he doesn't understand why he should. 'She's dead. Why should I come to a grave when I can talk to her whenever I feel like it?' I guess I can understand that logic, but every time I bring her up, he shuts down and won't talk for the rest of the day. Once he ignored me for almost a whole week. I backed off, but gave up on that quite easily. I don't have much time left with him, and we can spend the rest of our lives together keeping secrets from each other, but that's not in my plan.

Tugging on his hand, I rest my head on his shoulder. "I know you don't think this is necessary, but I do. You tense up and close yourself off every time I ask you about your parents or about Elizabeth, but I only ask because this is what couples do. They tell each other things. The good and the bad."

"Not all couples."

"Do you want us to be one of those couples?"

He sniffles. "Gods no."

I pull my head away and look up to him once more. His eyes are open now, but he looks straight forward, avoiding her grave marker as long as he can. "Is this the first time you've been here?"

He shakes his head, while his gaze finds me. "I came before I left for France, but every time I come back it hurts more. It reminds me of her funeral. There were only six people there. She and I were a lot alike. Neither one of us had much family or friends."

His eyes close again, this time they refuse to open. "I had to handle all the arrangements. Pick out the casket, the church. It was too much for a kid to handle. I made a vow that day, a selfish one. I promised myself I would never come back here, of course I didn't stick to it. But this place, it brings pain and that's the last thing I need right now."

I let go off his hand and wrap my arms around his waist, my face buried in his coat. He tightens his grip around me, his nose shuffling back and forth in my hair. Maybe I am asking for a lot, especially since he hasn't talked to anyone since she's passed.

"We don't have to do this. We can come back to it later if you…"

"She was my mum. I just find it hard now, living without her. Whenever something went wrong I would go straight home and tell her. I could cry, and yell, and she would listen. And as soon as I was finished wallowing in my own despair, she would make me a cup of tea, tell me to wipe my face clean and get over it. That no matter how bad life would get, I was still alive. As long as I still breathed, I had purpose. Of course, as a kid, you didn't want to hear that. You just wanted to be hugged and coddled, but she was right. Everything I have, everything I am; I owe it to her."

His hand slowly slides up my back and rest on the back of my head, pulling me closer. "Before you, I was alone. I had nothing. I know she's still here with me, but it doesn't feel the same. I feel like I was cheated, and it's hard to get over something like that."

"I'm sorry William."

He chuckles. "Don't be. Things have gotten much better since you've entered my life. I find myself smiling for no reason these days, like some idiot. Never be sorry for me

Liv, just know my life is a hundred percent better with you in it."

"Mine too."

He pulls away, just enough to find my eyes without letting me go. Tears slide down his face, but it's hard to ignore his smile. Even in the darkest of times, I can always find a way to get him to flash his teeth at me.

"You ready to go?"

He leans over, his kiss feels soft on my nose, but his hands are ice cold against my cheeks. "Just a few more minutes."

"This is your childhood home? Is there something you're not telling me?"

"Like what?"

"Like, exactly how rich are you?"

I hear a muffled laugh behind me, and in a flash two arms wrap around my waist, his breath on the back of my neck. "You never asked, so I never told."

"Well I'm asking now. You told me you were rich because of all the money Elizabeth left you, but you never told me your parents had money too. What did they do for a living? This place is massive."

He lets me go to close the door and set the alarm. I don't know why, there isn't another house for miles. "They had boring jobs, nothing to start a conversation on. And for your information, they weren't that rich, we just inherited this place when my grandparents died. I think you're too heavily focused on the rich part. Is that why you started dating me?"

I turn to him, his eyes light up, a wicked smile on his face. "You're an arse."

"I love you too." He sneaks a quick kiss before lifting our bags and walking past me, heading up the stairs.

"Are you sure you should be carrying all that." He stops in his tracks, turning, he gives me the same look he's been giving me since I found out about his cancer. "It just looks heavy, and I don't want you to get hurt, or tired."

"Olivia, it's just luggage, okay. It's not as if I'm carrying around rocks. I'm fine, really, and I thought I told you to stop..."

"Worrying about you, I know. Sorry, I'll keep my afflictions to myself from now on. Is that what you want?"

He's already halfway up the stairs. "It would be swell, thank you. I'll unpack us, why don't you take a tour around the place." He disappears behind a corner, a faint creak and thud of bags dropping follows.

I glance around the room, and come to realise I'm merely standing in the grand foyer. I mean come on, what normal house has a grand foyer. Not rich my ass.

There's a choice to either head left or right, or straight forward, and I can't make up my mind. This house is a maze, an utterly ridiculous dreadful maze that I will never have the time or energy to solve. I decide to head right; certain I will get myself lost.

The sitting room is oversized and crowded, which is unlike William, who loves to live simple and underwhelmed. It's not your average castle, no suits of armor or overused print on everything, including the furniture and walls. It's been modernized, the walls a light grey, with four sofas to match. The idea that they needed so much sitting space is beyond me, seeing as his parents were never home and only William and Elizabeth occupied this place. Not to mention the fact that there's two desks, an upright piano and a grand piano in adjacent corners. I'll never understand the wealthy.

A tiny door leads me from the sitting room and enter what looks like a study. It's so small, even someone my size could feel claustrophobic. It's dark too, the wallpaper a mix of black and deep red swirls, only making the room darker.

With four strides, I'm out the door that leads me back to the foyer, and out of the nightmare I call a room.

I turn to the stairs, my lips part, calling for William, but I choose not to. He's right about one thing. Ever since I discovered the truth, I've been watching over him like a hawk. Dr. Clark and his nurse Sebastian tell me not to worry, they say just because he only has a little under a year left, he is in perfect health for someone with his condition. Every time I hear them say that, a tiny glimmer of joy enters me, happy to know he's not in any pain, but that soon fades away when I remember he only has a year left on this earth. Worrying won't get us anywhere, but in the end, it's him who won't be here, and I will be left alone. Again.

Since the day I moved in, there's been no separating us. Some would say we're moving quite quickly, that maybe we're rushing into this, but I wouldn't agree with them. I think when two people are meant to be, they know. Sometimes there doesn't need to be an exchange of words, just one look at the person and you automatically know that this is the one you're going to be spending the rest of your life with.

When you meet someone, sometimes you just click. I've never believed in love at first sight, but if there's one thing I do believe in; it's that click. I think that's why I hated William so much in the beginning. It wasn't because he embarrassed me, it was because deep down I felt something for him, even though I didn't realise it then. And I think he felt the same way.

Thinking back to that night we spent in Hemingway Bar, and how he came clean and started naming off the things he liked about me. At first I was shocked, it felt weird to hear something like that again, after spending so much time and years alone. I automatically thought men didn't see me in that way. Possibly because I blow off everyone who looked in my direction, but nonetheless, when he told me he found my smile classically beautiful, I knew there was more to us than just teacher and student.

No teacher pays that much attention to one student unless; a) they are a massive kiss up, or b) they have secret feelings for them. Either way, I knew what I wanted when we spent the night together in my hotel room, and nothing, not even his horrible demise can ever change that.

I hit something sharp, and realise I've walked into the kitchen and right into the counter. The pain of jamming my rib fades into the background, when I come to realise how beautiful the kitchen is compared to the rest of the house. Okay, well the house isn't that bad, but leaving the sitting room and coming into a room like this is like entering a whole new dimension. A whole new dimension that's ten times better than the one I left behind.

Every time I walk into a new room, I stop myself and remember that only four people have lived here. Four people and yet it's just big enough to house the Queen and her entire family.

"By the look on your face, I can tell you weren't expecting anything like this, were you?"

William enters the kitchen through another door, one leading into what looks like a laundry room. Smiling at my shock, he strolls over to the counter and hops on top, patting the open space beside him. I obey, and with two short strides I jump onto the counter, my hand in his. "It's hard to picture your previous life, since you honestly believe in keeping it secret."

"It's not a secret, Liv, you know I don't like to speak on the past. And I don't understand why I should, the past is the past. Can't we just let this go?"

Staring into his eyes, I can practically see him begging me to move on from this topic, once and for all. A part of me doesn't want to, but another part of me can understand why one hates thinking about the life they left behind. I guess I can see his displeasure in my constant nagging.

I turn away from him, as annoyed with him as I am with myself. "Yeah, sure. I'll leave it alone." My hand jerks out of his, and I regret it as soon as it happens, but I stick to my guns. Maybe he doesn't want to talk about it, but what am I going to be left with when he's gone? I fell for a man I barely know anything about. I moved in with this same man and I still know nothing about him, nothing before the age of thirty anyways. I'm spending the rest of his life with him, and he can't see why I care so much. He'll be dead in months and what will I have when he's gone? Just the memories we made together. I would've spent a year with a stranger.

His fingers slip through my hair and pull me towards him, his lips kiss me softly. "I know why you're angry and you have every right to be. It's just going to take me a while, you know that. I'm not saying no; I'm just saying not right now. We're out in the country, with no other humans around for miles. Just you, me and this amazing house. Can't we just enjoy this, please?"

I reach up, my hand finds his and pulls it away from my hair. "I'm going to unpack." I slide off the counter and turn away, walking back in the direction from which I came and up the stairs. I already made a promise that I'd still be here when his day came. Isn't that enough for him?

He sits just outside our window, his old bedroom, and writes. He's been down there about two hours now, writing who knows what, regularly sneaking glances up at the window, hoping to see if I've cooled off by now. I haven't.

I don't want to seem like I'm selfish, and maybe I am, but just because he's the one who going through something horrible, doesn't mean I'm not either. Maybe it is best if we take some time apart. And I'm not talking about only a couple hours, I think a few days. No interaction of any kind. Just enough space for me to clear my head and to put some things into perspective. But I know that would never happen. Every time I'm away from him for longer than six hours, I miss him and find myself calling him to make sure he's okay.

And there's no way he'll ever let me leave again. I know he won't. Who am I kidding, I don't want a few days away from him.

All I desperately want is a lifetime with him.

He's stopped, his pen and notebook lay on the bench next to him and he looks on, his eyes resting on the pond right in front of him.

Yeah, they even have a pond.

He plays with his fingers, a thing he tends to do when he's scared or nervous, which leaves me wondering what he's scared of. Me storming out on him, or oblivion? I want to go out there, sit next to him and watch as the time passes us, but I'm not exactly over my frustrations with him, so I stay upstairs, curling into a ball at the window.

William turns around, this time I stay in my seat. No more acting childish and hiding when he turns to me. We have a staring contest; he tries to read my thoughts from all the way down at his bench. He waves up at me, apologising without using any words. It takes me a few seconds, but I wave back, my facial expression doesn't change yet. The wave reassures him I'm okay, but the look on my face tells him I'm not ready to talk. His hand drops and so does his face. He turns back to the pond, picking his notebook and pen back up. He starts writing again, occasionally looking back over his shoulder at me.

Something yanks me down into a bottomless black hole with no walls. I fight and spin, trying to find anything to latch onto. It feels like I've been falling for days now. An endless cycle of dropping without a hint of light. After the first couple of days, I stopped fighting it. No matter how much I reached, there was nothing to keep me from falling. And no matter how much I screamed, no one heard me. It was just an echo. Even the screams coming from my mouth sounded like an echo, like it wasn't coming from my mouth, but someone else. Someone trapped in this void with me.

I stop fighting and give in, and something catches me. Someone. Their arms wrap around me tight, holding me so close, I can hear their heartbeat. It's slow, but strong. Their warmth, I'm safe here. Wherever I am, I'm safe with them.

My eyes open and the first thing I see is a shirt. It's hard to see through my blurry vision, but the words stand out. *Star Wars*. That's not the only thing that stands out. The shirt is worn and ripped in random places. Whoever this is has worn and washed this shirt more than they probably should, causing it to be over washed, yet they won't let it go. They still wear it, as proudly as the day they first bought it. The first day I bought it.

My vision clears, the layout and look of the shirt pushed away in a repressed memory I hid years ago. It was my second summer job, I worked at a local up and coming clothing store only two miles from home. I got the job to help pay for rent in my new California apartment. Or what was supposed to be my apartment.

I went down to my favorite spot for lunch that day, a tiny pizza place that sold the biggest slices in all the United States. I had some time to kill before I had to get back to work, so I did some window shopping, all while trying to get a handle on my pizza, and that's where I saw it. A light grey *Star Wars* shirt. The title taking up most of the shirt, with a lightsaber wedged in the middle. I had to have it, but not for myself. I was a fan, but not as much as Niall. He used to be able to recite the entire dialogue to *The Empire Strikes Back*. I used to hate him for it. It was hard to follow the movie when someone is talking over the actors, doing his own one-man show.

As soon as my eyes hit that shirt, I knew it would be perfect. Niall's birthday was coming up and he was always a hard one to buy for. He never liked gifts, and always felt guilty when he received them, which in turn made me feel guilty. But not this time. This time I found the perfect gift and he wasn't going to take that from me.

I still remember his face when he opened his gift. It lit up, he was speechless. He may have been hard to shop for, but as soon as he held that shirt in his hands, his old beliefs went out the window. From that day forward, he wore that shirt at least twice a week, refusing to let me or his mother patch it up once the holes started to appear. He loved the ratty look, and I loved it on him.

My eyes wander, peeking at the face that belongs to the arms, and sure enough, there's Niall. His grey eyes on me, his smile as bright as it was the day I met him. "It's alright now, Liv. You'll never be hurt as long as I live."

I jerk out of my sleep, sweat slides down my face and back. I haven't dreamt about Niall since William and I started dating. This can't be good.

"You have a nightmare?"

I turn, William lays on his back, his eyes on the ceiling.

"No. Not a nightmare, just a bad dream. What are you still doing up, it's three in the morning."

He takes a deep breath, his jaw clenches up. "Can't sleep."

I sit up against the backboard with only one pillow to prop me up. "You want to talk about it?"

"Not really."

"Is this about earlier? When I walked out of the kitchen? If it is, then you should know, I'm not mad anymore. I just needed to let off some steam. I needed some time alone."

"To think about Niall?"

Where did that come from? I turn towards him, his eyes now rest on me, and they look all too familiar. Not the beautiful, soft blue playful eyes I fell in love with, but the eyes of my former teacher. The eyes that haunt me.

"Niall? What does Niall have to do with anything?" Holy shit, did he find my letter?

"Do you always dream about him, or was tonight the only time? Do you always smile in your sleep when you dream of him too?"

Dream? How did he know I was dreaming of Niall? I look away from him, shame and disgust flood my face. I didn't ask to have that dream, it just happened and now that it's happened I would love nothing more than to rewind time and fix this.

"How did you know?"

"You talk in your sleep."

That's right. I've totally forgotten about that. "Oh."

William goes silent, but his loud breathing tells me he's still awake, and from his constant moving, I know he's not done with this topic.

"I don't know why I dreamt about him. I haven't thought about Niall in a very long time, except..." why the hell did I have to say except?

He turns back to me, this time he's sitting up and he doesn't look happy. "Except what? Do you still love him?"

I need to fix this, and fast. "No. I haven't loved Niall in years, it's just..."

"It's just what Olivia?"

Might as well come clean. "He wrote to me. Back when the situation with Jade happened. I found his letter stuffed in a box with all my other things when we were unpacking. He was writing to tell me he was coming to England for work and he wanted to see me."

William throws himself back on the bed, his entire face red. "I was going to tell you, William, I was. But when I got home, the house was a mess and you were gone. Then that's when I found out about you and I forgot about the whole Niall thing. I don't know why he was in my dream, maybe I need the closure I thought I was never going to get, and besides that, it's nothing serious. I don't love Niall anymore. It was just a random dream, that's all." I look down at him, but his hands are covering his face, the rest of his body remains still. "William?"

"Were you going to meet up with him? Without telling me?"

"No. I wasn't planning on ever meeting up with him. I don't need to see him. I'm happy in my new relationship, the last thing I needed was to see my ex-boyfriend, or anyone from my previous life, and I wouldn't have done that without telling you first."

His hands drop, his face still red, but the anger has long faded away. He seems okay, like the last ten minutes didn't just happen.

"Have you ever thought about it, going back to him?"

This throws me back. "No. Is that what you're so worried about? Me going back to him? Do you honestly believe I'm that heartless?

He sits back up, turning his whole body to face mine. "I think you should go back to him. Just hear me out before you start yelling at me. He can give you the life I wanted to. He can promise you ten more years, and a family. All you're going to get from me is less than a year and a lifetime of heartbreak. I won't be here to take care of you, or to make sure you're happy, but he can, unless of course he's hit by a bus."

He trails off, a clear sign of tears in his eyes. "He can promise you a forever, when I can't even promise you a tomorrow. I should've left you alone, this way I would've died by myself, but at least you wouldn't be burden with the thought of me for the rest of your life."

He hangs his head in silence, his lips quivering, and seeing him like this doesn't help stop the tears from falling down my face. "Maybe he can promise me a forever, but I'd rather have one year with you, then a lifetime with him. I have never loved Niall the way I love you. No one will ever do for me what you've done and I wouldn't trade you for anything. I can live the rest of my life with a broken heart, as long as I get to spend the rest of this year with you."

My eyes flood, and my hands start to shake, but I ignore them. What I just said wasn't a lie, he may be dying, but he won't die alone. I won't do this without him. "I love you William. Infinity and always."

I toss the sheets aside, climbing into his lap, and wrap my arms around his waist, my head rests under his chin. I hate seeing him cry and can't stand watching as the water falls.

"I love you Olivia. Infinity and always."

"Loving you was worth every last heartbreak."

CHAPTER TWENTY

Tuesday, September 6th 2016

"I have absolutely no idea what I'm looking at."

A hand smacks up against my left shoulder, jolting me back into the real world. "That's probably because your eyes are closed."

I snapped out of my thoughts, my eyes fly open to see Emma flash her pearly whites at me.

"My eyes weren't closed, I was blinking. It's a natural thing to do, you know."

She turns back to her doctor, her hands on her stomach as she runs them along her belly. She feels for a certain spot and stops, breaking into a smile that could crack her face.

My hand reaches over, resting on hers.

"I'm so happy for you Em. You're going to be an amazing mummy, and I, an awesome aunt."

She crushes my hand, happy to hear me say those words, her eyes never leaving her stomach. Her hand pulls away from mine as she wipes a tear from her eye, shooting a quick glance at me, no doubt hoping I didn't see that.

"Try to get comfortable Ms. Harper, I'll be back before you know it."

Her doctor nods at us, before exiting the room, leaving Emma alone with me and my questions.

"So how are you Em? Everything good?"

She lets out a ragged breath, shifting back in forth looking for a comfortable position to rest.

"Of course, why wouldn't it be?" She tries to change the subject. "What about you and your handsome teacher boyfriend?"

I try to mask a smile, but fail. Something about the thought of William always brings a smile to my face. "He's good. We're good. Everything's good."

"That's it? Come on Liv, I'm pregnant, annoyed, hot and always horny. Give me something to go on. Have you guys, you know, shagged yet?"

My eyes grow wide. This isn't the Emma I remember.

"I'm sorry, but what happened to my shy little friend? Where the hell has she gone?"

"Oh, she died a very long time ago. Besides, I was sick of being the cautious, good little girl who never went out, or talked to men. She was so boring. I'm still shocked I was able to make friends."

"You weren't that boring. Okay maybe a little, but you were still fun. In the quiet, virgin type way."

She laughs, her expression from joy, then somber in two seconds. I look her over, attempting to read her, but every time I try she jerks her head to the side, hiding her anguish from me.

I stand, resting next to her on the tiny hospital bed, with just enough room to fit half a human much less a pregnant woman. "Em, honey, what's going on? You seem a little off today."

"I don't know what you're talking about. I'm fine. But enough about me, seriously, it's like every time we get together it's baby this, and baby that. Have you ever stopped to think that maybe, just sometimes, people are interested in what's going on in your life?"

Her failed attempts at changing the subject won't work on me. "I told you, everything's good. And the only reason I'm so concerned about you is because you're knocked up. I'm curious about how you and the baby are doing, isn't that what friends are supposed to do? Care about each other."

She freezes up, her fingers pull at the ugly grey blanket that rest beneath her. "Yeah, I guess."

Something's up and I never shy away from getting the truth.

"So how's everything with you and Jared? You two move in yet?"

Her body tenses up next to mine, her jaw clenched and her nails digging into the bed. "No not yet. I wanted to give it some time, deal with all the painful things that comes with getting pregnant. But, yeah, no we're good."

A single tear escapes her eye; this time she doesn't bother with wiping it away. Instead it falls, landing right between the two of us.

"Em, it's okay. You can tell me anything."

She lays back, the back of her hands covering her eyes. "Jared and Jade." She stops to look out the window. "They slept together."

As if all our friendships couldn't be more broken.

"What the hell do you mean they slept together? Like now, in the present tense?"

"Three days ago. I was packing up a few things, you know getting ready to begin the next stage of my life, and that's when I got the call. He asked me to come over, that it was urgent and it couldn't wait. As soon as I walked in the door, he went off. Told me that he ran into Jade, that one thing led to another and they spent the night together. In his house of all places. And after all the shagging, they had a nice long chat about how much they love each other and how much they missed one another. So, they decided to give love another go."

I freeze, unaware of what I should say or do. Jade has been the rock-solid foundation of our friendship. She was the mother, the one who threw out life lessons even when you didn't want them. She helped me with my parents and with Niall. She would give Avery 'the talk' every time she went out with a man or woman. And now there's this. I'm not saying I fully support the choices Emma has made, but what Jade has done is a million times worse. She knew that Jared and Emma were together, and she knew about Emma's new situation, and she goes and pulls this shit.

"It's okay, I had that same look on my face. I was stunned. I didn't know what to do besides sit there, staring into space. You know I wasn't even mad. I felt like I deserved it. I slept with her ex fiancé, what did I expect was going to happen? We all get what we deserve in the end. This is what I deserve. But I'll be okay Liv, really. I have my home; I have my education. I can do this."

"And what about the baby?"

"Oh, we'll be fine. No need to worry about that."

"No, what did Jared say about the baby? What's his brilliant plan on that?"

"He said he'll help. He still wants to be a father to his unborn child, but of course I told him to piss off. I don't want his help. I would rather do this on my own. I got myself into this mess and I'll get myself out. Without his help." Her smile fades. "I don't ever want to see those two ever again, for as long as I live."

Emma's face turns red, her eyes clouding up, but she doesn't cry. She's stronger than I thought.

I place my hand on her stomach and pull her closer to my chest. "You're never going to be alone. This baby is going to have an amazing mother and an even better aunt. Trust me Emma, there's no way I'll ever let you walk this road alone. I promise."

She pulls in closer, her head pressing hard up against my breast. "I ruined your friendship, why would you bother to stand with me?"

"Because you're my sister, and sisters don't let sisters raise their child alone."

"I'm an idiot, aren't I?"

I pull my head from hers and look out the window, a robin taps up against the clear glass, trying to find his way in. "Yes, you are. But you're my idiot. We all make stupid decisions, it's what makes us human. Your only mistake here was falling for the wrong man, and not because he was your friend's ex, but because he's not a real man at all. He left Jade at the altar, he went after one of her friends and got her pregnant, then he decides to go back to the woman he ditch once before, leaving his child without a father. He's the dumbass in this scenario. He and Jade, not you. Stop letting it consume you, it's only going to get worse over time if you don't let go. I can't begin to imagine how hard this must be for you, but I want you to know I'll be here. Every day, whenever you need me. Yeah?"

She sniffles, her head nodding in agreeing with me.

"I love you Olivia."

The locks have been changed, but there's no real point in using them. This door wasn't meant to keep anyone out. I lift the door up and turn the knob quick, my shoulder collides with it, and it swings open. Jade sits on top of our counter and jumps off, a knife in her hand, but lowers it when she sees me.

"What the hell are you doing in my home?"

"Our home, remember? Say whatever the hell you want Jade; this is my flat too. Put the knife down, you look like an idiot."

She opens her mouth to fight with me, but decides to shut up. She knows I'm right and there's nothing she can do to change that.

"What do you want Olivia? All your stuff is gone. You have nothing else here."

"A girl can't come home? Besides you can keep this piece a shit you call home, I'm not here to fight you on what's mine and what's yours. Our last conversation was cut a little short the last time we spoke and I think I want to finish it."

She places the knife on the counter and turns back towards me, her arms crossed and her head faced down. "I have nothing to say to you."

I close the door behind me and walk over to the kitchen. That doesn't mean I have nothing to say to her. "That's fine. I'll just do the talking than. I had an interesting conversation with Emma earlier. You want to know what she told me? Well she told me that you and Jared made up. And not in the let's be friends sort of way, no, more in the let's have sex and ruin someone else's life. Is this true Jade?"

"I don't have to answer to you, don't you remember what you did to me?"

I slam my hands on the counter and Jade jumps back. "Yes, I remember it clearly. I told Emma to tell you the truth about her and Jared and she did. You slept with one of your friend's boyfriend and stole him away, leaving her to raise her kid alone. What is wrong with you?"

"Jared was mine first Olivia, or did you already forget?"

"No I remember, but then he left you. Days before your wedding. Through voicemail! Did you forget that Jade? And last time I checked, Jared isn't a pair of shoes, you can't just toss him around, you idiot." I never in my life raised my voice to anyone, not even my mother, which makes this a bit of a shock. "You took a father away from his child. Can you live with that? Can you live with knowing you ruined someone else's life?"

The anger in her face dies away, and shame replaces it. I know she knows what she did was wrong, but I simply don't think she cares. I wasn't there when Jared and Jade were still together, but I was there every day after. I remember when we first met and she was in tears thinking about him. She spent an entire year looking over old pictures and reading letters he wrote to her. I know how much she loves him, but what she's done can never be forgiven.

"I hope you're proud of yourself Jade."

She cuts me off, doing anything she can to make herself feel better. "Emma brought this on herself Olivia. She was the one who went after someone who wasn't available. She went after the man I love. Please tell me, what kind of friend would do that?"

I can't do this anymore. I was such a fool to think I could come here today and try to get through to her. I've never been one to judge or throw my opinion out there, but maybe if I would've taken an extra effort, if I would've spoke my mind when I had the chance Emma wouldn't be pregnant by a man who walked out on her. Maybe Avery would've given up her old ways sooner and she wouldn't have to live with this disease. Maybe Jade wouldn't have turned into a heartless monster.

Either way, I can't change time, and I wasn't meant to, maybe this is just how life was supposed to go. Cruel, but honest.

Without saying another word, I turn away from Jade, my hand on the door, but I'm not ready to go just yet.

"You blame Emma for her situation, but remember this; it was Jared who made the first move and asked her out. She was an innocent girl who was played by the same man who left you. Jared started this, not her, but of course when it comes to a man, women are just too stupid and blind to blame the real source of the problem."

I don't bother turning back around, the one thing I never want to see again is her face.

My hand is on the knob and I'm halfway out the door when I decided to let her know her drama isn't the only bad news going around. "Just so you know, Avery has HIV and my boyfriend is dying, but of course if it has nothing to do with you, it doesn't matter, does it?"

Before she can say another word, I walk out into the hallway, slamming the door as I go.

Sort of expected this.

As you probably realised by now I got your letter, and in a way, I'm both happy and upset. They delivered it up to me a few hours ago, along with my room service. As I was writing my first letter, I had this strong feeling you would blow me off. Who would blame you? I did do some shady shit in the past, so there would be no hard feelings. Just heartbreak.

I didn't think you'd bother to respond to me, but seeing that piece of paper, with my name written in your cursive handwriting, I smiled. Truthfully, I didn't care what was in the letter, I was just happy to see that you had responded. My joy didn't last too long though. As happy as I was to see the letter, a part of me had a feeling that it wasn't going to go all that well. And of course, it didn't.

I know in my first letter I was asking way too much from you, but there's good reasoning behind it. You said you didn't want to relieve the past, and I can understand that, but there's always going to be this dark little piece of me that will never be able to move on with life until I'm able to come clean about everything. I'm not just doing this for you; I'm doing it for myself as well.

You told me you found someone new, and reading that brought a smile to my face. You found it. You found someone who could make you happy and that makes me happy, but what I did, it still haunts me. I can't move on from our situation, nor can I find it in myself to give love a try. If I can leave the only woman I ever love, then am I capable of finding another? I need to see you again, in person. I need to get this out in the air, and then we can both finally walk away and have new lives. Lives with people who can make us happy. Don't we both deserve that much?

If you don't want to see me, then I'll leave it at this. I'll go back to New York and you'll never hear from me again, I swear. I'll stop pestering you for good and you'll never have to think about me ever again. But please, if there was ever anything real between the two of us, just give me this chance. Please Liv, for old time sakes, you and I, one last time?

P.S. There's no way you could ever be a stranger to me. You were once everything to me, and that's exactly how I plan to remember you. As my everything.

I miss you.

Niall

CHAPTER TWENTY-ONE

Wednesday, March 14th 2012

"Where do you think we'll be in like, twenty years?"

I lay on Niall's bed; my focus has been lost on that exact same question for the past couple hours.

We've always talked about where we'd end up, but every single time it's a new state, new job, new life. Neither of us certain where this is going, but there is one thing we are sure of: Wherever we are, we'll be together.

Looking over at Niall, his entire body hidden beneath his bed, a loud noise coming from underneath me.

"What are you doing down there?"

His head pops up, blond hair standing up all over his head. "Um, nothing. Just looking for something. You?"

"What?"

"What?" His eyes look from the left to right, before landing on me again. He smiles his nervous smile, the one that makes his eyes disappear. "I mean nothing, sorry, little bit distracted. I lost my math book, and can't seem to remember where I put it. Did you ask me something?"

Niall has never been one to be so distracted. He's always been so alert, so on edge, ready to jump at any moment, which puts me in a not so easy mood.

I open my mouth to ask him my question once more, but my focus shifts to something else, something that throws me in a suspicious state. "You lost your math book? When?"

His head pops up again, eyes scanning me. "A week ago." His words sounding more like a question then an answer.

Something inside me shifts, my heart guarded and my brain fighting. "A week ago, yeah? Well that's strange."

"Yeah, how so?"

"Because your math book is over there, on your desk." He pops up once more, his eyes follow my finger to the nicely placed book that lays on top of four other books.

His eyes close, the look of defeat spreads wide across his face.

He throws up his hands in protest. "Did I ever tell you you'd make an excellent female Sherlock Holmes?"

I smile, but it doesn't last long. "No, you didn't. Why did you just lie to me? Horribly."

Niall stands, one hand rests on his hip, while the other covers his mouth. "I was looking for something, important, that I wanted to show you, but I can't find it anywhere. I mean how could I have lost it?"

Rage, still controlling my brain, won't allow this to slide. "Okay, then just tell me what it is, I'll help you find it."

"No! No, sorry, I didn't mean to yell." He lowers the hand over his mouth and it finds its way to his other hip. "This is important to me Liv, let me find it okay? Just give me a minute. Please?"

His words throw me off. Never has Niall ever raised his voice. At anyone. Even my witch of a mother, who has every reason to be yelled at. But if he's keeping something from me, then there's no point in waiting around.

I stand, heading straight for my backpack that's nesting in the corner by the door.

"Liv, where are you going?"

"Well seeing as you're so busy with your, secret project, I thought it best to get out of your way. I'll be home, ignoring you, if you need me." My hands on the knob, but so is Niall's, pulling me back into the center of the room.

"Okay, wait." He stops, contemplating rather he should tell me the truth or not. When I yank my hand out of his, he caves in. "It's a surprise. I didn't just want to tell you, I also wanted to show you the proof. I wanted to see the reaction on your face when I told you I was accepted into UCLA."

UCLA? My heart stops for a quick second; my brain soon follows. "You what?"

A smirk highlights his face. "I got in Liv. We get to go to our dream school." His arms open wide, and he does that silly face he usually does when he tries to get me to laugh. It works every time.

I jump into his arms and they close around me, tightly, spinning me around the room, his overexcited laugh matches mine.

"When? How?" I stop to catch my breath before going into all the nouns. "When did you get your letter? How could you lose something like that? Wait, does this mean we're going to California?"

The grip around my waist loosen, only enough so that he can look down at me, his eyes sparkle with glee. "We're going to California babe."

Whatever emotions that inhabited my body only seconds ago, have turn to dust, floating up in the air above us. I got my letter weeks ago, and the entire time Niall and I spent our days biting our nails and making alternate dreams. He sent out his applications way before I did, and when I found mine in the mail, he panicked. UCLA meant a huge deal to both of us, but more to him. Niall loves California. The heat, the beaches, the glamour. He would've sold his soul to move there, and now he doesn't have to.

"We're going to California." I repeat his words, ache in my face from smiling so hard starts to kick in. I don't think anything can wipe this smile from my face.

Niall wraps his arms around me once more, but this time not so tight. He inhales, taking in the scent of my hair and neck, and when he exhales, his breath feels cool against my skin, sending a jolt of pleasure through my body. "Married, amazing jobs, and kids."

I'm so lost in the moment I almost miss his words. "Hmm?"

"You asked me where we'll be in twenty years. We'll be married with our six kids and be working at our dream jobs. A perfect picture life. Niall and Olivia Parker, together till the end of time."

My chin digs deeper into his chest, my tears stain his favorite, faded shirt, but he doesn't seem to mind.

"Till the end of time."

Present Day

The ducks walk past me, ignoring the bread I throw in front of them. Maybe they're more drawn to William then me.

I look down at my watch, William's watch, I never did care for jewelry. The time reads four-forty-eight. Perhaps I came too early, but the silence between William and I was too much and I had to get out of the house. He told me he thought it was important and necessary for me to meet Niall in person, and he was right of course, but he wasn't happy with me doing it alone. He didn't say it out loud, but we've been together long enough for me to read his moods. He wanted to come and hover, but this is something I must do alone, and having my current relationship clash with my past one would not end well.

I look down at the watch again and only one minute has past, but my nerves haven't. Something inside me thought I was over Niall and his letter, but my sweaty palms speak otherwise. I wipe them on my jeans, but new sweat just replaces the old, so I give up.

The only way to get over this is to face him. Who was I kidding with that stupid letter, I need the truth. I need closure.

"You dyed your hair."

My heart sinks to my stomach, my knees seem to have gone numb, and my breathing becomes hyperventilating. But I look on straight, too frozen to move. His voice is different. Deeper, darker. He's not that boy I remembered and I haven't even seen his face yet.

A figure walks around the bench and stops right in front of me, chasing away the ungrateful ducks. My eyes shift up, and this is in no way the same boy I remembered.

He's a man now, inches taller than he was. His blonde hair darker, and a little longer, groomed and pulled back as he runs his fingers through it. A nervous habit he seems to not have broken. The bags under his eyes makes him look ten years older, his eyes heavy from lack of sleep, or something else that torments him. He manages a smile, but not like any I've ever seen on him.

This is not the Niall I loved.

"Niall?"

Crow's feet appear as he smiles again, this one as forced as the last. "Hey Livia."

I stand, I've lost all control over my body and look him up and down at least a hundred times. "You look different. Older. And taller."

He chuckles, his eyes haven't moved from me once. "You do too."

"Are you calling me an old giant?"

His face cracks into a wide smile, the old Niall makes an appearance, and in a way, it makes me happy. "You haven't change one bit, have you Liv?"

"Only in certain ways." I gesture to the bench behind me. "You want to sit?"

He waves a hand at me. "Ladies first."

I sit, moving over to give him and myself enough room. His eyes fall when he sees me scooting all the way over to the edge, and takes the hint, sitting on the opposite side of the bench. Avoiding his gaze, which I can feel on me, I toss some tiny pieces of bread, but there are no ducks. They all ran when Niall showed up, but right now I'd fake a heart attack to get out of this awkward situation.

"Feeding your imaginary ducks, are we?"

"Haven't lost your terrible sense of humour, have we?"

"Oh, and the old giant thing was supposed to be what, hilarious?"

"I thought it was." The bread slides from my hand and I sneak a glance at Niall, who still has his focus only on me. I turn back to my bread. "Let's just say we both have a possible career as standup comedians, and move on from there. Deal?"

He chuckles under his breath. "Deal."

The silence between us lasts for minutes, neither of us sure on how we should start this long overdue conversation.

"I fucked up." I turn to Niall, his fingers run through his hair on repeat. Old habits die hard. "I let you go, and still to this day I can't understand why I did it. Maybe, at the time,

338

I thought I was doing you a favour. She got in my head. She made me think I was useless, and I believed her. I thought you were wasting your time and energy on me, and maybe I was right. After ten years, I dump you with a letter. What kind of prick does that?" He pauses, his hands turn into fist, grabbing a strong hold on the bench. "We had a plan. We had it all figured out, and I ruined it. I let it all go, and I still can't see the good in it."

He looks back up; tears dance around in his eyes. "You were the greatest thing that's ever happened to me, you know? I'm sorry Olivia, for everything. I'm so sorry."

Our eyes lock, the pain in his brings me pleasure. For a while, I used to think his letter was real. That maybe he did stop loving me, but seeing him as he is now, damaged and destroyed, a piece of me is relived.

I thought I was alone. I couldn't have been more wrong. "She? My mother?"

He nods, his eyes never blink. "You were right. That woman is Satan."

I knew it. I blamed her for years, but hearing the truth gives me the closure I needed. Mother set this up, and Niall took the bait. "You chose her words over me. Why?"

"Because I was a stupid, little boy, and you deserved a man."

That's not enough for me. "I hated you. For years, I hated you. The thought of you. The idea of you. I wanted to hurt you so bad." Now I'm crying. "I loved you Niall. All I wanted was you. Just us; till the end of time, remember? Do you even remember your promise to me?" My voice has raised higher than I thought it could. "Did you even love me?"

In a flash, he's by my side, careful not to get too close or touch me. "Don't say that, you know I did. I did, I just…" His head shakes, back and forth, like he's trying to forget everything he's done. "I don't know what I was thinking then. I wasn't thinking."

"No, you just walked away. And the fact that you left a letter. A fucking letter, that, that is what killed me. Ten goddamn years, and that's what I get? There were so many ways you could've gone with it, but you chose the worse. You told me you didn't love me anymore, you made me feel like some sort of idiot. I gave everything to us, my relationship with my family was ruined because I loved you and here I thought you loved me the entire time, but you didn't. We planned a future together, we picked out the country we were going to settle down in. Our kid's name's, all six of them, first and middle. We had everything set, and I thought it was what you wanted too, but I was wrong. I was such an idiot."

I pull the sleeve of my jacket up, wiping away the river that flows down my face. I thought I could be strong. I thought when I first saw his face, I would lash out and get angry, not become an emotional wreck. I didn't want to give him the satisfaction of seeing me cry.

"You didn't love me. No matter how much you claim you did, you didn't. You don't purposely hurt the ones you love, or give up on them. Not after a decade together. You just don't. So please, don't insult my intelligence. I'm no fool, not anymore. You may have sold your little fairy tale before, but not again. I will not let you make an arse out of me."

He pulls back, from the look on his face he didn't expect our chat to go down like this. If I know Niall, or who I thought he was, then he came here thinking with the time that's passed and the people we've grown into, that maybe he had a chance at fixing things without them falling apart first. But he was dead wrong. The old Olivia would've forgiven him, because she was so in love with him, but the person I am today, well let's just say she had a very heartbreaking, stressful half-year, and the last thing she's going to put up with is her ex.

"Is that all, or did you want to give me some more big news? Did you kick an innocent puppy on your way here?"

"Italy. Venice, or Rome. We still hadn't made up our minds. Thomas, Heath, Tristan, Jordan, Lily, Ariel and Aaliyah. We weren't sure if we should name one of our daughters Jordan or if we should give her a normal female name like Ariel. You didn't want her to be bullied for her name. We'd wait, until about around the age of thirty, then we'd get started on our first child. Hopefully twins. You always wanted a set." He remembers. "Neither one of us cared for a big, fancy wedding, and with your parents not being invited, we made up our mind to go simple. Courthouse wedding, save our money for our first home." He looks down at his hands, regret feels his voice. "I remember everything Olivia. I may have screwed it up in the end, but you must believe it was real for me too. Do you think I would've wasted all those years on a woman I didn't love?"

Something white in the corner of my eyes catches me off guard, but it's only a piece of paper. Ripped, damp, and losing its color, Niall passes it over and I take it from his hand.

I turn it over in my hands a few times before giving into my curiosity. The note unfolds, carefully, and I look at it in disbelief. It's a picture, a stick figured drawing of Niall and I hand in hand, three kids on each side. Two dogs stand in front. I remember the day he drew this awful picture.

"You kept this?"

"It was our future. I never wanted to let it go. Even after I let us go. Do you remember when I drew that for you? We were in…"

"Sixth period, junior year. We almost got in trouble for passing notes. I stuffed it down my bra so our teacher wouldn't find it. He must've searched my notebooks for twenty minutes. Persistent one, that Mr. Cunningham." I run my fingers across the two dogs. Two huge circles, with sticks for legs. "John and…"

"Sherlock. That's what I get for letting you name them." He smiles, looking down at the picture as if it would pop off the page and become our real, everyday lives.

"Because if I would've let you name them, it would've been CP30 and R2D2, and I couldn't live with myself if you tortured our dogs like that."

"And what's wrong with the names I picked out?"

"What's right with them?"

His glare meets me, his eyes soft and tired. "You look beautiful Olivia. Did I tell you that yet?"

I shake my head, turning back to our tiny home, with our tiny family and our large dogs. Our future was set.

"Well you are. As beautiful as the day I met you. Not one thing about you has changed."

"My boobs. I had only nipples when we met."

His laugh even seems sad. "Your sense of humor hasn't changed either. But your hair has. It's longer too."

"I'm not the only one who's changed. You grew a beard. Back then you couldn't sprout any hair anywhere. You look skinnier too, and your eyes, they're sad. You look so much older than you are, Niall. What's happened to you?"

He turns to the ducks who decided to creep back on us. "I lost you."

"Whose fault was that?"

"Mine, and I'll live with that on my shoulders for the rest of my life."

"Don't Niall. Don't do that to yourself. Something's were meant to be and some weren't. We fall under the latter." I look him over once more. Even under that burly coat, I can see how skinny he's become. His eyes tell me how much he suffered in these past years

Was this all because of me?

"I don't hate you. I did, but not anymore. We were together for so long. So much has happened between us that no bad choice can take away. I loved you once Niall, and I still do, in a way. You were my first love, you taught me everything. I am who I am today because of you, and I'll never forget it. But this is us now. I live in England and I go to Cambridge, and you live in California and go to UCLA. We're not those kids anymore. And we never will be again."

"New York."

"What?"

"I live in New York now. Photographer. I thought I mentioned it in my letter."

"What happened to web development? You had your heart set on that."

"I also had my heart set on us, but we don't always get what we want, do we?"

My thoughts shift to William, slowly wasting away at home. Counting down to the day where we'll have to say goodbye. I had my heart set on the two of us too.

Maybe it was I who was never meant to be happy. "No. No we don't."

CHAPTER TWENTY-TWO

Sunday, September 18th 2016

"I think you've already made up your mind. You're only asking for my approval without actually asking for it."

"I am not."

Niall folds another set of black shirts and stuffs them into one of his drawers, shifting his attention to his socks now. He rubs his chin, trying to find matching pairs.

"Olivia, you always do this. When it comes to making up your mind, you do it in an instant. You only ask because you like to say it aloud to others and see what their opinions are. And once you get those opinions, you totally ignore them and stick by your gut choice. It's a classic Olivia Fitzgerald move. Trust me, I've known you for ten years, I know more about you then you know about yourself."

I sit on the edge of his bed in the middle of his hotel room. Since our first conversation, I've learned to forgive him. A part of me remembered how much he once meant to me, and no amount of heartbreak could've ever taken him out of my life permanently. It took a few days, mind you, hearing the words come out of his mouth was the relief I've been waiting for, but knowing I was right about my mother interfering in my relationship took a massive toll on me. I didn't leave the bed for days. William finally tricked me into coming downstairs, he did that dance with his eyes, the stare that could make you forget all your troubles, all your suffering. Eventually I stopped ignoring Niall's calls and forgave him, a weight detached when I did.

It feels weird, being alone in a room with him. Like a blast from the past, but a thousand times more awkward. Well maybe not awkward, but strange. Genuinely strange.

After I left for England, I just assumed that was it. I never thought I'd hear his voice, or see his face again. It all seemed to be over. Ten years flushed down the drain, and I had to watch as everything that once mattered so much to me, be stripped away. Slowly and painfully.

My hands move along the bed, searching for his other silk sock. He has like four pairs, all black, but they all must belong to the original set that he bought them with.

Old habits die hard.

"It's nice to see your paranoia in regards to your clothing hasn't changed a bit." I pick up a random sock and hand it to him. He turns it in his hands before throwing it back into the pile. "Seriously Niall?

His concentration breaks. He looks at me as if I haven't been here for the past two hours. "What? Come on Olivia, even you can see that didn't match this one. And I'm not paranoid, I'm driven."

I pick up another black sock and hold it up in front of me. He shakes his head at me. "You're paranoid Niall. Accept it. I did. It was one of the quirks I admired about you. Most of the time."

He looks at me through hooded eyes and manages a sly smile. The next sock I hold out for him to inspect, he looks at my reaction to his OCD and sighs. He takes the sock from my hand and rolls it up with the one in his hand other, tossing it aside and moving on to the next pair.

"So exactly how long does it take for you to get dressed in the morning. One, two, eight hours?" He smirks at my sarcasm, hitting me with a white sock, inches away from hitting my face.

I lean back on the bed, my hands propping the rest of my body up, giving up on him and his wardrobe. Two hours we've been doing this. After the first few minutes, it becomes tedious.

My hands slip, throwing my body back against the bed, but I don't attempt to regain myself. Instead I lay against the soft, warm hotel sheets, my fingers tangled together above my head, my eyes closed. Besides Niall's constant breathing, I can hear the telly going off in the background. Something about a bus crash, and a movie star I could care less about. My thoughts teleport me back to Paris, and the late night visit to the botanical gardens. The drunken night I spent breaking the law, and falling asleep next to William on the grass. Who would've thought that night would help set up an everlasting relationship.

I can feel my lips move, a smile now on my face. I try to keep the amazing memories filed first in my brain. Remembering him as the man who was full of life, and always so happy. It keeps me going.

"How's William doing?"

My eyes shoot open and I prop my head up to see Niall's facial expression. He looks worried, scared even.

353

He's took on the role of guardian when I told him about William. I don't know how it happened, sort of slipped out after William had another episode.

We were downstairs. I try forcing him out of the room every now and again to give him a different scenery then the four walls that make up our bedroom. He tends to stay in bed a lot these days, his energy drained from his fight. He still looks like himself, which is good, still has color in his face. It's his body that gives up on him. Making a trip to the bathroom, which is only a few feet from his side of the bed, exhausts him, forcing me to have to help him back in the covers. He's become a bit distant too, his mind sometimes gets away from him and it's caused a strain on us. I know he doesn't mean it; I think it's just the reality of his situation is starting to kick in. His doctor told us he might have a good six months left, but who knows, maybe it'll be longer, maybe it'll be shorter. Only fate can tell.

William caught me one day, after I've given him his meds and watched as he fell asleep, I broke down in my pillow. The sight of him, worse than any heartbreak I've endured throughout my entire life. I cried for hours, couldn't bring myself to sleep until my body was emptied of all fluids and I had nothing left to give. When I woke, his arms were around me, his ribs piercing my skin like a set of knives. He's lost some weight, nothing too drastic, but you can see it in his face. Just like Niall, he no longer looks like himself, but through it all, I can still see those eyes. The same deep blue that stole my soul, and his smile, even with his never-ending battle, he always manages to keep a smile on his face.

As bright as our first night together.

I force the tears back. "He's good actually. Been walking on his own lately, which is good. Still don't like leaving him for too long, you know. He's doing well now, but his health can change as quick as the weather."

Niall gives up on his socks and plops down on the bed next to me, laying side by side, our shoulders touching. "I'm sorry, Liv. I never would've imagined this as your life. You deserve so much, after all I put you through, and your family. You would think the world would stop screwing you over by now."

I feel his hand bump up against mine for a split second, then wrapping itself around mine. Instead of pushing it away, I squeeze onto it, as if it were my life preserver. I can feel his eyes on me.

"You know, no matter what happens, I will always drop whatever I'm doing, book the first flight I can get and stay with you until you had enough of me. You won't be alone, Olivia. I'll never leave you. Never again."

I can feel something hit my ear, sliding down inside and leaving a moist spot. It's followed by a few more drops, tears streaming down my face and falling sideways. I take my free hand and grab onto his arm, digging my nails into his flesh. "I don't think I can do this Niall. I can't watch him die. I just can't." I turn to the side, laying my head on his shoulder. The same position we always found ourselves in when my mom pissed one of us off. "I don't want to live without him."

He takes his free hand and wipes the tears from my face. "I know, Liv. I know."

"Olivia?"

I shut the door behind me, forcing a smile on my face before turning around. "Who else would it be? One of your mistresses?"

William is out of the kitchen and lifting me off my feet with only a few quick movements. It's good to see he has his strength back. His hand is on my chin, lifting my head so his lips can find mine. He kisses me the way he used to, when we first starting dating. Forceful, yet playful and sweet. I stumble on my heels, and fall back against the wall, but he doesn't seem to notice. His teeth have a tight grip on my bottom lip, his hands cradle my neck.

"They know better than to drop by. They always call first." He whispers into my mouth; he tastes of herbal tea and mint. He kisses me again, first my forehead, then nose, each cheek, and back to my lips, his hips pressed up against me, pinning me to the wall without an opportunity to break free. Not like I would want to. "I've missed you. What took you so long?"

I reach up, my hands move along his middle, digging underneath his shirt, rubbing against his skin, until they find his back. I pull him closer, the pain of being stuck to the wall disappears as I stand on my toes, my turn to kiss him. "Niall had a sock panic attack. I forgot how weird the man was."

His hands tighten on the back of my neck. He said he was okay with Niall and I being friends, but I don't think he likes the idea of us being alone.

William's head drops, his forehead against mine, his breathing fast and rough. My hands leave his back and move up to his face, forcing him to look at me. I kiss his chin, then his nose, each cheek, and end with his lips.

"You don't ever have to worry about Niall, babe. He's not you. And I don't want anyone who isn't you. Okay?"

He nods, but his eyes are looking down at our feet. I push myself off the wall, making William stumble back this time and falling against the dining table behind us. I wrap my hands around his neck this time and pull him closer to me, our noses touching.

"I love only you. Infinity and always?"

Those three little words cause him to smile. The crow's feet on each side of his eyes grow deeper, and I kiss him once more, the smell of his hair, coconut and something else, something strong, fill my nose.

He leans his head against my shoulder, his hands, bare and warm beneath my shirt, trace my hips before resting on my thighs.

"Infinity and always."

"No Olivia, I'm not going to drop it. Why would you do something like this without talking to me about it first?"

I stick my head out of the bathroom, annoyance in my heart and a toothbrush in my mouth. "Oh I'm sorry, how about from now on, I go to you first to beg for your permission before making any decisions. Would you like that?"

William hunches over the bed, his head down, his eyes closed. He's doing the breathing exercises I taught him so he wouldn't get tired, or winded so quickly. He raises a hand to his head, his palm pressed against his temple as he bends down a little more. He looks as if he's going to collapse at any moment.

I drop the toothbrush on the floor, rushing over to his side. "Get in bed. Now William." I help lift him onto the bed pushing him over just enough to get the covers from under him. He throws himself back, tired and frustrated. "I told you, you need to stop this. You're working yourself up for nothing, and you pay the price in the end."

"You quit both your jobs and school, Olivia. How was I supposed to react? Do you think this is what I wanted? For you to give up everything for me? That's why I didn't want to do this. That's why I wanted you to move on. You would've had a much better chance if I would've left you alone."

He covers his face with his hands, his breathing loud and irregular. Swiping away the covers, he attempts to sit up, but my hand is there to stop him. "I wish I would've stayed away from you."

I don't like where this conversation is going. "Are you telling me you think life would be better without me?"

"No, I'm not saying…"

"Why are you telling me this now? Six months later and now you tell me?"

"I'm not saying I regret you, Liv, I'm saying I regret ruining your life. You'd still be in school, you'd still have your work, but no. Your cancer riddled boyfriend had to take everything from you. Including your freedom."

"Exactly, my freedom. Not yours. I made the choice to love you. I chose to stay even after I found out the truth. It was my decision, not yours to make and I don't regret my choices. I'm allowed to love who I want and I'm also allowed to decide if I want to quit working and temporarily quit school, to take care of you."

I stop before I say something I might regret.

"You have less than a year, and then you'll be gone, and you're never coming back and I'm the one who's going to have to find a way to cope with that." The tears fight their way to my eyes, but I fight back. I can't spend the rest of our lives together crying. "You're going to die and it's going to hurt, but I'll get better. I have to. I don't know how, but I'll figure it out when the time comes."

I stand, putting on a smile, and walk up to his side of the bed to put the covers back over him. "So, until that day comes, I'm going to be here, taking care of you like any person in love would do. From this day forward, it's going to be me and you, every day, attached at the hips. So, deal with it, yeah?"

My lips stop him from starting a fight neither of us will win. His kiss is soft and empty, mine doing all the work. I pull away, my finger on his mouth. "No more fighting. We can't keep doing this, it's not getting us anywhere."

I walk back to the bathroom, closing the door behind me so he can't see me. Once the door slams behind me, I turn on the faucet and collapse onto the floor, my face inches away from the toilet seat, everything I consumed today coming back up and disappears into the water below me. I sit back up, resting against the wall behind me, tears running down my face.

"Olivia?"

The bed starts to squeak, and before he can open the door, I flush down the mix of two tuna sandwiches, an oversized plate of fish and chips, a few pork pies and a whole lot of trifle. Niall over spoiled me today.

"Yeah I'll be out in a minute."

I can hear a knock. "Open the door Liv. Now."

Wiping my mouth, I toss back some mouthwash, allowing it to disappear in the sink, and splash some water on my face and take one last look at myself in the mirror before opening the door. William stands before me, leaning on the dresser to keep himself up. He looks me up and down, his eyes scan the bathroom behind me. I know when he knows that somethings up, so I change the subject.

"Come on, back in bed with you." I push him, weakly, and he obeys me. I help him back in bed, avoiding his eyes so he can't read the pain behind mine. Once he's safely lying down, I turn to the unfolded laundry and try to keep myself busy and hope he gets the message.

"I'm sorry. I know how hard this must be for you, I just wish you wouldn't have made this decision without coming to me first. Maybe we could've found a way around it. I wanted you to finish school, Liv. I know how important it is to you."

I refuse to turn. "Yes, it is, but you're more important. Besides I have the rest of my life to finish school. I don't have that same luxury when it comes to you. Now get some sleep, will you."

"Olivia, it's four in the afternoon, and I'm not tired."

"Well just rest your eyes then. You look like hell."

"Thanks, sweetheart. I always love getting compliments from you."

I smile. I always found it funny how we could go from being angry with each other, then it turns depressing and we come back to a silly idiotic couple who still loves one another. "Anytime love."

I've given up on the clothes, it was only meant to be a distraction, but the last thing I want is for anything to come between us. Especially at a time like this. He can be gone any day now, and keeping secrets is not something I want.

"William?"

"Hmm?" I think he must've fallen asleep.

"I love you."

"I love you more."

"Infinity and always?"

He chuckles, the sound muffled by his pillow. "Infinity and always."

There's another silence before I decide to be brave. "William?"

"Yes love?"

"I'm pregnant."

CHAPTER TWENTY-THREE: *WILLIAM*

Saturday, March 19th 2016

"I can't believe you actually took that! Wasn't it bad enough that we committed one crime today?"

She cradles the poppy in her hand, the look of someone who's just done a crime and has gotten away with her spreads across her face.

"Oh you just don't know how to have fun." Looking up, she places the flower behind my ear and gives me a wide, closed eye smile. "There, now you look pretty."

"Apparently not." I slide my hand into hers, using all my energy to keep her up. I'm starting to think glass number four and five were huge mistakes. "Olivia?"

"Yes Mr. Edwards?"

I decide not to ask. "Never mind."

She lifts her head off my shoulder, leaving it cold and lonely, longing for her touch. "No you started, now you must finish. Isn't that what you taught me?"

Her eyes are on me now, her chin poking against my arm, but it bothers me none. To be this close to her cancels out all pain I've been feeling this past year. "I don't think I've ever said such words."

She reads my expression and shrugs. "Must have been my history teacher. Or was it my eighth-grade teacher?"

I squeeze her hand tighter, never wanting it to leave mine again. "Okay, before we go down the long journey of who said what, I wanted to ask you something. It's a little random and out there, but I'm just a wee bit curious, so answer it, don't answer it." I sneak a glance at her, and she blinks sleepily at me, wonder shines in her eyes. "Do you have a bucket list of things you've always wanted to do, before you know?"

"You mean before I die? Wow, way to bring an amazing night to a depressing close."

"I'm serious. Just answer the question. Please?"

She pulls away again, studying me before saying anything else. "Well, I've never actually created a list, so to speak, but I guess mentally I've made a list of a few things worth doing before I croak. You know, things like see my favorite artist in concert, or learn a new language. I always wanted to live in a different country than the one I was born in. Who knows, maybe after school I'll do just that."

"Olivia, you're an American living in England. You've already completed that one."

Her head jerks back up, a confused look on her face. A laugh soon follows. "Oh yeah. Well hey, that's something to knock off the list. I must make a mental note of that."

I can't help but laugh with her. This Olivia is so much different from the Olivia back home, the Olivia who sits in the very back of my class and keeps her head down for the full two hours. She's human and funny. And she can definitely make a night interesting. "I think it's time we get back, before you talk me into something I might regret. Or you know, get us thrown out of the country."

"Well now that's a thought." She beams up at me, the street lights illuminate off her bare shoulders, her skin the color of coffee and her hair dark chocolate, and then there's her smile. I think I unsold just how beautiful she truly is with nothing overcrowding her breathtaking features besides her burgundy lipstick.

"I don't know if I like you like this."

She looks offended. "Like what then?"

"Plastered? Off your arse drunk?"

"Now that was just rude. I happen to think I'm a joy like this. Very loveable. It's not my fault you're such a prude."

I take a step back, my hand on my heart, pretending to be insulted. "Me? A prude. Well now who's the one being rude." This gets a laugh out of her. Or it could just be the drink. "I'm not trying to be a prude, it's just weird to see you this way. Makes me wonder what's really going on up there." I raise my hand and tap twice between her eyebrows and she playfully swipes my hand away. "I'm serious though, having you in class gave me a perception on who you really are, and I just find it shocking that you're nothing like the woman I imagined."

"Is that a good thing, or a bad thing?"

"Both."

She grins at me, moving back in closer to fill the hole between us. We walk down the dimly lit street, the back of our hands touch but don't interlock and a piece of me yearns for it. Something about having her hand in mine makes me feel safe. It makes me feel as if I'll never be alone again.

Her hand, her touch, makes me feel like I've finally found a home. A proper home, one I never want to leave. One I can cuddle up and hide in forever.

"What's your name?"

I look down at her, a little lost. "What?"

"You know my name, but I still call you Mr. Edwards. It sounds weird, you know. It sounds almost dirty. The good kind of dirty, not the boring kind."

I wonder if she'll remember any of this when she wakes tomorrow. "Yeah, you are nothing like the woman I imagined."

"Good. The woman you imagined sounds boring. Which in turn makes me sounds like an absolute square, and I refuse to be one of those shapes. Wait, where was I going with this? Your name? No more changing the subject mister, I want to know."

I laugh, my eyes scanning the sky. A beautiful day. "William. You can call me William."

She smirks, a little too proud of herself. "William, eh? William. William. William Edwards. Very British name you have there, William."

"Thank you, Olivia Fitzgerald. A very literary name you've got."

"Why thank you. I've always thought so myself."

Her other hand slips around my arm, pulling me in closer as she closes her eyes and leans on my shoulder. Her breathing comes to a rapid slow, her hand slips from my arm slowly and I fear she's either fallen asleep or passed out.

Her voice puts me at ease. "Do you have a bucket list?"

"Hmm?"

She pulls away from me, forcing her hands into the pockets of her skirt, a shiver shakes her entire body. "You asked about a bucket list earlier, I believe. Why? Do you not have one, because everyone should? It doesn't have to be anything major, you know, it can be something as simple as riding a roller coaster, or trying an authentic cuisine. Which by the way, I would not recommend eating anything French, besides the bread. The bread is delicious, but everything else is just god awful. I puked for like two hours straight."

I slip off my jacket and slide it over her shoulders, my fingers brush against her neck and she trembles under my touch. She slips her arms through the sleeves, smiling up at me as she does and I find myself reaching for her hand again. Choosing to not let it leave mine again until we get back to our hotel rooms.

"I have a bucket list; I was just curious to see if you've actually completed any adventures on yours. I haven't."

There's a small yank on my hand, but I hold on tight, not letting her go. Her hand stays in mine, but her face drops, shocked at my admission. "You haven't done anything, like at all on your list? Oh my gods, you have not lived. How old are you exactly? Never mind, look the nights still young, I still have like maybe a little more than four hours left before I give in to a massive hungover. Hangover? Hungover? Anyways, let's do something, anything on your list. It can be something tiny, or something huge, either way I'm ready. So what is it, what are we doing?"

I look down at her, she has taken both my hands in hers and is staring up at me, waiting for my answer. The only thing I want to say is spend the rest of this night walking beside her, hand in hand. But drunk or not, I don't think it's the right thing to say. Then again, I also don't want the night to end, so I improvise. "I want to watch the Parisian sunrise. I don't think I've ever watched an actual sunrise, come to think of it."

She leans her head back a little more to get a glimpse at the sky, her neck reaching the stars and I find it hard to not stare. The simplest things about her make me smile, and we've only just met. Officially.

I lift my hand up, my fingers brush loose strands of hair away from her neck and she looks back down at me. A smirk spreads across her face.

She leans in closer, her breath, the smell of wine and sweet mints on my chin.

"Well then, we should get a better view, shan't we?"

Present Day

"William I'm going to fall."

"No you're not babe, just hold onto me, I'm not going to let you go."

"Why can't I just look, it's safer than walking down a hallway in four inch heels, having no idea where I'm going."

"It's a surprise, Liv. Would you just trust me please?"

"I trust you very much, just not right at this moment. I would trust you a lot better if you'd let me see where we're going. I feel like you're leading me into a trap."

He lets go of my hands and takes me by the waist, spinning me ninety degrees to the left, then letting me go.

"William? Are you still there?"

"Of course, where else would I go? You ready?"

"Depends on what awaits me beyond this blindfold."

He kisses me softly on the cheek, his nose strokes against my nose until his lips find mine, kissing me six times quickly and playfully. I bite my lip to keep from smiling.

I can hear him fiddling with the key, pushing it into the lock. Once it beeps, he grabs my hand and leads me into our room and let's go of me once again to pick up our bags and to shut the door. I find myself fumbling around the room, looking for anything to help me figure out where I am. A pair of hands are on my waist again, pulling me back up against him, his lips on the back of my neck. "Am I ever going to find out where we are, or do you plan on keeping this thing on me the whole trip?" His breath shudders against my skin, and for a second I forget I'm blindfolded and reach behind me, my hand on his thigh. "Or we can just keep this blindfold on and stay in this vey room until they kick us out."

He spins me around, I know I can't see anything, but I can sense the smile on his face. He pulls me closer; his hands rub the small of my back. "As lovely as that sounds, there is a purpose to this trip. Although, I won't say no to spending at least one day in bed with you. The curtains shut, the lights on, and more crap movies to lighten the mood."

"Well I'm not going to say no to that." I pucker my lips and wait for him to lean over to kiss me. He does, but it's too quick and I find myself wanting more. "Should we get this over with then?"

"Alright just stand right here. No Olivia, just let me lead please." I obey, loosening up so he can move me right where he wants me. "You ready?"

I nod. I was ready like thirty minutes ago.

William pulls the blindfold from my eyes, and I blink a few times before my vision comes back to me and when it does it takes me a while to realise what the surprise is. I look around the room, and it looks like your average, every day hotel room. Bed over there, telly right in front of it, a sofa off in the corner.

Wait, that sofa, I know that sofa. And the bed. Everything is starting to look so familiar. I walk into the middle of the room and spin around slowly, trying to figure out how I know this room. Then it hits me like a sack of bricks.

I run out to the balcony and look down at the pool, right beneath my room. My room. This is my room.

I spin to face William, a goofy smile on my face. "Is this my room, from our holiday?" He nods, his one-sided smile brings a glow to my face. "You booked my same hotel room?"

"Well of course I did. It wouldn't be much of a celebration if we couldn't sleep in the same room we fall in love in." He strides over to me, pride spreads across his face. "I thought it'd be nice, you know, us spending our holiday here, just like our last one."

"Yeah, except that time, you didn't get to see me naked."

"Funny how fast things change, huh?"

I smile, my arms wrapped around his neck as he lifts me off the ground and spins me around. "Thank you, William."

"Don't. You don't ever have to thank me for anything, love. There isn't anything on this earth that I wouldn't do for you, Liv. You know that."

I bury my face in his shoulder, hiding the tears from him. They're tears of joy, you know, happy tears. But I've grown so accustomed to hiding my face whenever I cry, I think it's just become a regular old habit for me.

This Paris holiday was an amazing idea. And it's just what the both of us needed. Some time away. Time away from the doctor's appointments and the constant calls from the hospital. It's become an endless cycle of nurses coming in and out of our home, checking up on his health since he refuses to spend any time in any hospitals.

Can't blame him, once upon a time I hated hospitals just as much as the next guy. After watching my papa slowly diminish behind those drab pale pink curtains they have at hospitals, and then one day he was gone altogether. I made a vow that day, both Delphine and I, to take care of ourselves and remain in perfect health. I kept my promise to myself, but I never imagined I'd be going through this horrible process again with someone I planned on spending forever with.

"Don't do that to yourself Liv."

I sniffle in his sweater. "Do what?"

He tries to pull me away, most likely to get a look at my face, but I fight against him. My arms refuse to loosen their grip. "I know when you're crying love. You hide your face and hope I'm stupid enough to not notice, but I do. Hey, Liv. Liv." He tries another failed attempt at pushing me off. "Livia, we said we'd try to have fun. Just us. You, me, and the baby. Please, for us, let's try and enjoy ourselves."

I nod in his shoulder but still won't let go. "They're not tears of sadness, they're of joy. I always did want to be knocked-up in the city of lights with the man of my dreams."

"Well then good, as long as you're happy." He tries his best at sarcasm, but it doesn't work. We've already entered that state of mind that this will be our last real holiday together, seeing as he's not supposed to be traveling anywhere anyway. His doctor voted against it, but he ignored him of course, and lied to me.

The three of us on the only trip we'll ever take together.

William finally manages to wiggle out of my arms and bends down enough to kiss my stomach, before kissing my forehead. He turns and picks up our bags, carrying them over to the closet to unpack. I sit on the edge of the bed and kick my heels off, my head resting on my knees, I watch as he takes his time. Carefully folding and hanging up our things.

I find myself watching him a lot these days. Maybe it's my mind telling me his days are limited and I should take advantage of every opportunity I can while he's still here. Niall gave me one of his overly expense cameras, telling me it makes up for all the birthdays he's missed. And so far, I've put it to good use. At every turn, I'm capturing a new photo of him, of us, and adding it to my collection. I used to be a picture hoarder. There was something so nostalgic about them. I loved going through old albums with Niall, looking back on the days the photos were taking and smile. It has a sense of purpose in it. I find myself doing that every day with William, since he's health is getting worse and worse, and he's only getting skinnier and weaker.

He has his days. When he doesn't take his meds, he usually is his happy, old, upbeat self. Laughing and joking around. But whenever he's on them, he mops around all day, sleeping and crying. I know they're supposed to help, but in my opinion, I think they're only doing harm.

William looks down at his suitcase, a wide, toothy smile on his face. He pulls out a notebook, the one he bought a few days before we left. His hand rubs the worn leather, flipping in over back in forth in his hands as if it were to change colors right before his eyes. He still won't tell me what the book is for, just that it's important and that one day, when he's gone, we'll look back on it, our child and I and smile. Remembering him only as he was; happy and madly in love with me.

He cried the day I told him I was pregnant. For days, he cried, both tears of joy and sadness. Neither William or I thought this day would come. We never thought we'd fall in love with anyone, not after my ordeal with Niall, or his fear of ending up like his parents, but now that we're here, everything seems so wrong. I wasn't supposed to get pregnant. We haven't been safe either, but I didn't care. I didn't think about anything but him and I. That's all that mattered, it's all that will ever matter.

But now, here I am, pregnant and waiting for the father to pass away is possibly one of the hardest things anyone will ever have to go through. For both of us.

When I told him, he cried and laughed, but it soon faded once he realised there was a hundred percent chance that he wouldn't live to see our child's birth. And then I cried, because there is nothing I want more then to wake up the day after I give birth and roll over to see him holding our baby. Looking down at its rosy cheeks and smiling, knowing we both got the one thing we never thought we'd have; a family. A real proper family. But it's pointless now, we both know that's impossible, and we decided not to talk about it. For my sake and the baby's.

I wipe my face on my sleeve. "Why can't I see what you've written in there? Is it love letters to your other sweethearts?"

"Of course not, I email them all the good stuff." He looks up at me and smiles, his eyes as red as blood. Seems I'm not the only one thinking on our situation.

"Then why can't I see it? I thought we promised no secrets."

"It isn't a secret, love. It's just not ready yet, okay."

I choose not to start a fight. "Okay. I'll let it go."

He stands and walks over to me, kneeling so his face is aligned with my bine. "There is something I've been wanting to ask you, but thought this would be the absolute worst time for it."

"Trust me William, the time, when it comes to us, will never be right. You might as well get it over with."

"No, I know, I just didn't want your answer to be obvious because of my condition. But you're right. I don't have much time left and I want to do this while I still can."

"Well go ahead then. I'm all ears."

He takes a deep breath and looks me dead in the eyes. "I know this is all happening so soon and sudden that it's hard to get a grasp on reality and I'm sorry for that. All of this is my fault and I'm going to take that to the grave with me." I open my mouth to speak, but he raises his hand to my mouth, cutting me off. "Please don't try to talk me out of it, you and I know it's true. None of this would be happening if I stayed away from you. But a huge, selfish part of me is happy I didn't, because I can die saying I knew true love and it was worth it. And I want to thank you, for everything you've done for me in such a short time. You helped me find love and hope and happiness all in less than two months and I'm grateful. I finally found a place I could call home, with you. Home was never a place to me. Home is a person and my home is wherever you are."

The tears fall from both our eyes, and we don't try to stop them.

"I love you Olivia, and I knew from that night, the night after the bar, when we walked around and broke the law, and spent the early hours of the morning watching the sunrise hand in hand. I knew you were the one I wanted to spend an infinity with, and as long as you still want me, we can. We can have our infinity." My head collapses in my lap, the pain on his face too hard to bare. "What I wanted to ask you is…, is will you marry me Olivia Fitzgerald. Not in reality, but in spirit. You and me, forever. Infinity and always?"

I look back up and see him holding his Nana's ring before my eyes and break down. A marriage proposal. In Paris. Every woman's dream, and maybe, in a different lifetime it was mine. But things are different now. We only have less than six months left together and as much as I wish this was all some sick dream and I'd wake up any day now and William will be laying right beside me, fast asleep, healthy and happy and living a long, beautiful life. But it's not. It's not a dream. This is all real and any day now, I'm going to be in a room, probably back in our home, just me and our child looking through photo albums so it could know what it's father looked like. How his eyes shined, no matter what mood he was in. Or how he had a smile that could stop traffic. The kind of smile that could make you forget your troubles, lifting your spirits without trying.

I'll be alone again. Left by another man to pick up the pieces, but this one is different. He didn't choose to leave me, fate made that choice for him. Fate screwed us over in the end. Again.

My eyes move from the ring and back to William, and this would've been perfect in another lifetime. The man I love, down on one knee, promising to love me forever, even after he's gone. A tiny little fetus swimming around inside me, an amazing gift given by the greatest human being I've ever had the privilege to meet.

I love him, and he's right, everything is moving fast, but it feels so right. Everything that's happened to me since that night here in Paris, has been the very best and I wouldn't trade it for anything.

I would never trade him for anything.

I'd rather have our one year then a lifetime with anyone else, and that right there gives me my answer.

I lean over, my head resting against his as the tears stream down our faces. My hands cup his cheeks, wiping away the tears before placing my left hand in front of me. My ring finger exposed.

"Infinity and always."

Olivia Grace Fitzgerald

My beautiful, lovely wanker.

Bet you never thought you'd get a letter from me, eh? I guess sometimes we can shock ourselves.

There is so much I would love to say to you, but there's no point, right? You already know. Jade, Emma, you; the three of you are the greatest friends a loose, stupid girl like myself could ever ask for. I felt at home when I was with the lot of you, and I will cherish that until the day I die.

I want to thank you again. You were there for me when no one else was and you have no idea how much that means. Even though the two of us were so indifferent to the other, deep-down we love each other and I wish we could've been better friends. It would've been fun; the slut and the prude! We could've been amazing together.

I thought it would be easier if I wrote down my feelings, since I won't be able to tell you to your face. As you read this note, I'm already settled in my old comfy bed in Holmes Chapel. I decided to move back home. This has all been one massive wake-up call and I need to get away from it all. I need to be home, with my parents.

I told them. Told them everything. My dad didn't say a word for an hour and my mum cried. Spoiler alert, she still hasn't stopped.

I'm not going to let this mistake change me. I own it, it was my bad decisions that got me here, and I'm not ashamed. This is my chance to start over, to start making life choices I could be proud of.

Don't you feel sorry for me, nor shed a tear. I know the kind of person you are. I'll be fine, Liv. I have my family. I have my girls, and I still have my life. I'll make it through this, and I'll bounce back; happy and healthier than ever.

Thank you, Olivia. There will never be a better person in this world or the next who will ever measure up to you.

B.T.W. I hope you and William find it. Find the life you deserve. Time may be limited, but that doesn't mean you won't find your happy ending. Some people find it in a mere couple of months.

Oh yeah, before I go; he is really, really gorgeous. Don't screw it up, yeah.

Love forever and always,

Avery

CHAPTER TWENTY-FOUR

Thursday, October 18th 2012

"Why can't you just tell me where you are? I swore to you that I wouldn't tell anyone, Liv, and I meant it. If you're afraid that I might tell mom and dad, then you shouldn't. You know I would never, ever betray you like that."

I rest my head against the inside of one of the many phone booths that line the street, the receiver dangles at my side. Even with the phone down near my thigh, I can still her high-pitched voice. Puberty has yet to creep up on her. I tried to be compassionate, but right now isn't the best time for a heart to heart conversation with anyone from the Fitzgerald family. Not after what's happened.

Her voice grows silent as I place the phone up to my ear. "Now's not a really good time Delphine. I have a few things I need to take care of. I'll phone you when I get the chance, yeah?"

"No, Olivia. Why can't you talk now? Where are you? You just up and left, took your things, and forgot to mention exactly where you were going. We all know about UCLA. Mom called them. She knows you declined. Does this mean you're still in Colorado at least? Please, just give me something? Anything?"

"I'm sorry Fe, but I've got to go. Love you."

"Wait, Olivia, please don't hang up."

"Talk soon." I slam the phone, but it misses and swings back and forth beneath me and I walk out into the cold, bitter air of Cambridge.

My eyes scan the street, confused on what to do next. So, I just walk. For hours.

I could always go back to my hotel, but being alone, stuck in a room depresses me. I could always ride the tube wherever; I mean I am in a new country. An amazing and beautiful country, but I can't seem to focus. I wasn't supposed to be here. I should be in California right now, starting my first semester as a college student. Instead I'm in England, a place a million times better, and I find myself mopping about.

But I can't keep this up forever. School starts soon and I still don't have a place to live. I'll allow myself one more day of this bitter misery, then it's off looking for a flat mate. A proper one too. Not like the first one I met.

"In the hallway?"

I chuckle, my smile returning for the first time in months. "In the hallway, the bathrooms. Even the kitchen. The woman had no limit."

"Oh my god. I can't believe someone would just hang their knickers up about. Bloody hell. I'm sorry, I'm not laughing at your awful unfortunate luck, it's just…" She trails off, her eyes scan the room, as if she were looking for someone. "It's just, I don't think I've ever heard of such a thing. Most people wait until they've lived together for about a year before they've gotten a proper view of their dirty pants. I'm sorry you had to endure that."

"Oh it's alright. There's nothing like saying 'Welcome to England, now here's a first-class seat to all my flaws and disgusting habits.'"

She laughs. Her green eyes fade behind heavy, and dark eye lids. It seems I'm not the only one who hasn't slept in months. She opens her mouth, but her mobile stops her before she can get her sentence out. "Oh, I've completely forgot. I took a night shift today, hate working nights. But listen, I like you Olivia, a lot. You're probably the greatest candidate I'll ever meet, so If you want it, the flat is yours too." She stands, tossing down a couple of quids and gestures towards the door.

We stand and walk out into the warm air, the first day since I've been here where I didn't need three pounds of layers or an umbrella. "I'll be home around nine, most likely ten, but you're more than welcome to make yourself at home, for the time being anyways. Tomorrow we'll go look at the new flat together and sign it off, yeah? My gods I'm excited. Sorry, just happy to move out of that rundown flat and into ours. You remember where everything is right, of course you do. Well here's my key then, I'll phone you when I'm close to home. Have fun, do some shopping, and I'll see you later."

She turns, ready to run to the bus turning around the corner. "Jade, wait. I just wanted to say thank you. Really. Meeting you has been the best thing to happen to me in a long time and I'm very grateful. Thank you."

She smiles, the dimples on her face deep and clear. "You're always welcome mate. Besides, I think you and I will be the best of friends, yeah?"

I wave her off. "Yeah."

She turns, waving behind her as she runs off, screaming at the bus to wait.

I may have lost my family, I may have lost Niall, and I may have lost my dreams, but it seems things are finally looking up for me.

Present Day

"This is a stupid, dumbass idea William, and I can't believe I let you talk me into it."

He plays around with his food; his appetite fades more and more each week. "It's a brilliant idea Olivia, and you know it. And I didn't hear you making any complaints before we left the house?"

"I made many, you chose to ignored them."

William finally drops his fork, making faces at his food. He looks over at me and smiles. "Everything's going to be fine, love, you just can't see it yet. You're too emotional invested. And it's not like you have anything to worry about, I'll be right here the whole time. You're not alone anymore, nor are you stuck with these people. I'm here. Yeah?"

He gives me that look, the one I hate loving. The one that can make me do whatever it is he wants me to do.

I turn from him, annoyed and defeated. Sometimes I hate being in love with him. "I just think this is waste of everybody's time, that's all. I know they haven't changed. It's not in their DNA."

The sound of a screeching chair startles me, but I'm calm once his arms are around me. "If you won't do this for you, then do it for me. Do it for the seventeen-year-old Olivia?" His hand is on the back of my neck; his warmth sends a cooling sensation throughout my insides. "I never got to fix my relationships, but you still can. You've already repaired one, with an ex none the less, but still, I'm proud of you. And you shouldn't stop there. Liv, I need to know that once I'm gone, you won't be alone. You can't be alone, I know you, and I know what this is going to do to you, so please, for me, just get through this."

"And what if it fails?"

"If it fails, I'll do the dishes for the rest of the year."

I scoff at him. "You already do the dishes."

He stops to think on that. "Oh yeah, that's right. Well I'll find another way to make it up to you. By the way, you can do a dish or two every now and again. Would save me a lot of energy."

I turn to him, leaving a kiss on his nose. "Why would I take away the one thing that makes you happy?"

He laughs under his breathe. "You're the only thing that makes me happy. You smart arse."

I turn away, looking out at the Thames in hopes they won't show today, but I'm no idiot. Dad's been desperate to see me again since I've disappeared and Delphine seems as if she's dying of guilt and has this anxious need to make me forgive her. Which I have, I've even forgive my mother. I think.

If being with William has taught me one thing, it's that life is short and one day, unexpectedly, life is going to take the things you love the most.

"Stop worrying love, it will all be alright."

"I know. I know. It's just been a long day, and I'm not feeling too fabulous at the moment."

I rest my hands on my stomach; todays lunch ready to come back up. William's hand is over mine, his head on my shoulder.

"Everything's going to be fine, just breath. It's just panic you're feeling, not the baby. The baby's fine."

"And how do you know?"

He kisses my shoulder. "I just do."

His lips make their way up to mine, and I kiss his right back. "I hope you're right."

"I always am."

I kiss him once more, before backing away, my eyes franticly searching the faces passing by. I've always wondered what this day would be like. Seeing my parents and sister again. In person. I've imagined it ending disastrous. Me threatening mother, her threatening me. Dad being the spineless man he always was and sitting back as mother and daughter attempt to kill each other. Delphine and I, two loyal sisters, separated by horrible circumstances that could only change us into two entirely different people.

These days I wonder if mom has finally gotten to her. Has she turned her into the very person I fought hard to not become? Or is she still that little girl I used to protect. The one who, every night, I would tell to listen to her own heart and gut. To never do the things mom wanted from us.

We're our own people, and we don't have to listen to anyone.

"Honey?"

I hope so. I pray that she didn't become that person...

"Love?"

...Because if she did, I would never forgive myself. I left her behind, unguarded and unprotected. I left her alone with two of the world's worst parents.

"Olivia, honey?"

William's hands cup my face, forcing me to turn to him. His eyes are wild. "Olivia, are you alright?"

My eyes shut, the last mental images slip away to the guilty parts of my brain. The parts I try to forget.

When my eyes open again, William seems to be looking at something off to the side, but with his hands tight on my face, I can't move. "William, what's wrong?"

A deep, monotone voice speaks up from the opposite side of the table. "Hello darling."

Now I know why William has that look on his face, I have it on mine now as well. Looking at him, he nods, his smile fake, but at least he's trying.

I nod back, the sudden urge to grab my steak knife washes over me. "Mother. It's been a long time." I reach up to loosen his grasp on my face, and look up, my family towering over us.

Delphine and dad have a wild excitement in their eyes, but mom on the other hand, has that same look she's always had. The 'I'm judging your boyfriend and life choices' look.

I knew this was an awful idea.

William stands, offering his seat so that they can sit closer to me, but my hand grabs on tight to the back of his knee, not letting go until he sits back down. He obeys.

"Please, everyone, sit. Olivia, honey." He grabs my hand, shaking it so I loosen my grip. I don't. "I thought maybe it would be a good idea if I let the four of you have a proper chat, but I don't see that happening today, so why don't we all sit and have a nice talk then?"

Ugh, I hate the fact that he's so proper. Gets on my nerves sometimes.

"Or not. Perhaps the three of you should just catch the next flight back to Aspen." I whisper under my breath, but it comes out louder, and harsher then I imagined.

William pinches my side, leaning in so only I can hear him. "Olivia, I thought we talked about this."

I turn to him and pinch him back, pissed he brought me into this situation. "No you talked, I said yes to make you happy. Doesn't mean I have to be nice to these people."

"These people are your family."

"Says the man who let his parents die without ever telling them his true feelings. Perhaps you're not the one to be throwing out life lessons, especially when it comes to family. Or telling people the truth, for that matter."

I regret the words before they even leave my mouth, but they're out there now, lingering in the empty space between us. No amount of apologising is going to fix this. "I'm sorry William. I didn't mean it."

"It's fine, but this is a conversation best to have at home. Alone."

I nod, my eyes pull back up to my family, still standing awkwardly above us. "Are we going to have this talk with the three of you standing the entire time, or would you prefer to sit?"

On command, Delphine and dad sit down, their hands crossed in their laps, their eyes glued to the tablecloth, but mom stands there. Her body erected, her head held high, with her hands proudly resting on her hips. All this time has passed us by and she's still just the same bitch I remembered. And hated.

William stands again, his body language matches hers. "Would you care to join us Mrs. Fitzgerald?"

I toss my napkin on the table, my hands guarding my stomach. "Yes, please mother. Join us why don't you. You're ever so welcome."

William looks back at me, his eyes telling me to dial it back. "You're not helping Liv." I turn away. If she can act like a child, why can't I?

He tries again. The man's persistent, I'll give him that. "Please, join us. It can't be enjoyable to stand while the rest of us are comfortably sitting. Please?"

She turns her deathly glare on William, judging my newest choice of a boyfriend. Inviting them to come down was a stupid mistake. One I don't plan on sitting through. But before I can make my move, William has his hand out, putting me back in my place before I can even stand.

"Oh Keira, would you just sit down please? You're only embarrassing yourself and us." I look up, my father sits in his seat, looking up at mom. He's never talked back to her. Ever.

Dad turns his eyes on me, sadness and fatigue have made him look years older. "Enough Keira, this idiotic tantrum of yours is what made us lose our daughter in the first place." He hangs his head in shame before returning his gaze towards me. "This has been a long time coming, and for years I believed I would never get the chance to redeem myself to you. So, imagine my surprise when I get a call, telling me my little girl wanted to finally make-up." He looks over at Delphine and she nods to him, never looking up from the table.

"I'm sorry Olivia. I…we were horrible parents, to you and your sister, and you have every right to hate us. We're bad people, I've always known it, but I was afraid. Of your mother, of what she would do…" He trails off. Observing the whole table, he fixates his attention back on me. "You were never like us. The only Fitzgerald to have a mind of her own and I've always respected you for that. I always thought you were so brave, and you are. Just look at you.

You've started a new life here in a new country and I've never seen you so happy. You moved on, a new life, a new guy. You're practically glowing."

Dad stands and walks around the table, taking the empty seat next to me and attempts to grab my hand, but I wind up yanking it away. He pulls back, giving me my space. "This is the life I envisioned for my girls, I was too much of a coward to protect you, or to tell you that your mother was wrong. She was, and always has been a selfish individual who only cares about herself."

"Elliot!"

He looks up to her, for the first time in years he doesn't shy away. He sits tall, his eyes as wrathful as her. "You're smart, and better than us. You and Delphine, the both of you are going to do amazing things in this life. I just wish I was man enough to help you when I had the chance. But I'm here now. If you ever need me, which you probably won't, just know I'm here. As a father and not as that man

410

you grew up around." He looks behind me, his eyes scanning William. "I hope you can find it in your heart to forgive me one day. If not, I'll understand."

A pair of hands grip onto my shoulders, holding me firm as dad looks around the table, his eyes now look over Delphine, who still hasn't moved an inch since she sat down. Reaching back, my hands rest on top of William's as I try to bring myself back. I've finally gotten my apology. Not from mom, which is never going to happen, but from dad.

I hated him for so long. I hated the way he would sit in the background and watch as she talked to us the way she did. The way no mother should ever talk to their child. He stood there as she tried to primp and pimp us out to available, rich men with potential. She used to be so ashamed, marrying a tenth-grade science teacher. Her own mother disowning her after she did just that. I guess it runs in my family; forcing the woman to marry for money, not love. 'You'll learn to love him,' grandma used to say. So glad she died while I was still young. The last thing I needed was two Keira Fitzgerald's in my life.

"I'm sorry too." Delphine's head sinks lower, making it hard to understand her.

Looking at her, I wouldn't think she was a day over fourteen, but here she sits across from me. Seventeen-years-old and still resorts to the fetal position. "I was supposed to keep your secret, but I cracked under mom's pressure. I never meant to tell them you were in England, or your address. They made me believe I was protecting you by telling them where you were. You left without a real goodbye, just an I'll see you later and you were out the door. I was a kid, I thought I was doing the right thing. I know now I was wrong. I only made things worse, and you started to hate me for it, but I hated you too. You left me with them. I became mom's new target, I watched as dad sank lower and lower, aching to say something, but never doing anything. You walked out. I was jealous, and angry, and spiteful. But I still loved you. I still love you, and even after everything, I'm glad to see you happy and with someone. It's good to see you haven't fallen for someone who can only provide for you."

Her fingers trace the table cloth, tears rolling down her face. She's right. I left her alone with these people. At least when I was still there we had each other to lean on, but then I was gone, like a thief in the night.

Now it's time for me to hang my head. I used to think, poor me, poor Olivia. Forced to live with an awful mother and a useless father, but I never stopped to realise Delphine was there too.

"Never apologise to me. I left you, you didn't leave me. You were still just a kid; you didn't know right from wrong. We didn't have great role models to teach us either."

Delphine finally looks up, her black hair stuck to the side of her face, her tears acting as the glue. She smiles at me, then hangs her head back down, not yet ready to forgive me.

The chair flies back with a screeching sound. Mom sits down, her hands crossed before her as if she was in some sort of interview, her eyes move from dad to Delphine. "Well, it seems we all have a lot to say, although none of us could say it to each other's faces back home."

I won't let her attack anyone else. "How could they, you never gave any of us a chance to open our mouths, unless we were sticking your horrible cooking in it."

She turns on me, her smirk as wicked as ever. "Oh now Olivia, let's not be childish, shall we?"

"No one's being childish. Besides you of course."

"Why don't you…"

"How about this, why don't you apologise to every single one of us for all the crap you've pulled over the last

414

twenty years. Better yet, why don't you just own up to how much of a terrible person you are and let's be done with it. Because, I'm just going off how you're acting right now, but it seems like not a damn thing has changed about you. Not one thing. So why are we here? If you didn't come to speak the truth, or own up to your faults then why did you come at all? To annoy me? Because you could've done that from the safety of your own house."

William speaks up, his voice soft and tired. "Olivia, honey."

"No William. I told you I'd try to get through this. I never said anything about playing nice. Not with this woman."

"You still hold a grudge towards me darling. Well that's just sad. I thought with time, and this bitter cold air you have out here, you would've gotten past all this. Since you're so much better than we are."

"Are you kidding me?"

"Olivia, think about the…"

Too late to try and calm me down. "Shut up William. Me? Hold a grudge. You sent my boyfriend away. You forced him into thinking I was too good for him. That I didn't love him. He left me on the day we were supposed to leave! What kind of mother does that to their child?"

"A mother who…"

"I swear if you say 'A mother who loves her child,' I am going to flip this table over on you."

William stands up, pushing me back down into my seat. "Olivia, that's enough!"

"Are you protecting her?"

"No, I'm protecting you and our baby, now stay seated."

Gasp follow around the table, three sets of eyes on me. "Baby?" Delphine has her hand over her mouth, the other one pressed up against her stomach. "You're pregnant?"

I don't answer, my frustrations currently boiling my blood and cutting out any of my common sense.

"I want to go home."

William turns to me; his face softens after he sees the look on mine. He sits back down, rubbing his temple while waving our waiter over for the check.

"Olivia, baby, you're pregnant?" Dad leans in his seat, his eyes full of wonder.

I just nod, the shame of letting that woman get to me spreads across my body, bringing me back to my right mind. "Can we go? I want to go."

"Let me get the check, then we can go, yeah?" He grabs onto my hand, clenching tightly as we wait for the stupid waiter to slowly make his way over to us.

"Wait, how far along are you? Do you know what you're having?" Delphine finally looks up from the table cloth she's ripped into tiny pieces with her sharp nails. "Are you okay?"

"I'm fine." I blurt out, my emotions all over the place. "I just don't want to be here. Maybe the three of us can get together, without her, and talk, but right now I'm not feeling too well and I want to go home. William?"

"Go, take her home. I'll pay for this one." Dad pulls out his wallet, throwing up his hand as William tries to protest, but I grab onto his hand, yanking it away from the table and away from my family.

"Infinity and always."

CHAPTER TWENTY-FIVE

Wednesday, January 30th 2013

Her eyes are bigger than ever, the green shines through the red veins crowding the white. She lies back, her head hanging over the back of the sofa.

We sit here, in silence, watching as the ceiling fan slowly rotates around. We've been flat mates for three months now, and the whole 'awkward phase' most people go through hasn't happened with us.

Since the day we met and agreed to rent a flat together, Jade has become like a sister to me. More like a twin. We've been inseparable since the day after we officially moved in together. Something about having shitty exes and horrible families brought us closer together than either of us realised.

My head shoots up, eyeing the ceramic owl jar on the counter, hidden behind a mountain of dishes the both of us agreed to leave while we sulked in our drama. "You know what will make you feel a lot better?"

Jade brings her head down, the moisture in her eyes have faded. "Alcohol, sex, or junk food? Because I'll take either, or all right now."

I throw her a smile and hop off the sofa, my feet move over to the kitchen, carrying the heavy jar back over to Jade. I plop back down and open the jar, revealing the vast goodies of biscuits.

I slide the jar back and forth under her nose, trying to tempt her. It works.

"I knew this would blossom into a beautiful friendship." She jams her hand into the jar, pulling out a handful of mini biscuits and stuffing them in her mouth. "Could really use some milk with these. That would really hit the spot."

I smile up at her and push the jar into her lap. "Now you're talking." Hopping off the sofa once more, I skip across the room, and swing the fridge open. My smiles fade's a little as I scan the contents of the tiny white box, with little food in it. "Bad news love, I think we ran out of milk last night, along with all our ice cream and cereal."

Jade lets out a loud sigh, mumbling to herself. "As if life couldn't get any worse, we've run out of milk. It's like the gods are cursing us, and for what, I'll never know."

"You know, one of us could always run down to the little shop down the road and get a few things."

"But neither of us wants to put on clothes. Nor do we want to deal with the humans in the outside world." I never thought I'd find my better half. "This day is just not going well for us, is it?"

Looking around the kitchen, then back inside the fridge, I'd have to agree. I know maybe we're egging on our situations, but I don't care. I've dealt with my family far too long, dumped by my boyfriend unexpectedly, and Jade abandoned at the altar. I think we have every right to sulk, just for a little while longer.

"Fine then, what do you want to do? We can sit here and complain about our lives while eating biscuits and washing it down with water, or we can do something productive today."

Jade turns to me; another handful being tossed in her mouth. "I'll take the water."

Reaching for two cups, and the pitcher of water near the sink, I stride back over to Jade and drop the cups on the sofa next to her, being careful not to waste any water on me as I sit. She holds both cups out for me to pour water into, and we sit in silence for a few minutes, wolfing down more biscuits then one person should consume.

"Olivia?"

"Jade?"

"Do you think I'm an idiot? For still crying over him? It's been a while, I should've moved on by now, shouldn't I? I know he has."

"And how do you know that, mate? Maybe he's just as sad and depressed as you."

"He goes to Uni with us Liv. I see him. I see him with other girls. He's moved on, but here I am on a Wednesday, in the middle of the bloody day, getting fat and going on about someone who's no doubt forgotten about me." She looks down in the jar, rolling her eyes when she notices we've reached the bottom. "Why can't I move on? Why is it so easy for him to find someone new, but I sit here, thinking about the day he proposed and then the day he left me that voicemail. Voicemail Liv. The man ended our engagement with a missed call. What is it you Americans say, 'Piece of dog shit?' Because that's what he is, a huge, smelly piece of shit. The kind you get stuck on your shoe and walk around the whole day smelling like you slept with a mutt."

I bust of laughing, and she soon follows. I know she's being serious, but it's still hard to not laugh at. "You should tell him that. Call him up, and this time you leave the voicemail. Tell that bastard that he's a smelly piece of dog shit and then just hang up and be done with it. He doesn't deserve your pain, and you deserve way better than that dick. Oi, I just remember, I have something that's going to make this day a little better."

"Yeah, what's that?"

"I think I still have some vodka stored for a rainy day, you want to tear into it?"

"Don't lie to me Liv, do you really have alcohol you've been hiding from me?"

"Not hiding, simply waiting for the perfect moment to bust it out and get drunk off our arses. Shall I find it?"

"Yes, why are we still even talking about this, whip that out mate."

She takes two long sips before handing the bottle back over to me, wiping her mouth with the back of her hand as she jams her hand into the bag of crisp. I take one small sip, one of us should be in our right mind.

"You know, I think we've eaten and drank everything in this flat. Besides our variety of spices, I don't think there's one drop of food left to devour."

"Then we'll drink and pass out on the floor and wake tomorrow with massive hangovers and pass out again in class."

Her hand reaches over to grab the bottle back, I let her.

"Sounds like one hell of a plan."

I let the silence calm her down a bit before I say what I've been dying to say since she told me all about her and Jared. "Jade, don't get mad, but have you ever stopped to think maybe the two of you were too young to marry? I mean, you were only seventeen. That didn't come off strange to you, the fact that you guys were still just kids? You had your entire lives before you, why get married so soon?"

I can feel her eyes on me, and when I turn there's realization in them. She nods, taking four more sips straight from the bottle. "I knew; believe me I knew. But I was just a stupid girl in love and Jared was perfect you know. Like a modern day, real-life Peeta Mellark, or a Mr. Darcy. In other words, he was like one of those boys from the books. The one every girl surpasses for the bad boy, or the one who's just too perfect to exist. I thought he was the best the world had to offer, he was my knight in armour. Boy, was I wrong?"

Taking the bottle from her, I swallow one long, hard sip, wiping the tip and passing it back. "I used to feel that way, about Niall. I knew we were going to get married and have kids one day, but I wanted to wait until the both of us were out of school, with our dream jobs. I wanted to be smart, you know. We knew we'd last forever, but just in case I didn't want to rush things. If we were truly meant to be, why rush? We had years to plan our future. But it turns out I was right not to rush into anything in the end. He left me with only a letter to sum up ten-years together. I guess nothing's certain, is it?"

"No, I guess not." Jade lays her head on my shoulder, wrapping one arm around mine, while keeping her free hand clenching the bottle. "Women, eh? We can be such morons. Believe anything a man says because they love us so much. Bloody hell, I never hated myself this much. I held onto someone who walked out on me, and not even in person. I mean what kind of person does that to another? A piece of garbage, that's who, and I won't let it bother me anymore. No, I'm not going to sit around the flat all day, crying over someone who never loved me."

"Don't say that Jade, he…"

"No, if he loved me, he would've married me, regardless of age. If he loved me, he would've never ended it the way he did. There's no way you'd do that to someone you were truly, madly, deeply in love with. There's just no way. This is how things are going to go from now on, first off, I'm going to put this down, because getting drunk isn't helping the situation." She tosses the bottle behind her, and it shatters into a million pieces, the remainder of the drink left inside now soaking up the shoddy tile in our kitchen.

I throw my hands up in protest, but she ignores me. "Second, I will not cry, or think about that bastard ever again, and if I do, I give you the right to punch me, as hard as you can in the face."

"After that idiotic stunt you just pulled, I feel like punching you right now. Why would you throw half a bottle of alcohol on the floor? You could've just placed it, safely on the table right behind you."

She turns around and looks down at the coffee table right behind and laughs. "Forgot that was there. Sorry, I'll clean it up later. And the last thing, I plan on getting laid, by the hottest guy I can find. You know what, let's go out. Like right now and find us some dates."

"Yeah, no, I don't think so."

"Oh come on Liv. You have been worse than me since that Niall broke your heart, you deserve to be happy too. Screw em, I say. They aren't worth are time."

"Okay drunky, as much as I agree with you, I'm not exactly looking for anything now, especially some random man at a bar. And even if I were, it's a school night and we both have classes early in the morning. What we should be doing is taking our asses to sleep and praying were not as plastered in the morning as we most likely will be. And excuse me, me worse than you? I'm not the one drunk and throwing bottles across the room."

Her body hunches over, and she sticks her tongue at me. "Oh you are such a wanker sometimes. I'm going to call Avery, let's call Avery."

I jump out of my seat, lunging for the phone before she can. "Oh no, no, no, no, we are not. I'm sorry, but no Jade, we are not calling Avery. That girl is bad news. I know she's our friend, more your friend than mine, but all she cares about is sex and alcohol and more sex. We are not going anywhere with her."

On cue, there's a knock at the door, signaling our take-out is here and we no longer need to have this conversation.

"Fine, I'll get it though. Your self-righteousness might taint the food." I stick my tongue out at Jade and she stumbles over to the door. Instead of asking who it is, or looking through the peephole, she opens the door wide, to reveal Emma and Avery, wide grins across their faces. Jade throws her arms up, pulling the two in for an embrace.

"Speak of the devil. Liv, look who's here. Avery. Fucking Avery. Come in, come in."

"Hello Avery. Emma."

Emma bounces over to me, her pigtails jump up and down as she moves. "Hey Livia." She gets closer, whispering in my ear so only I can hear. "What's wrong with Jade?"

"Drunk I'm afraid."

"And the glass and water on your floor?"

"Vodka bottle. She's really drunk."

"Should I be worried?"

"Only if she convinces Avery to go out with her tonight. She's determined to get laid."

Emma shakes her head. "Bloody hell."

"Bloody hell indeed."

Jade and Avery tip-toe around the shards of glass, arms locked together with mischievous smiles on their faces. This can't end well.

Avery turns the Emma and I, her dark glare rests on me. That woman has hated me since the day we met, doesn't bother me none, she's a hot mess and not one I want to get involved with.

"What do you girls say we go out and meet some men? Or women?"

Present Day

"When did you hear this?"

Emma bites on her straw nervously, hormones and stress do not go hand in hand. "Two weeks ago. Those two haven't been the best when it comes to decency. I suppose I shouldn't be shocked, should I? The two of them getting married? It's what she always wanted, so glad to see her dream come true. It's alright though, I don't care what those two bastards do with their rotten lives."

She sits across from me, her busy hands pulling at her hair. If she doesn't care, she's doing a horrible job at showing it.

"I'm sorry Emma. I know this must be the last thing you wanted to happen. The worst part is knowing a friend did this to you."

"She's not my friend Olivia. No friend does what she did. Although, I'm no better than her. I went out and slept with her ex without telling her, and now I'm stuck with having his baby. Let's just chalk it up to were both terrible people and friends and leave it at that, shall we?"

"You're not a terrible person. You've just done some bad things, that doesn't make you a bad person. Just someone who should think before they dive into any situation. Or maybe you ask your friend next time if it's okay to go out with their ex. Yeah, definitely do the latter. Just to be on the safe side."

Emma chuckles, but her smile fades fast. Defeat becomes her new emotion. "What's happened to us?"

I look off at a framed photo of William and I, our second visit to Paris. We did all the things we did before. The gardens, the bar. Disneyland. This time around no breaking in. It was better the second time around. This time we were more than just two strangers who found company with each other. We're two idiots in love. And that's always better.

"What was that?"

"I asked about us. All four of us. What's happened? Everything was so simple before the Paris holiday, then it all came crashing down on our heads. Fast. I still can't wrap my mind around it. We were so good together. The lot of us, then it just went to hell from there. I wonder where we all went wrong."

"Well you slept with someone way off limits. Still not judging. Avery thought herself invincible and that ended badly. Very badly, poor thing. Jade became green with envy, with you dating her ex. and having his child. That had to sting. And well, I fell for a cancer patient with about four months left to live, so we all have made messes of ourselves. No point in obsessing over the past, can't take it back, but we can control what we choose to do from here on out. No more stupid mistakes, no more acting before we thought things through. From here on out, the two of us need to start being smarter. We're both pregnant, we're both going to have to do this without the help of our baby's fathers. We need to grow up, help each other, start making the right choices. Yeah?"

She smiles, scooting over so she sits only inches away from me. Her hand rest on my stomach. "I still can't believe you're pregnant."

"Right. I still don't know where it came from. Scratch that, yes I do. We weren't very careful, or smart. Sort of heat of the moment type thing."

"Are you happy at least?"

436

"I am. In a way. I'll always have a piece of him with me, even after he's gone, and it's a big piece too. It's a part of him and a part of me. I couldn't ask for a better miracle. Well I could, but that's already been decided, so no reason crying over it anymore."

"I'm sorry Liv, truly. If anyone in this friendship deserved a better life, it was you. We all made our mistakes. I knew what I was doing and I still did it. Avery knew the consequences on having multiple sleeping partners and she still did it. Jade knew she was breaking up a family for her own selfish reasons and she still did it, but not you. You had no idea what he was going through. You thought you finally found someone and you did, but it just wasn't meant to last. Your story is the saddest. The rest of us will live on, trying to repair the mistakes we made. Given time to think our decisions over and see where life takes us. All you can do is love him until the last breath leaves his body and try to pick up the pieces and move on."

Her hand moves up to my face, wiping away tears before they reach my cheeks. "You both deserved so much more than this."

"We did. Too bad the world had much worse plans for us, eh? I guess no matter how good you are, or how much shit you've already been through, sometimes things just weren't meant to be. I just wish with him it could've, you know. I wanted this to work. I wanted him. Forever."

My hands clutch onto my stomach now, gripping on tight so the world can't take the last thing I have worth living for. "I just don't understand Em. Why me? Why him? Of all things that could've gone wrong in my life, why bring him along for me to fall in love with, and then snatch him right out of my hands? We were so good. So happy. He's all I ever wanted. He was my dream that somehow turned into a goddamn nightmare."

My head is in my hands, my shirt drenched. For these past few weeks, I managed to keep all my anger and sadness inside, especially whenever William's around. Finding out I was pregnant helped, a lot. Too busy thinking of possible names, and school districts and paint schemes.

We started a book. A baby book of sorts, I want our baby to know who their father was, and not just from my soon to be many tales of the man I remembered.

William got this idea to record videos of himself and his voice, reading books and telling stories. He wanted the baby to know his voice, and his face, and not only in the thousands of pictures we have all around the house, but a real life moving person. I thought it was an amazing idea, but I can never stay in the room too long, it hurts more than I show.

He isn't stupid. I know he knows I'm in pain and that I try to hide it, but it's not enough. We know each other too well, there's no hiding anything from one another anymore. It's impossible. But he doesn't say a word, he stopped doing that months ago. He knows it's as hard for me as it is for him.

In four months, he'll be burned and scattered, and I'll be coming home to this very house, alone. A baby on the way and nothing but images and videos and letters of the man who once meant everything to me.

He is going to die. He's going to die.

I fall apart in Emma's lap, her hands resting on my head as she strokes my hair. Water drops near my ear and I know she's crying too. Two pregnant woman. Two shitty endings.

There's a creaking in the background, but we ignore it. Nothing can pull me back from my current state of mind. I've spent too long holding it in and I'm really getting sick of acting like everything is just fucking perfect. William's going to die, and just like before, I'll be left alone in this world. Only this time, I'll have a child to occupy most of my time.

"Olivia? Emma?"

I can feel Emma shift from under me, her hands leave my hair, leaving this longing feeling of comfort from anyone besides William. I love him and want to spend every minute with him, but right now I'm dying to be with someone else. Someone who won't tell me it's going to be okay, or that I'll find love and happiness again. That it just takes time.

My head is lifted, two hands, two tiny hands, hold my head up as a weight is elevated from the sofa and another weight is brought back down. My head is back down, resting on a new lap, a familiar one. A set of hands are on me. Bigger, but leaner, hands. One on my stomach the other brushing my hair out of my face. Another pair of hands down by my ankles, rubbing my leg back and forth, before resting their head on it.

A whisper tickles my ear, but brightens my heart. "It's okay love. Let it out. You're owed that much."

William places my loose hairs behind my ear and kisses my cheek, his nose touches mine. "Just let it out."

Emma leaves my leg, and crawls up to me, her face next to mine. She gives me a weak smile and kisses my forehead. Her hand, William's, and mine all on my stomach.

"One day it'll all be alright. It may take one year, it may take a decade, but someday you'll see. Even though this has a bad ending, at least you'll live knowing you had the privilege to love someone worth your tears. He is worth it, right?"

I close my eyes. A million memories flash through my mind, all of them experienced in just under a year. The many times I got caught staring at him from the back of the classroom. The many times I would catch him peering at me through those glasses that hid away his striking features. That night in Paris where he caught me as I stumbled out of that shop and into his arms. The look in his eyes when I caught my footing and looked up to thank him. Our night after the Hemingway bar, when we broke into the gardens and I stole that flower. He still has it. Dead and wrinkled in his favorite journal.

The night in my hotel room. The night we fell asleep side by side after a binge of awful movies. I watched him sleep for some time, it's the only time he doesn't feel pain anymore. The only time he's safe and sound. I knew that night. I knew I wanted him, and not just in the sexual way. I wanted all of him. Every last piece, and I got it, just got a little more than I asked for.

After that sleepless night, I knew I didn't want to go another day without him, and I'm not. Even after he's gone, I refuse to let him go. He was the best I ever had, and that's more than most get in a lifetime.

"Our last class together. The one where he acted like an ass, I thought he hated me, and a part of me was hurt because of the feelings for him I didn't know I had. But then Paris happened to us, and in the short span of two weeks, everything changed." I look to Emma, and for a minute I forget William is in the room with us and I'm just talking to my best friend. "The way he looked at me that day changed everything. What I thought was hatred turned out to be something worth suffering for."

She smiles, her lips turn down and start to quiver. I look away, my eyes and hand on William's knee. "You are you know? Your worth suffering for."

He leans over again, his cheek against mine. "And you're the happy ending I never thought I'd have."

My hand shifts from my stomach and latches onto his, pulling it towards my lips. He pulls on my hair, turning me towards him. His lips kiss mine, soft and wet, just like the first time.

"Thank you, Olivia. For my happy ending."

CHAPTER TWENTY-SIX

Tuesday, March 14th 2017

This has got to be one of the most awkward walks I've ever been on. And the worst part about all of it; it's with my own father.

One would think after years, almost your entire life of growing up in a house with your father, the two of you would be closer. Father, daughter. A relationship that means everything to little girls, but not me. I had a father, without having a father. He was there, yet managed to not be there. I grew up alone, just a sister and a boyfriend.

We walk side by side and I occasionally point out a few notable sights, a couple of my favorite places, and it goes back to an awkward silence.

I told him. Him and Delphine. She called me one day out of the blue, none of us had spoken since that disastrous lunch date William set up. We went back home, they went back to their hotels, and things just kind of ended there. I got a few messages from Delphine, congratulating me on my pregnancy. Dad left a voicemail, but that was it. They were gone like the wind.

After sobbing, grossly into the phone, Delphine handed the phone off to dad, that was only after she told him why I was crying. And I finally got what I wanted; a father who takes an interest in his daughter. He cried with me, said he was sorry about a billion times and vowed to be on the next plane back to England, and that we would stay as long as I needed him. At first it sounded amazing, things had been getting harder with William, watching as he slowly fades into someone I can't even recognize. Being around him 24/7 hasn't been easy on me, or the baby, but leaving him scares me. I always think, what if this is it? What if he's gone by the time I get back? I wish I wouldn't, but anytime he doesn't answer his mobile, I panic.

Every time I come home and call out for him, and he doesn't call back, I panic. These days, anytime he goes downstairs for something, I freak out, and wind up following him all around the house. He's sick of me, I know he is, but look at it this way, he'll be dead soon. And I won't.

"You're looking different these days."

"Is that an insult dad?"

"No. I don't know. I never was good at these kinds of things. I never was a father to you or your sister. I wish I was better at this. Especially at a time like this. You really shouldn't be alone honey."

"I'm not alone. I have William, remember?"

"I know. It's just…"

I pause in my footsteps, dad follows. I give him the look I give just about everyone these days, warning them to change the subject. Fast.

"I'm fine dad. We both are, and so is the baby. Everything's going to be alright in the end. It's just going to take some time, that's all."

He throws his hands up, backing off from the topic and we start walking again. "I know you'll be fine honey. You are the one who packed up and jetted off to a whole new country and made a life. There's no way I could ever do that."

"Must be something I get from grandpa."

He smiles. He always smiles anytime anyone brings up his father. "Yeah you are. That man was unstoppable. Did I tell you about the time he took his entire savings of two hundred dollars and headed off on a bus and train to New York. Didn't tell anyone, just disappeared. He was a wonderful man. I miss that old guy."

He has told me the story, so many time I can't even count that high. But I let him talk. Anything's better than speaking about William and I. But after a while, I doze off into my own mind, thinking about everything that's happened to me in the past twelve years. Never have I ever thought that far back, which is a little weird to me, but standing here, with dad, takes me back.

We were once close. I think it might've been the first six years of my life. After that things fell apart. Mom started in on me, training me, just like her mother trained her. I used to look to him for support, my eyes would beg him to help me, to save me from her, but he sat there in his favorite chair and did nothing. And somewhere along the way, we grew more and more apart. His face would sell him out every time. He hated the fact that I stopped talking to him. Or that I would walk right into the door after school, or after work, and speed past him, heading to my room.

I can still see the look now. Heartbreak. Disappointment. But the old Olivia didn't care. She used to think he had his shot and he did nothing with it, so everything that's to happen to him in the future is his own fault. Don't blame me if you never see your own grandkids.

That Olivia died years ago. I think Niall helped kill her. Once I moved to England, started school, and found Jade and the rest of the girls, things started looking up for me.

In a haste decision, I moved out here. Tired of living with my family, I made the choice to run away and start over. To a place where not one person knew me, and I could be free to do whatever it is I wanted. And I did. And it helped me forgive them. Never forget, but forgive.

"You alright there, sweetie?"

I look up from my feet, dad's eyes hopefully look down at me. "No, I'm good. Just listening."

"I stopped talking minutes ago."

Caught. "Did you?" I give up the charade. "I'm sorry dad, I was just wandering. But I have heard the New York story many times, so it's not like I'm missing out on anything."

He smiles. "I do tell that story a lot, don't I? Sorry. It's just…"

"You miss him. I know dad. You don't have to explain yourself to me."

"How did you get to become so perfect? You're nothing like your mother or me. I'm proud. I may not have said anything back then, but seeing you today like this, it makes my heart smile sweetie. I'm glad you found the life you wanted and not the life that was forced on you." He grabs my hand and pulls me off to the side, away from hoarding groups of people walking all around us.

"Thank you, Olivia. You showed me there was a better path. A happier path." He lets his hands fall to the side, his head shakes back in forth like he's trying to erase something that just won't go away. "You gave me the strength to start over. To be happy. I once thought the world was this simple place. You're born, you go to school, you finish school and then you find a job, and you work that job until you take your last breath. And somewhere in between it all you find someone to spend the rest of your days with. Someone you'd learn to love, you have kids and make a life. I believed that was the only outlook on life, and I fell for it. I married your mother because I thought it was what needed to be done. But I was wrong. The world was wrong."

He looks up, scanning the dozens that walk among us. "Look at all these people. So many of them, so many to choose from. So many to love. Why settle for someone you don't love, when the one you were meant to be with is out there, waiting for you. I settled sweetie, and I hated every single day of my life. The only thing I had that kept me going was you girls, and I failed with the two of you also."

Dad looks around, grinning at the many citizens of London as they pass us by. "You were the first Fitzgerald to defy your mother and you've become the only Fitzgerald to live a happy life. You're my inspiration. Secretly, you always were."

I lift my shoulders up, my mouth covered behind my scarf as the cool air starts to hit my face. "Why did you never say this to my face?"

"Afraid. I feared her. I wasn't a man, not the man I wanted to be. My only goal back then was to make the wife happy, and try to do right by my kids. Neither of those happened."

"Is that why you left? Why you filed for divorce?"

Dad nods. His smile comes back. "I couldn't do it anymore, and once Delphine hit seventeen, I knew what I had to do. I had to live for me."

How do I say 'I'm proud of you?' without sounding like an ass? I am. Proud of him, but my parents are now divorced and I don't feel the least bit sorry. But that also makes me feel like some heartless bitch who's happy that they're no longer a couple.

"I'm happy for you dad. In the end, we all deserve to be happy. Even the wicked ones. Even her." I don't say her name, but we both know who I'm talking about. "I'm even happier to know I inspired you. I'm thinking I should write a tell all book. What do you think?"

He throws his arm around me and I don't flinch. Instead I let him walk me back through the traffic of bodies as we head back home.

"I honestly think I'd love to read that."

"So, it ended well then? With you and your father?"

William passes the thermos back over to me, changing his mind. He pours more cocoa in my mug and screws the top back on, leaving it between us. We sit out in the backyard. His health has been up and down these last few months, but today it's back up. He was even able to get himself out of bed today.

He told me he wanted to do one last thing with me and we both know he doesn't have much time left. Any day now will be the day, so we're doing everything we can to prepare ourselves for it.

One of his last wishes was to watch the sunset. Sit out back, eat junk and watch as the sun went down with me by his side. I was happy to give him this. And he was excited to give me another precious memory.

"Yeah. Shockingly. I thought it would end... To be honest, I'm not sure how I thought it would end."

He starts to cough and I'm on my feet, jumping to his side, but he places his hand on my growing belly. "It's okay, love. Just a cough."

"William that's more than just..."

"Olivia baby please. Just let me have this. I don't want to spend this last month with you worried about me. I just want to be with you. I don't want to talk about my health, or anything else. Can we just be happy? Please?"

For him, I will. I take my seat, adjusting so I can find a comfortable spot that won't kill my back. I sit back against my chair and lift my feet up, my eyes forward. I'll do this for him, but I won't pretend to be happy anymore. I don't have the energy for it. I can't carry his baby, and act like I'm okay with his impending death. I refuse to fake a smile.

"Olivia, don't ignore me. Please."

I turn to him, a clear forced smile on my face. "Does that make you feel better?"

Looking at him these days gets harder and harder. His beautiful, stunning eyes lost, sunken under dark circles. The grey-blue encircled with a faint yellow that's starting to become brighter and brighter. His clothes don't fit anymore. These days I spend most of my time hemming them to fit his body.

The coughing gets worse and worse. Once I found blood on one of his tissues and cried for two hours straight.

He grabs my hand, and I'm tempted to yank it away, but that would just be childish. I'm mad at him, that doesn't mean I still don't love him. "I know this is hard for you, I know, but please Olivia, please. I just want a peaceful night with you. A night where we're not fighting, or crying."

Too late. Tears start to form and he sinks lower in his chair. "I don't want to leave this world thinking you hate me."

"I don't hate you William, so stop saying shit like that."

"Really? Why wouldn't you? Look at what I did to you? I lied to you in the very beginning of our relationship. I watched as you started to fall in love with me and I sat back and let you. I let this carry on. I got you pregnant. I'm leaving you to raise my son alone. My son." He trails off, his hand on his throat as he struggles to speak.

I'm at his side, my hands hold his face, forcing him to look at me, smacking him a few times to bring him back to reality. "Oi! William, look at me. Hey breathe, breathe, please don't do this. Not now."

I smack him a view more times, his breathing comes back slowly. Gasping breaths turn into steady ones. Taking deep breaths, he tries to calm down himself down. "William? Hey look at me."

He takes one last deep breath, gulping it down and choking on the aftermath. "I'm fine. Sorry."

Panic spreads through my body, a tiny sign of relief washes over me. "Goddamn it. Don't do that again, you hear me?"

"Yes. Sorry, I just needed a minute."

"Can your minutes not consist of you scaring the hell out of me."

William lays back against his chair and I prop his legs up, keeping him as comfortable as I can. His bony hand wraps around my wrist, pulling me down into the empty spot next to him.

I let him lead me, my arms wrap around his shoulders and pull him close to my chest. He obeys me, resting his head just above our son. There was once a time when he'd do this to me. I'd lay on his chest, listening to his heartbeat. It was beautiful, it was alive. Now it's my arms he falls asleep in. The arms he feels safe in.

We sit in silence for what seems like an entirety, his breath on my hands are the only sigh I get warning me he's still here with me.

I can feel something on me, something cold and hard. Sharp and strange. It moves back and forth, all around my stomach. His hand, of course. These days his touch feels so unfamiliar, I catch myself flinching every time he touches me now, and the look on his face kills me. He knows his body is slowly giving up, fading right before our eyes, and he knows what it does to me. I guess my poker face isn't as great as I thought it was.

I try to change the subject, lift both our spirits a little.

"Look at us, a set of star-crossed lovers who didn't quite get the happy ending they deserved. But it's okay. I'll be okay William, because you gave me a happily ever after in only a year. And no matter how much pain I might be in for the next forty years or so, I can look back on us and our son and know that loving you was worth every last heartbreak."

Another cough escapes his lips. "I wouldn't hate you. If you wanted to get up and walk away right now, I'd still love you. I don't think I could ever stop loving you, but I'd forgive you. I would. I had the fortune of getting to know you, and that's more than I ever asked for in this life and I'm going to die knowing I loved you and you loved me back. I'll die knowing I have a son. A beautiful little boy and he'll be raised by a perfect woman. A woman I was never worthy of."

His hand grips my stomach, bunching my shirt up in his fist as he kisses my bare belly. "I'm so fucking sorry, Olivia. I'm so sorry. I fucked it all up."

"Yes, you did." His head snaps up, his eyes even more sunken. "But it was worth it. All the pain and heartache this past year, it's all been worth it. There have been days when I hate the sight of you, and the sound of your voice, but then I remember the walk we took. I may have been semi-drunk but I knew. I knew that my ban on men was about to be lifted and I didn't care, or try to hold my feelings in. I knew something extraordinary was about to happen, and it did. Just look at us. Almost a year later and we're engaged and having a baby. That doesn't happen to most people. Then again, we're not like most people, are we? No, we're so much better." I pause, the sudden shift within my belly stuns me.

"I'm going to miss you, gods you have no idea how much I'm going to miss you, but I'll be okay. I'll survive. I have to, I have a little boy counting on me."

He lays his head back down, and I'm grateful. I couldn't stand seeing the pain in his face anymore. "Anytime I'm feeling sad William, I'll think of you, and all the things we did together. I have a lifetime of memories, astounding memories that will keep me going. It'll be hard in the first couple of years, but somewhere down the timeline, I'll learn to smile again. A real proper one. I'll leave the house and make new friends. I'll have pricey, ridiculous parties for our son, parties he won't even remember. I'll go back to school and graduate and dedicate my diploma to the both of you." I trail off. I need to stop before I say something that will only end up making me cry again.

"You'll move on? Find someone who can make you happy. Promise me you will?"

I shake my head. I wish I could, but that's not something I can promise.

"I'm sorry, but I can't. That's not something I can just promise you. It took me a very long time to find you and the world is just ripping you away from me so fast…"

I feel something bump against my stomach, but calm myself when I realise it came from the inside again.

"I don't think there will ever be another man out there for me. And even if there is, I don't want him. I got what I wanted with you and I'll die knowing I was happy and I lived well and was loved by the most outstanding man in the universe." I turn my eyes to him, but he's still looking down.

"I don't want anyone else. Not while I have you."

"You shouldn't be alone, Olivia. I don't want you to be alone."

A smile somehow makes its way to my face, and it's real. Didn't know I could manage those anymore. "What's our son, a cockroach?"

He chuckles, his laugh bounces off my belly. "You know what I mean."

"I do, and I'm putting my foot down. It's my life William, if I want someone else, then I'll find them, but I don't. So get off it."

"You're not going to change your mind, are you?"

"Nope."

He looks up at me, studying my expression before giving in. I can be stubborn when I want to.

William scoots his head back up to my chest and we watch the stars. Now would be a good time to have that talk about how to raise our son, or what his name should be, but every time I bring it up, it only brings tears. William hates talking about a subject he'll never be able to take part in. It kills him knowing he won't see the birth of his one and only child. It kills me too, doing all this without him, but we both know there's nothing either of us can do, so we chalked it up as a waste of tears.

"Remember when I asked you about your bucket list?"

I smile. Although I was a little drunk, I remember the conversation well. "I do."

"Remember when you asked me what was on my list?"

"I do."

"Well I think now's the time to be honest. I never had a bucket list. I tried to make one, but every time I looked it over, it just reminded me that I was going to die and none of the things on it mattered. So I would toss them out."

"So watching the sunrise with me that day, was made-up?"

"Yeah, kind of a spur of the moment type thing. But then I got to know you, and then I fell in love with you. We became engaged and now we're having a baby and with all else that's happened to us, I finally realised something. I

465

never needed a bucket list of amazing things to die before I died because all along, my bucket list was you. I wanted to be happy and I wanted a life with someone who'd love me as much as Nana loved her husband. You know, she once told me that the right girl would stumble into my life one day, and that's exactly what happened. You fell right into my arms, and as I looked down at you, I knew. I knew there was no way I was ever going to leave you alone."

"You really mean that?"

"I do. I found you, and I'm all the more better for it. Thank you, for teaching this selfish arse how to love."

Screw it, I'm pregnant and hormonal and I'm about to lose everything. I can cry if I want to. "It was my pleasure."

We go silent again, the sun peeking out just enough to light the night sky. This could be it. This could be the last day we spend together.

And you know what? It would make an amazing last day.

"Olivia?"

"William?"

"You're never going to let me go, are you? Even when you're in your sixties and playing bridge with your other old friends? You're still going to love me?"

"Infinity and always William. Just the two of us. Together forever. Till the end of time."

Kissing the top of his head, I notice his hair has grown back quicker than we expected.

I reach down near my stomach and place my hand on top of his, our fingers intertwine. There is just no way I could ever let him go.

My hands ruffle his hair, taking in the scent of him. "I told you forever, didn't I?"

Olivia,

I was hoping our reunion could've lasted a little longer, but your mother has always been one to ruin things for everyone. But for what it's worth, I'm glad you decided to give us a chance. I know it must've been hard and we're all very grateful. No matter how stubborn some of us were acting.

I forgot just how beautiful you were. Haven't seen any pictures of you during your four years here, so I could only imagine how you looked these days. Don't get insulted, but you look just like your mother. Before the devil took over her soul and turned her into one of those dance mom like monsters. I'm so happy you chose to live a life of your own. A life that makes you smile. I know things got rough back there and you were holding everything back for your sake

and the baby's. Oh my god, my little girl is having a baby.
You're having a baby. I'm sorry, I just can't believe it. It's
just... It's wonderful Olivia. If there's anyone who deserved
this life, it was you. You've dealt with enough, it's about
damn time you found happiness.

I hope this isn't the end, honey. Your mother was wrong,
yet again, but that shouldn't have to come between the rest
of us. I was a bad father for most of your life and, believe it
or not, I've been trying to do the right thing since the day
you disappeared, and now that I have a grandbaby on the
way, I would literally do anything to see him or her. You
didn't get the chance to tell us. That's if you wanted to tell
us. Probably not. Wouldn't blame you if you said no.

Anyway, if you can, or want to, call me, or write,
whatever's best for you. I really miss you, sweetie.
Delphine does too. Your move has been harder on her than
anyone else.

Love you baby,

Dad

P.S. I think William is amazing, I didn't get the chance to say it back there, but he is. He definitely passed the boyfriend test.

P.P.S. The three of you are going to make a beautiful family. Just you wait and see.

CHAPTER TWENTY-SEVEN

Tuesday, March 21st 2017

It's like some awful nightmare, you know, like the one you keep having repeatedly, and there's nothing you can do to stop it.

No matter how hard you try, it keeps coming back. Haunting you, torturing you. You pray, to anyone who'll listen, to make it stop, but it never does. It just keeps coming back.

Just like yesterday, and the day before that, and the days before that.

Every time my eyes burst open, I half expect him to be there, his arms suffocating me, not letting go until I've calmed. But he's not, and he never will be again.

My eyes water again. Like they do every six minutes, and I find it hard to breath. This past week, I catch myself hyperventilating and knocking things over as I try to breath, but it doesn't work, and the entire room goes dark once again.

William went in his sleep. I told him I'd love him forever, and that this wasn't the end, and then he went to sleep. Just like every other night before.

He went to sleep with a smile on his face, a kiss from my lips and laid his head down on my pillow, curling up next to me. I slept for only a couple of hours and when I woke to check on him, he was gone. Like a thief in the night, free at last from his suffering.

It was one of the best ways to go. He was at peace in the end, and that's all I wanted for him.

I watched him, a part of me really believed his eyes were going to open at any minute. I just needed to give him some time, and I did. I don't know how much, but I waited.

Emma came over to check on us, like she did every day when she found out I was pregnant. She found me staring down at his lifeless, cold body, my eyes refusing to blink. The other part of me, the realistic thinking one, knew he was dead, she just didn't want to let go. My mind and body finally caught up when I watched as the many paramedics and EMT's ran through the house, checking on me and my son before running upstairs. Everything came into view when I saw them carry his body down, a sheet blocking my sight of him. He was under that thing; he was really gone. I lost it, and the next thing I remember was waking up in a hospital. Doctor Xavier hovering over me.

A soft voice speaks up from behind the sofa. "Olivia, honey you awake?"

I shut my eyes, eager to not have a talk with anyone, not even Emma. She means well, but right now, the only thing I want is to sleep. No dreams, no nightmares, just some rest. Some quiet. My mind has been on since that morning, and I would give anything to shut it down.

"Olivia, honey, are you awake?"

Sometimes I wish I had no one. That way I can be alone and bathe in my sadness without interruptions.

"I made you something to eat. You haven't eaten in days. That's not good for either of you Olivia, you need to eat. Please?"

She starts to say something else but stops. I can hear the hesitation in her voice. "William wouldn't want you to do this to yourself. Just eat something, okay, anything. If not for you, think about the baby. Olivia?"

She's right and I hate it. I'm not just torturing myself, I'm hurting his baby too, and I can't lose the both of them in the same month.

There will be nothing left to keep me alive if they're both gone.

I sit up, wrapping the blanket around my shoulders, I nod at her and she jumps from her seat, taking light steps around her son, who's fast asleep on the floor and paces into the kitchen. She comes back with a plate full of food I know I won't eat, and I reach for the easiest thing.

Forcing down some carrots and apple slices, I can feel them coming back up before they have the chance to enter my stomach. But I keep it down. Leaving that bitter nasty puke taste in my mouth.

"I did some cleaning and made the bed if you want to…"

"No! No, I won't sleep in there, I won't."

Emma places the plate between us, her hands on my shoulder. "Hey, hey, it's okay. You don't have to; it was only a thought. You've been sleeping on this sofa for days, I just thought it would be more comfortable."

I close my eyes and shake my head. I can't sleep in that bed. Not again. He lived and died up there. I can't be in that room.

Her hands grab my head, stopping it before it flies off my shoulders. "It's alright. You don't have to go up there if you don't want okay? I'll bring you down some clothes and I'll try to make it a little more comfortable down here for you. Alright? I'll be right back."

Without another glance, she forces the plate in my lap and hops over the sleeping Ethan, skipping every other step on her way up the stairs.

He looks like his mother. Emma's rosy cheeks and bright pink lips, even those mesmerizing light hazel eyes of hers. I'm glad he looks nothing like his trash of a father.

I force down a few more apple slices and slide the plate away, lying back down, I try to keep my mind blank, but can't. William isn't just one of those people you could ever forget.

In a fit, when I got back home from the hospital, I was ready to pack up my things and leave. This isn't my house, it was his. Well technically it is my house. He made sure to leave it to the both of us when he first found out I was having a baby.

Doesn't mean that should make me happy.

Staring up at the ceiling, I watch helplessly as a fly float's back and forth before me, taunting me as it lands on my belly then flies away again. I keep my eyes straight, doing everything in my power to not look down. I hate the sight of my stomach now, I know it's there, but knowing and seeing our two very different things. Whenever I catch a glimpse of it, I start to cry.

I stay awake most days now. Besides the nightmares, anytime I close my eyes, he's there. His smile, his annoying, stupid blue eyes. His dimples. That messy hair I loved. I'll never see any of it again. Not in real life. Just in my memories and the pictures that now lie on the ground.

The son of a bitch left me, and I know it's not his fault, but I hate him so much. I wish I could see him right now, just one last time, so I could punch him in his perfect face.

I start sobbing uncontrollably, and before I can calm myself down the room goes dark.

"Look I don't like this anymore then you, and seeing your face right now only reminds me why calling you was a terrible idea. But for now, let's put our bullshit aside. Olivia needs us. All of us. Whatever we have between us can wait. Alright?"

"Yeah, sorry."

"Yeah whatever. Just sit with her while I change my son. You think you can do that?"

"Is this what getting along looks like?"

"I'm doing this for her. You can die for all I care."

The room is still a little blurry and my head is pounding. The cushions beneath my face are sticky and warm. I must've been crying in my sleep again. The shades are open and I can see the moon from here, bright and depressing.

I blink a few more times, my vision coming back and try to make out the voices I just heard. One of them was Emma's, no doubt, but the other one doesn't sound at all familiar. It's deeper and sounds a bit tense. Not that I care anyway. The last thing I want right now is a babysitter.

Footsteps, the sound of heels, walk around to me, and I shut my eyes. I can't stand to hear anymore 'I'm sorry's.' I think they're worse than the pain of losing… No, I can't keep doing this. I have to stop. I'm only making things worse on myself.

A pair of hands lift my head and set it back down in their lap. One hand grabs my hand, the one I keep by my face to wipe away the tears, while the other hand strokes my hair. The touch feels so familiar and I don't want to push whoever it is away. Maybe I should let someone in. This isn't the kind of thing you should go through alone, and I don't want to be alone.

"Olivia? You're probably sleep, so I'll let you, but there are some things I wanted to get off my chest. I should start with an apology. You were right, about my situation. It had nothing to do with you, and I made the mistake in driving you away. I think about you every day. Ever since the day you moved out, I couldn't stop thinking about you."

Jade?

"I had no right to throw your things out and that was just me being a child. It was between Emma, Jared and I, and I suppose I just wanted to take my anger out on someone and I chose you."

She sounds so different, so broken. Her voice isn't even her voice anymore.

"I felt like you broke our trust. If you were a true friend you would've told me. But it wasn't you. It was never you. It wasn't even Emma. Jared went after one of my friends and made me give up another. That bloody bastard ruined my friendships and I blamed you. Like a stupid jealous woman." She pulls the loose hair floating near my eye and puts it with all the others.

"I wanted to call you. I did a few times, from the phone at work, but hung up before you could answer. I didn't know how to fix it. I was in way too deep and couldn't figure a way out. And then you showed up, yelling about Jared and I getting married. I was going to apologise, but you were just so angry, so I kept my mouth shut. I knew I deserved every word and shouldn't say anything. I needed those words. I needed your frustration. It put me back in my place."

Jade stops talking when she hears Emma's footsteps shuffling around upstairs. Another door closes and it goes

481

quiet once again. "When you told me about William."

Please don't go there. "I cried. You finally found someone to love and then you get a bombshell. A horrible one too. I wanted to run after you. To throw my arms around you and cry for hours, but couldn't. Not while you hated my guts."

Drops of water hit me on the side of my face, and a few more follow. Jade sniffles and lifts one hand to wipe her face before grabbing my hand again. "I'm so, so sorry, Liv. He was an amazing man and I know he loved you. More than he loved himself. He was everything I pictured in a perfect guy and you scooped him up."

We hear feet trotting down the stairs but Jade doesn't stop. She doesn't care if Emma hears this part. "The two of you belonged together. It was meant to be, and even though he wasn't here long, this one year the both of you had, was the greatest year of both your lives. One day you'll see. Meeting William was never an accident, or a mistake. He was born to be the love of your life and no matter how much pain you're in right now, a few years from now, when that beautiful baby of yours is starting school, you'll see. William was the best thing that has ever happened to you and you owe him everything, including your happiness. He gave you a love story in just a year and you must pay him back. You have to find a way to be happy. You don't have to move on from him, and I personally think you shouldn't, but you must find that place where you can be happy again. The place where you can smile and laugh, and go to sleep with a smile because although he may be gone, he'll live on forever in your heart."

My eyes betray me. Rivers of tears pour down to Jade's lap and she holds on tighter to my hand. "It's going to be okay love. Someday, you'll look back on this day and smile because William left you with the greatest of gifts. A baby and a happily ever after. Don't hate him, thank him. He didn't have to love you, but he did. He chose you, day after day after day. He chose to live the rest of his life with you, and that means something."

Ex friend or not, I don't really care anymore. "I miss him." My hand grips onto her knee and I bury my face in her lap.

"I know, love. I know. You should. He was your fiancé, and the father of your son. Not to mention the love of your life. You should miss him, but you should also smile. He's still here. He'll always be here. For as long as the two of you need him, he'll be right here with you. Infinity and always, right?"

Emma knows what those three big words do to me and she's sitting on the floor in front of me, her hand wiping my face. "It's going to be okay, don't cry. We'll always be here with you too."

"Morning sunshine."

484

Jade sits on the floor, a bowl in her lap and a smile on her face.

"Morning."

She sits the bowl down on the empty spot beside her and helps me sit up. Once I'm propped up against the grey pillows William and I picked out, she scoops the bowl back up and sits next to me. "It's your favorite. Thought you might be hungry. Here, I even chopped up a few carrots and tossed them in there."

"Well how can I say no to the carrots."

I take the bowl from her hand and eat, no force this time, I honestly feel like I haven't eaten in years. "You know if you're really hungry, I can make you something proper. How does a whole chicken sound?"

"You cook me a whole chicken, I guarantee you I'll eat that whole chicken in one sitting."

Jade laughs out loud, looking more and more like her old self.

"You two seem to be getting along quite well."

Emma opens the doors that was once William's study. He never spent much time in there. At least after I came along he didn't.

A woman, a familiar looking woman walks out behind Emma. Her expression a blank canvas.

Jade's posture changes, her face tightens. "Work everything out, did we?"

Emma never meets my gaze. "Yep, Eva here was just leaving."

I know that name. "Eva Thomas?" My eyes widen. "You were William's lawyer."

She gives me a weak smile. "Yes. Lovely to see you again Ms. Fitzgerald."

"What are you doing here?"

She looks between Emma and Jade. They pass along secret messages without talking.

"I asked you a question. What are you doing here?" I'm on my feet now. It feels weird. I haven't stood since William died.

She exhales and takes a few steps towards me. "I've come to see you actually. There was some business Mr. Edwards and I talked about before…"

She stops before she says anything she knows she'll regret. "He wanted some business handled right after he was gone. I know this is a bad time, so I was going…"

I put my hand up to silence her. "What kind of business?"

She looks between the two other girls in the room once more. "It's about the matter of his estate and belongings."

This is not a conversation I wanted to have. "What estate and belongings? We've already talked about this house. He put it in my name before he died. Don't you remember?"

"I do, but this house wasn't the only thing he owned. He had many other things he left you."

I can't breathe. What other things? What else did he have?

"What do you mean other things?"

"Ms. Fitzgerald, we can do this some other time. it's really not that important."

"If it wasn't important then you wouldn't be here, now would you? Just out with it. What did he leave me?"

She caves in and places her briefcase on the dining table. The latches click open and she pulls out a view documents. "Well first things first, William didn't want a funeral. He said he knew it would be too hard on you, and he didn't want you in anymore pain. So just a cremation and a headstone right beside his Nana."

This I know. We had a talk back when we stayed at his family's home. "I already know this part."

Another set of worried glance bounce around the room. "There's the matters of his birth home. It now belongs to you."

My mouth drops open. "What?"

"The home was left to him after the death of his parents and he wanted to pass it down to you and your son."

This we didn't talk about. "The manor? He left me that big ass manor?"

"Yes ma'am."

I grab onto my stomach, the pain too much to handle. Jade is by my side and helping me sit back on the sofa as I grow lightheaded. I never thought about that place. What was to happen to it after he passed never crossed my mind. What the hell am I going to do with a manor?

"I'm sorry, but there is more."

"More? He just left me two houses, what the hell is left?"

"His car, as well as all his money."

Money? What money?

"I'm sorry." I try to talk between breaths. "But what money?"

"All his money. The money he made from years of work. The money left to him by a Ms. Elizabeth Knightley, and there's his family's money, of course."

"Wait family money, what family money? He never said anything about family money."

The look on her face tells me she doesn't want to say what she's about to say.

"You know what, I think that's enough for today. Olivia's already worked up and she should get some rest."

"Shut up Jade. What money? Tell me?"

Emma cuts in. "Olivia, don't get worked up, okay? Try to calm down."

"What money, goddamn it!"

"Mr. Edwards was left a very sizeable amount after his parents passed, and…"

"How much?"

"Ms. Fitzgerald…"

"Just tell me how much?"

She looks to Emma, her eyes begging for help.

Emma answers her prays. "Olivia, the amount shouldn't matter. All that matters is that the both of you are protected for the rest of both your lives."

I'm really getting sick of being treated like a child. "Emma, I lived and loved this man for a fucking year, and he never once told me his real parents were rich. I figured from the huge manor, but he never said what they did or who they were and I want some answers. Now I don't know if any of you noticed but he's dead and gone, so you three are the only people I have left to tell me the truth. So please, tell me just how much that bastard was worth?"

"Tell her. She won't stop until one of us answers." I turn to Jade, thanking her with a simple nod of my head.

Emma turns to Eva and nods as well. She takes a deep breath before speaking. "Four-hundred million dollars."

What?

"What?"

"Before his death, William was worth a little over four-hundred million. And now it's all yours."

I try to speak, but there are no words. I try to cry, but feel too betrayed. So I do the only thing I can do and the room, for the fourth time, goes black.

CHAPTER TWENTY-EIGHT

Friday, April 21st 2017

"Yeah well I happen to think he's a beautiful pink little thing. Just look at those cheeks. Such bitable cheeks."

Delphine cradles his tiny little head in her arms, his dark wavy hair smoothed down. I've only held him twice. The first to breastfeed, and the second when he cried for me.

For almost an hour, dad did everything in his power to get him to calm down, but nothing seemed to work. Not until I reached out for him. As soon as my arms extended, he stopped crying. Holding him hurts. I don't know why, but it does.

2 pounds, 4 ounces. For a while I thought I was going to lose him too. I panicked for days. It got to the point where I

couldn't feel anything. Physically or emotionally. I was just numb to all pain. But when they brought him in, bundled up in a dark grey blanket, the one William and I used to keep flung across the sofa.

It's the same blanket I wrapped around his shoulders the night he…

I've got to stop this. It's been more than a month and I still can't find it in my heart to let go. Doesn't much help when I'm surrounded by things that once belonged to him. Or the fact that I'm now the not so proud owner of his house, or that I'm the mother of his new born baby. This should be a time of happiness, a time of celebration and non-stop smiling, but it's all a simple reminder that I'm going through all of this without him and there's a huge hole in my heart that will never be filled.

"Olivia, look, he's opened his eyes. Look. You have your daddy's eyes, you lucky duck. Not like your mummy's boring brown eyes. Yeah, she has boring eyes, doesn't she? Yes, she does."

"Delphine?" Mom folds another round of William's tiny onesies. It's hard to believe anyone can fit in those.

"You know, I'm not the only Fitzgerald with boring eyes Fe. Your eyes are pretty dull compared to mine."

Everyone in the room jumps up, even little William seems startled by my voice. I pull myself up, still a little irritated that dad put me in the bed a week ago.

"Not to mention your hair is starting to lose its shine. And you're looking a little thick around the middle these days."

Delphine smiles. This is the old Olivia and Delphine Fitzgerald. The one's who would purposely insult each other for fun. Just like real sisters. "Well, look who's awake? And here I thought you were dead, which by the way, I called dibs on this precious little thing."

"And what do you know about being a mother? If anyone was going to raise that little bundle of joy it would be me darling."

I chuckle. "You? The same person who did a bang up job raising us. Yeah, I think I'd rather leave my son in the hands of a vicious and hungry wild pack of wolves."

Mom throws down the basket of socks and crosses her arms. She has a staring contest with me, before rolling her eyes. "Okay, even I admit I deserved that one. I deserve way more than that actually."

"Well if you want, Liv and I can read off the list of things we hate about you. Gods, let's see, do you have about twenty years to spare?"

I laugh harder than I've ever laughed before, and it feels amazing. The last time I felt this good was the first night William and I spent together in France. Why does that seem like it's a million miles away now?

"Oh, you see that. Auntie made mummy laugh. Score one for me. You think we can get her to change your smelly diaper?"

The bed is pretty much clean, except for the thousands of pieces of clothes William, Emma and my family went crazy on and a photo album. It's marked, 'Our Year.' William. He spent most of his energy on that thing. Putting in some of our best pictures, so his son can see what kind of man he was.

I pat the empty space in front of me, and reach for the blanket that's wrapped around my shoulders and lay it out flat in front of me. Delphine looks at me like I'm crazy and turns to mom. They both looked stunned.

"Hey he's my baby and I want to change at least one of his diapers. Delphine?"

She nods, a smirk on one side of her face. She stands and carries William over to me, every step slow and

497

careful. Climbing on the bed, she lays him down between my legs on the blanket.

"Now Olivia, I'm going to walk you through this, so there's no need to panic. Just listen to my words and follow my hands, yeah?"

Cheeky little asshole. I unwrap his blanket and throw it in her face. Looking down at his almost naked body, I notice he has the same birthmark as his father. Just above the belly button. I find myself smiling.

"Okay, so this little white thing wrapped around his bum, what the hell am I supposed to do with it?" I sneak a glance at Fe, and she's smiling from ear-to-ear. We haven't been real sisters in years. It feels good to pick up where we left off.

"Well, my inexperienced sister who randomly happened to get knocked up, that thing is called a diaper. It's where his pee-pee and poo-poo goes."

"That's disgusting. I change my mind; I don't want to do this."

"No, it's quite easy, the real hard part is getting the poop out of your nails."

"You're gross, Fe." I remove his diaper and play toss it in her face, and she jumps off the bed, knocking over two rows of footsie p.js.

"Delphine! It took me forever to get those right. Good god girls, you are too old to be acting this way." Mom points at the floor and Delphine bends over to pick up all the clothes she's drop.

"How come you don't make Olivia clean?"

"Because it wasn't my gigantic foot that knocked over the clothes. And what are we, eight?"

"What are we, eight?" Delphine mocks me, and I hit her with one of my pillows. "Oh, and you're not acting like a child."

I turn from her and snap fasten a new, clean diaper on William. "Heads up."

I fling the diaper in the air, aiming it for mom, and she has a mini heart attack, jumping out of the way as the diaper plummets to the ground.

"Really? It's seems you're the one acting like a child, Olivia."

"Well I haven't seen any of my family in many, many years, so excuse me for reverting back to my childish ways. I was also aiming for Delphine, not you."

"Nice to know you still have your fathers throwing talents."

The room goes so silent you can practically hear it. Since I gave birth to little William, mom and dad haven't been able to be in the same room. They managed to put their feelings aside for me, but once we were able to finally go home, they begun taking turns. One stays for a few days, and then switch. It's awkward and a little bit sad, but as much as it pains me to say this, especially since mom and I have made up, she brought it on herself. You can't assume that everyone is going to be okay with the crap you put them through.

"You alright mom?"

She turns to Delphine, her eyes water. "Fine darling, just thinking, that's all."

"You're my mom, and I appreciate you flying all the way over here for the third time, to be with us, but you did kind of screwed yourself in the end. What did you expect? That you could've stayed the same rotten person all your life? You've ruined many lives mom, karma is only doing its job."

"Olivia?" Delphine gives me a glare that could kill me.

"You want to know the worst part about this, girls? I knew. The entire time, all those years, I knew what kind of person I was slowly becoming and I hated her, but my mother did it to me, and her mother did it to her. I thought it was the right thing, ruining your kid's life so they could get ahead. But I didn't just ruin your life, I ruined your dad's as well. The three of you deserved better than me."

"No, you were perfect mom. You taught me that no matter how low life may get, make sure we never turn into you. I kept that promise to myself for years, and after you did what you did to me with Niall, I knew I could be better, so I left and I lived. And I loved. And the pain has all been worth it."

I reach for one of his pajamas and cover him up, scooping him in my arms, I lean back and rock him to sleep.

"I hated you. For a long time, I would think of the things I'd say to you if ever we met again, but now, there are no words. I buried them all the day William found me." I never told anyone about the day we met. I think I'm finally ready to.

"I ditched my friends on holiday. They were partying and having a good time, and I wanted nothing to do with it, so I went for a walk around the city. Don't say a word, I know what you're thinking, and no I was in no danger. Believe it or not, I took a few self-defense and boxing classes while I lived here, and I know how to defend myself."

Little William's eyes start to close, so I lift his head, pulling him closer to my chest, letting him fall asleep the way his father used to. "Three men followed me for a while, but William was there. I didn't need him, but he was there anyway. He didn't want me to be alone so we went to this bar and talked for hours. I got drunk, not stupid drunk, but free drunk. I stopped moping about my life and just went with the flow. He helped me forget my anger with you and Niall. I was just happy to not feel alone anymore."

My heart starts to beat rapidly in my chest and little William opens his eyes. His father's blue eyes.

He looks up at me. This tiny pink thing in my arms, looking more like his father then I realised. I place my thumb on his cheek, stroking back and forth until his eyes close again.

"We committed a felony. Broke into the botanical gardens and stole a flower. I placed it behind his ear that night and he kept it, even after we went our separate ways and came back home. I woke up with a hangover, but didn't care. I was too busy trying to wipe the smile off my face, but it never worked. I was free with that man. I was myself again. The old Olivia. The fun Olivia. And only he could give me that. Give me my real self-back."

His eyes are closed now, and he's snuggled tight and warm in my arms. A place he feels safe and loved. Just like William.

"I knew that day. I didn't want anyone else, not even Niall crossed my mind in that way ever again. Even after he came back in my life and we patched things up, I still didn't think about him, or us anymore." William raises his hand up to my chest, a tiny little fist rest on my heart. "I wanted to hate him, but I couldn't. Something about the way he looked at me that night, it made the downsides worthwhile."

Mom and Delphine are around me now, their hands in my hair and playing with his soft, brown hair.

"Thank you, mom. I hated you for taking Niall from me, but all you really did was remove him from my life so that I could meet William. I love that man; you know? I love him with every part of me. He was my greatest tragedy and even after his death, he made it his life goal to give me everything I ever wanted, and things I never cared for. He gave me a safe future and a home. But I could be broke and homeless as long as I have this perfect little sweetie right here."

I smile like an idiot. For the first time since I found out about his cancer, life is starting to make sense again. "He gave me a son. He gave me a husband. He gave me a few houses, and a car, along with a lot of money, which I have no idea what to do with." My smile grows wider thinking about him. "Mom, he gave me the happy ending I wanted with Niall, in only a year. A year. I found everything most people dream of in just one year. How could I possibly ever hate that man?"

I lean back and rest my head against the headboard, my eyes watching the ceiling. "It was hard in the beginning, but I know now. I know it was all worth it. I needed that pain to help me realise just how wonderful you were. I know it's going to be tough and on a bad day, I may slip back into hating and blaming you for everything, but somewhere, hidden in a large portion in my heart, you'll always be there. You gave me an eternity that somehow still feels real and alive. You may be gone, but you're still here, I know you are. That's just the kind of person you are.

You'd never leave me, especially now that little William is here."

I look back down near the foot of the bed, because I know he's still here. He always will be. "I won't say goodbye, you're not gone. You live in me and a piece of you lives within our little boy."

No tears. This is new. "No, you're not gone. But one day I swear, we will meet again. And when that day comes, well not even the gods can tear us apart ever again."

Mom's wet face presses up against mine as she kisses my cheek, and Fe buries her face in my shoulder. I lean back once more and notice the picture of the two of us the night we became engaged. His smile as big as the night in the gardens, his eyes as blue as the bluest ocean. And then there's me. A look on my face so bright, a deer would stop and stare. "Wherever you are William Thomas Edwards, you better be waiting for me."

How the hell are you supposed to start letters like these????

Olivia, dear god, I'm so sorry. I know you're probably getting sick of hearing that repeatedly, but I am. Very much. God, I can't even find the right words to say. There are no words but sorry.

I knew this day was coming, but now that it's here, I don't know what to do. I wish I was there, I wish I was with you right now, but I can't because of this stupid ass job. But I will be wrapping up by the end of the week, then I'm free to do whatever the hell I want, and as soon as I'm out of that building, I'm hopping on the first flight to England and I'll run all the way to your front door if I have to.

Your dad told me he went in his sleep. That's good, at least we can say he was at peace. Oh, Olivia, I can just see you now. I hope you're not alone. Please tell me you're not alone? You shouldn't be. Not at a time like this. God I wish I was there with you, Livia.

Okay, I'm going to go now. The more time I spend on this shoot, the quicker I can get things done here, and be over there with you.

I love you. Always. Be strong, Liv. For you and the baby. Congratulations by the way. Heard it was a boy.

Love you forever and always.

Niall.

CHAPTER TWENTY-NINE: *WILLIAM*

Sunday, March 20th 2016

"You can be a real son of a bitch; you know that right?"

"Me? This coming from the drunk woman who was ready to break every law in the book two nights ago."

"Oh my gods, you do one stupid thing, one, and you spend the rest of your life paying for it. It was only one flower. I'm most certain they won't notice."

"And if they do?"

She pulls her fingers up to her chin, playfully tapping them in a pattern as she thinks of something smart to say. "Then we'll put the blame on you and you'll go to jail. Look at that, problem solved."

I let the conversation drop, there's just no winning with her. "Why are you such a difficult person. Nothing like that nerd who sits in the very back of my class."

Olivia's hand grabs me, stopping me in my steps. The look on her face in priceless.

"Nerd? Did you just call me a nerd? I am not a nerd, thank you very much. One might refer to me as a thinker. Or a lover of the simple things, like books."

"Olivia, sorry love, but you're a nerd. And there's nothing wrong with that. Own your geekiness. It's adorable."

She lets go of my arm, and I already regret the things I just said, but instead of being pissed off, she gives me this 'just you wait and see,' look, which really frightens me.

"What was that?"

"What was what? You ass?"

"That look. What are you thinking?"

Olivia smiles with the corner of her mouth, turning her face slightly so I can't see it, but it does no good. "Olivia, what are you planning?"

"Now what makes you think I'm planning anything?"

"Because you have that suspicious look on you face. That's the same face you made when you tricked me into going with you to the gardens."

Olivia takes a step back from me. The space she occupied now feels like an empty void. "I tricked you? If anything, you talked me into it."

I take a step back myself. "Me? That whole thing was your idea. Oh, that's right I forgot, you were way to plastered to remember, but lucky for you, I have an astonishing memory."

"Exactly. I was wasted, you were the sober one. You could've talked me out of it. You could've thrown me over your shoulder and took me back to my room, but you didn't, you followed me. No, you encouraged me. You see, you're the bad influence. I was simply the innocent young lady trapped in your web of tricks."

"Oh, piss off."

"Oi, don't you tell me to piss off. You piss off."

She's so goddamn adorable when she's upset. "Alright, alright. I'm sorry, I didn't mean it."

"And?"

There's something about the way her lips curl up into that little smirk of hers. It makes them a hundred times more kissable. "I don't want you to piss off, I want you to stay right here with me, until I get bored of you."

Her smirk turns into that enchanting smile. "That's what I thought. Although, if were being open here, I'm sure I'd be the one ditching you. I mean, who wants to hang out with a dull college professor all day. Not quite the interesting one, are we?"

"Did you just call me dull?"

"I calls it as I sees it."

"Yeah, well, maybe you should pay more attention in my class, your grammar and work is utterly horrendous. The only reason I've been giving you good grades is to get you into bed, but you still haven't caught on."

Her reaction is priceless. Her face beaming. "You, ass. You better be joking with me?"

I decide to play along, her body stands firm and strong, but her eyes deceive her. She's enjoying this. "You kidding me? Your essay on the works of Shakespeare alone had me ready to fail you out for the whole year, but I thought if I played my cards right, then eventually... you know."

Her smile drops and her eyes scan me. That irresistible smirk is back. "You know, for a while I actually thought maybe if I did screw you, I could get out of doing work all year. It's what I did with my other teachers. Especially that Professor Wales." Okay, now I'm getting a little worried. And a little bit jealous.

Who am I kidding, a lot jealous. "My gods you should've seen the body on him. And don't even get me started on his big…"

"No. No. That's enough. I don't want to hear anymore."

She puts her hands behind her back, proud she got under my skin. Seems she's won another round. "But I was getting to the good part. You know Professor Wales, yeah? Isn't he a fellow English buddy of yours?"

Olivia takes a few steps closer to me, her energy and cunning personality rubs me the wrong way, and the only thing I can think about right now is punching Wales in the face.

I can feel her toes on mine, her face so close I can feel the touch of her nose on my chin.

"Don't you want to know about our little escapade? Or perhaps you'd like to hear about Mr. Cunningham and I?"

"I swear to god Olivia, if you don't stop talking…"

"You'll what?"

I think on it, and know just what will get to her. "I'll fail you."

Her eyes grow wide, her lips part only slightly, but I can practically taste her mouth.

After a few seconds of us standing so close, she gives up. I win this one.

"That's not fair. You know how I feel about my education."

Olivia starts to walk again, and I'm right by her side before she can get to far, my arm around her shoulder, keeping her close. She doesn't say another word, and I feel as if I've done something wrong, scrambling my brain to try and fix it. Olivia doesn't seem like the kind of person to get offended too easily, but I've only known her a couple of days, even though it feels like it's been a lifetime.

I rest my head on hers, her shampoo intoxicating. Just like the rest of her. My grip on her shoulder tightens, squashing her into me, the warmth from her fills me like nothing on this shitty earth has ever done. Not since Nana.

"I was only kidding; you know? I've never once tried to get you to sleep with me. The idea never crossed my mind." That I can proudly say is the truth. I found her stunningly beautiful, but never took it beyond that. "I'm sorry if I upset you. I was only joking."

She shakes me off a little bit, her arm draped across my waist so I don't go too far away. Her eyes meet mine. "I don't care about that, it's just…"

I never once look away from her. "What then?"

"It's just… Do you really give me good grades because you like me, or because I'm smart?"

"That's what's bothering you? I just made an awful sexist joke, and you're upset over who's the smartest student in my class?"

"Well yeah, of course. You think I cared about that joke. Come on, I'd be lying if I said I didn't think you were hot, or screw-able. I don't care about your joke either. I make sexist jokes all the time. What I want to know is who's the smartest? Me, or that annoying little witch Tristan?"

I try to suffocate the grin on my face, but fail miserably. Hearing her call me hot brings a feeling I've never dealt with before. I smile even wider knowing it came from her.

"Yes Olivia. You are the smartest student in the class. Hands down."

"No lie?"

I kiss the top of her head. "No lie."

She pulls away from me to read me for the last time and then smiles, her hands clasp together as they find their home around my waist.

"Glad we got that settled then."

"Me too. Olivia?"

"William?"

"Did you just say I was screw-able?"

"You know; I can hold onto one of those for you."

"What, are you calling me weak? Do you think it's impossible for a woman to hold two tiny little bears in her arms without needing the help of a man? Well, for your information, I am perfectly capable of carrying around a couple of stuffed bears, and I don't need help from the likes of you. Thank you very much."

Why is it that everything she says or does, is extremely attractive? "Whoa there, lady feminist, I was only trying to help. Mainly because I'm sick of catching you every time you stumble over because you can't see what's ahead of you."

Her face is buried behind the oversized Donald Duck bear I brought for her. "I can see just fine."

"Oh yeah, do you see that garbage bin you're about to crash into?"

Olivia jumps back, her elbow jamming into my rib, as she tries to shift the bears out of focus. "Where, I don't see it."

I snatch the bears from her grip, tucking them under each arm. "Because I lied, and so did you, you can't see anything ahead of you."

She gives me a dirty look and takes a sharp turn down a busy alleyway.

"I hate you William."

In a few large steps, I'm right next to her again, zipping our way through the smoke induced alley, the Goofy bear bumping up against her as I try to make her smile again. It works.

"I hate you too Olivia."

We continue down the alley, passing shop after shop, person after person, the silence between us comforting. I've grown to love these moments. The two of us, side by side, with not one word spoken. I don't need words, neither does she. We can stay like this forever, in complete peace and quiet. As long as she's right here beside me, the rest of the world can cease to exist. It already sort of does. I wish we could stay like this. Right next to each other in beautiful silence.

Nana must be happily rolling in her grave right about now.

"William?"

"Olivia?"

"Are you alright?"

"Of course. Why?"

"Because you're unusually silent. That's new coming from you."

"Ha-ha."

"I'm serious though, are you okay, you seem, I don't know, not here. I mean your body is here, but your mind is lost somewhere else."

I stop to stuff the Goofy bear under the same arm as Donald, and reach over, the familiar touch of her hand sends my heart into overdrive. "I'm fine, really. Just thinking."

Her brown eyes glow in this evening sun; her lips perk up into that smirk I've come to worship. "Alright then, stay right here, I'll be back."

I find myself clinging onto her hand as she tries to wriggle her way out. "Whoa, where are you going?"

That smirk turns into a playful grin as she grabs my face with her free hand. "I'm just going into that thrift shop right there. I'll only be a few minutes. I just want to see if they still have this thing I was looking for."

"What thing?"

"Now you're getting suspicious. It's fine, it's not like I'm going to ditch you or anything. Just stay here, okay? I'll be right back."

She breaks the hold I have on her and turns towards the shop. She turns back once more to give me a reassuring smile as the door closes behind her and I suddenly get this vile feeling in my chest.

Since that night after the gardens we've become attached to one another and being without her makes me feel like I'm already dead. Sometimes I find myself wondering what this all means. How did we both get here, hanging out on holiday, when my plan was just to come here and complete a bucket list?

Mentally, I've created a new list, well not really. There's only one thing on that list now; Olivia. In just a few days with her, I've done more things then I have in my entire life, and I loved every second of it. The walks, the felonies, the spontaneous trips we take around the city. I haven't smiled this much since Nana, and every time I'm with her I forget about my situation. But when I'm alone, when I'm thinking about her, I start to remember real life, and the crap I'm going through and I start to hate myself. I don't know what is really going on between the two of us, or if this is just something that's meant to last for a week, or two. But if it's not, and this turns into something beyond my understanding, I must tell her. I'm dying in a year, and she hasn't a clue.

I wanted to break down that night at the bar, but she sucked me in, made me forget the troubles of the world and nothing else mattered except her. But now, I sit in an alley waiting for her return and all I can think of is how selfish I've been. She opened up to me, and I haven't told her a damn thing about myself. I avoid the questions with my parents, or Nana. And then there's the big bombshell I hide away.

I have to tell her. I will. Tonight.

My focus stays on the door, waiting for her to step back out, and when she appears, my heart lights up again. She waits as a bike zooms past her and skips over to me, my heart beats uncontrollably. My smile stupid and wide.

Her hands stay behind her back as she looks up to me, her teeth bite on her bottom lip. There's something mesmerizing about it. And sexy.

"Guess what I have behind my back?"

"What have you got behind you back, Olivia?"

"That's not guessing William, that's demanding, which isn't attractive on you. So guess."

She always manages to win me over. "Fine. Is it clothing?"

Her head shakes playfully, her bottom lip red from the biting. I look away.

"Okay. Is it some little trinket?"

"Nope."

"Is this game going to go on forever?"

She lets her lip go to think about it. Her eyes look at something far down the alley, and I'm immediately jealous.

"It will end quicker once you get the right answer."

There's no way she's going to let me ruin her surprise, so I start to think. If I were Olivia Fitzgerald in a thrift shop, in Paris, what would I buy?

I know exactly what it is. "Is it a book?"

Her head jerks back over to me, her eyes smile. "It is."

I read her expression and start to smile. "Is it for me?"

She's biting her lip again. "Yep."

Now I'm the excited one. "Is it an F. Scott Fitzgerald novel?"

Olivia nods, her tongue tracing the bottom of the top row of her teeth.

I'm breathless now, holding on as her bears almost drop from my grip. "His short stories?"

Her hands spin around in front of us, the book hidden inside a brown paper bag. She opens the bag and faces it toward me so I can pull it out and I do, and there it is. The book of his complete short stories and I can feel a couple of tears cloud my eyes.

"How did you? When did you? How…"

"I remember when you told me just how in love you were with his stories and you would die for an earlier edition, so I did some searching, and found that this very thrift store had only one left, so I asked them to hold it for me."

"You did all that for me?"

She shrugs her shoulders; her expression has softened a bit. Happy that I'm happy. "You did a lot for me in two days, so I wanted to repay you. You are very welcome."

I sit down on the bench right outside a coffee shop and set the bears down, my hand slides across the cover as I flip it back and forth in my hands. The inside of the book is a little worn, the pages have faded a bit, but I don't care. That's what makes a book a book.

"I don't know what to say."

527

Olivia sits right beside me, her hand patting my knee. "You don't have to say anything. It was my pleasure. Besides, the look on your face says it all."

Maybe I don't have to say anything, but I'm sure as hell going to do something. I throw my arms around her, my face concealed in her neck. Her arms drape around me, her hand resting on the back of my head.

"Thank you, Olivia."

"You're welcome, William."

I pull back, my tears residing on her neck. Before I get to far from her face, I kiss her cheek, inches away from her lips. My lips lingering there, wanting nothing more than to kiss her, but I pull away and our eyes meet. Maybe it's just the heat of the moment, but looking at her makes me want to grab onto her chin and jerk her over to me, our lips wedged together forever, never letting go. And I know I'm very emotional right now, but I swear she has that same thought hidden in her expression.

But I waited too long, and she's on her feet now, her hand out in front of her, waiting for me to take it. I exhale, angry that I let the moment pass, and take her hand as she leads me out of the alley.

Another night, another memory with her.

She lays right beside me, yet I still can't manage to get her off my mind. Even when I feel her hand slip into mine, she still feels a million miles away, and all I really want is to run to her and never let her leave again.

I pull her hand up to my chest, as I look down at her. She's fast sleep now. After the canal mishap, we rode back to our hotel in a taxi, dripping wet. We couldn't stop laughing, the driver thought we were nuts, but that didn't stop us. Olivia disappeared in her room and me in mine, and for that hour and a half, a piece of me felt dead. I don't like being without her. It's strange and awkward and I literally don't know what to do without her here with me. I can't even remember what I used to do back before we met.

I sat outside on the balcony, clenching my new book in my hands, hoping she'd come out, but she never did and things seemed lost.

But then there was a knock at my door, and my heart, lungs and brain dropped down into my stomach. Every step I took towards the door, I was silently praying it was her, and once the door opened I didn't even try to hide the idiotic smile on my face.

"I thought you were going to sleep?"

"I was, but decided I didn't really feel like sleeping alone. Can I come in?"

I take a few steps back, inviting her in. She steps inside, a pair of owl pajamas cover her from head to toe and I can't contain my laughter.

"Love your pajamas."

Olivia twirls around, not the faintest offended by my joke. "Don't you though? Aren't these adorable owls just precious?"

"I can't believe you sleep in that."

That smirk returns. "I don't. Usually I sleep naked, but I don't think we're there yet, so I threw this old thing on. Oh, by the way, I call the left side of the bed."

She half runs, half walks, over to the bed and hops on top, kicking of her slippers as she climbs under the covers. She stokes the spot next to her, doing hand gestures like those women on the game shows who tell you what you've won, and pulls the covers back. I bite my bottom lip to keep from smiling and walk over to the bed, jumping on her side before rolling over.

"Ow, William, you weight like two hundred pounds."

"That's just more of me to love."

She lets out an annoyed grunt as I crawl under the covers and shift my body a couple of inches to the left until our shoulders touch. Reaching up, I pull my shirt over my head and throw it on the floor next to me. That's got her attention.

"Trying to seduce me Mr. Edwards?"

"Is it working?"

Her shoulder digs into mine. "Maybe."

We take turns laughing, her hand moves up to her stomach and her elbow pokes me in the ribs.

"If you must know, I'm not a huge fan of wearing clothing in bed either, and I wouldn't be wearing anything right now, but it's not my fault you're so extremely in love with me that you can't sleep without me."

She jerks up, staring me down. "Me? In love with you? This coming from the guy who's managed to pop up everywhere I just happen to be. If anyone here is madly in love, it's you. Stalker."

I sit up and face her. "I am not a stalker; you just happen to be in the same places I happen to visit."

"Uh huh, that's what a true stalker would say."

Olivia lays back down, her hands clasp together as she stares up at the ceiling. I stay seated, looking down at her as she gets lost in space.

The lights are out and it's pitch black out tonight, but I can still see her. Her coffee colored skin, smooth and glowing by the only light source in the room; the clock. It reads two thirty-two, but I still can't find it in me to fall asleep. Especially now that she's here with me.

Her eyes move to me, her head cocked to the side. "What are you looking at?"

I look away, only realizing I've been caught staring at her.

"Nothing. Why?"

"No, don't lie to me. Is there something on my face?"

"No, Olivia, there's nothing on your face. I was just looking at you."

"Oh? You checking me out?"

"You're conceded, you know that." I throw myself back on the bed, my head facing away from her, embarrassed.

I can hear her chuckle lightly, making fun of me, but who cares. I have something I need to get off my chest.

"You remember when I said you were beautiful?"

"Yes. I remember how weird and awkward I felt after too. Why?"

"I never seen you without make-up. Or dressed down like you are now. You look so, human. So stunning." I've been dying to say these words all day, and nothing is going to stop me now. "And you're not just beautiful, you're gorgeously beautiful, like the classy women from the forties. You're charming and idiotic. Magnificent and bubbly, and I can't get enough of you. This trip, it was sort of a promise to another person. To my Nana. She always wanted to go to Paris, but after her husband died, she lost all excitement. I wanted to complete her bucket list, her dream, but a part of me expected this trip to be boring. And it was, until you crashed into me at that shop and then the bar, and the night in your hotel. I don't know, I guess I just really appreciate you, more than you know, and I'm honored that you chose to spend your holiday hanging around with your hot-headed English teacher, instead of your wild friends."

I can feel her eyes on me, but I don't stop. "I guess I just wanted to say thank you for making this trip interesting."

The bed moves under me, and before I know it, her lips have found my cheek, her hand pressing my face closer to her.

She pulls away, and all I can think of it wanting her closer.

"You made this holiday interesting for me too. I never would've done half the shit I did if it weren't for you. I think you bring my fun side out, and I'm grateful for that. So thank you, for one hell of a journey."

Her breathing has gone silent, a whistle coming out of her nose every now and again. I move a little closer to her, listening to her sleep. Her leg wraps around mine, her head on my shoulder.

"Olivia?"

"Hmm?"

"Do you ever find it weird, the two of us? How close we've become in just two days?"

Her hand falls from mine and she moves in closer, her breath blows slightly on my neck.

"No. Why, do you?"

"No, that's just it. Somehow this all feels right, you know? Like we're two old friends who've know each other for years."

"Exactly. Why else would I be sleeping in your bed?"

"Because you can't get enough of me. And women throw themselves at my feet."

She laughs at that. "Sure, whatever you say William."

There's a silence between us again, and this time I leave her alone. I squeeze my arm out from beneath her and wrap it around her shoulder, holding on so that she can never leave.

I don't really know what this is, but I think I finally know what Nana was talking about. She always told me the things that happen unexpectedly, are the things that should be treasured. Life can change in the blink of an eye and there's no point in sitting around and waiting for something amazing to happen.

My amazing just happened and I'm eager to hold onto her. I know this can't become what I think I want it to become, I'd only be hurting her in the end, and I care way too much about her to ever put her in pain. I should cut my loses and run far away from her.

She'll be okay. She has her entire life ahead of her. She'll find someone to love and have children with them. She'll get married and forget all about me, but I'll remember her. There's no way I could ever forget a person like Olivia Fitzgerald. You just can't. Nor should you want to.

She made life worth living again and I'll forever cherish this week with her, but I need to let her go. Let her live a life she can be happy with.

Maybe in some other time, in some other alternate world, we could be together. Up until four in the morning talking about nothing, obsessively chatting about our favorite books and authors. Kissing her lips whenever I want. But we can't, no matter how much I may wish on it, we can't.

I'll hurt, but in less than a year, I'll be gone and she'll be living her life to the fullest. I hope she does. I hope she can find someone who wants her as bad as I do, and I hope he treats her like every man should treat the love of his life. Like she's the only person in the world and just the thought of living without her makes your heart skip a few beats.

"Olivia?"

She lifts her head a little, her hair brushes up against my face. "William?"

"Goodnight."

"Home was never a place. Home is a person and my

home is wherever you are."

CHAPTER THIRTY

Thursday, March 14th 2019

"I hope you're not mad at me. It wasn't intentional you know; I just didn't know how this should go. These past two years have been harder then I realised. It's been hard on all of us."

"You were gone; you are gone, and things haven't gotten any easier. I thought with enough time, maybe things would start to look normal again. I would be able to walk down the street without everything reminding me of you. It hasn't worked yet. I passed by Goldsboro Books the other day, and found myself smiling yet crying at the same time. We spent what, almost four hours alone in there, searching for book after book, then got lost at the nearest thrift shop, looking for things for the house and got distracted looking at vintage books and trinkets."

"It's not what you think, the tears, they were happy tears. Every time I think of you, I cry happy tears. It's hard to hurt anymore. We were given such a short time together, but in that time frame you gave me a forever that no one or nothing can ever take away. In one year, you made me feel loved, you made me feel wanted. I felt like I mattered for the first time in my life and I owe any happiness from here on out to you."

I look around, the rain has let up, giving the sky this perfect blue shine, with a fade of a rainbow. Looking back down, I smile, my heart beating a little faster than usual. "I know you're here, right here beside me, watching over as you always said you would. You promised you'd never leave me, and you kept it."

Before I sit, I push a few scattered leaves out of the way, clearing an empty and clean path for me to rest. I lay the flowers to the side, not ready for them just yet, I still have so much I need to get off my chest.

It's been more than a year since I last visited William, our son only a few months old. It didn't end well. I passed out midway through and woke up in the hospital. It was harder for me then. I accepted the fact that he was gone, but still couldn't find it in me to move on.

Losing William, it's still hard to cope with. I wake up, expecting his arms to be wrapped around me. I go downstairs thinking he's in the kitchen, cooking his famous eggs, while our son watches. There are nights when I think he's coming home late. That any minute he'll walk through the door, and there I'll sit, waiting to hear his voice and see that smile. The one he does with his eyes. I still sit up at midnight, wishing, hoping that somehow he'll wander in our home, his arms spread wide open, waiting to greet me.

I hate myself for it, thinking and wishing he'd come home, I wish I could just come to my senses and accepted that he's never coming back. I wish I could let him go, let him finally rest in peace. He deserves that much, after all those years of suffering, all those years of hiding his cancer, and fighting his fight alone, he deserves rest.

Deep down in my heart, I've only wanted the best for him, and even now that he's gone, I still want what's best for him. But that doesn't mean I'm ready to move on. I spent ten long years with Niall, thinking he was my beginning and my end. We were childhood sweethearts who had the whole world ahead of us. We planned for the future, we planned for after the future, when the two of us were gone from this world.

I used to think that was my only future. That Niall would always be the only man for me. Never did I think another man would come out of nowhere and give me a second chance at life.

Niall was the only route for me. Of course, I was young and naïve then, but I thought I loved him. I thought no one else could ever make me feel the way he did. Was I wrong.

In one week, William showed me a new world, a world

where anything was possible and love could come from

anyone and anywhere. He gave me everything I've ever

needed, and there's no way I can ever repay him.

I wipe the tears from my eyes. I promised myself I

wouldn't cry, not today. I need to get through this and it

doesn't help if I can't get through a sentence without

breaking down in the grass.

My hand finds the flowers lying beside me. Forget me

nots. What other flower can better represent my love for

him. I kiss every last one of them before laying them down

on his grave.

"Oh William, you gigantic ass. I miss you, you know?

Everyday. I wish you were still here. And not just

spiritually William, I want you here with me. Right here,

right now. I want to feel your hand in mine again. Gods I

miss your touch. I miss your smile and your laugh. I miss

those beautiful, beautiful eyes and that sweet voice of yours. I miss you. I hate you. You promised me a forever remember? I wanted my forever with you, not anyone else, just you and me and our son. Goddamn you for this, for all of it." My eyes are clouded, the tears taking over. I wasn't supposed to cry; this was just supposed to be a visit. It wasn't supposed to be like this.

I lean forward, my head resting on his gravestone, the cold from the stone freezing me over. I thought I could do it. Come here today, sit down and have a chat without breaking down and lashing out. I don't want to do this. I don't want to blame him anymore. None of this is his fault, none of it. Yes, he chose to fall in love with me, while keeping a very big secret to himself, but I don't care. He loved me, and that alone gives me reason to keep going on.

If it weren't for William, where would I be? Still obsessing over an ex who chose to leave me because my mother told him? Still swearing off men because I couldn't find it in my heart to trust anymore? Still hating my family for the role they played in ending my first relationship?

If it wasn't for my mother's constant nagging, I would've moved to California with Niall, went to college at UCLA and who knows where it would've went from there. Maybe we'd still be together, maybe not. Overall none of it matters anymore. I didn't go to California, I'm not with Niall anymore, I'm someplace better. Someplace safe. Someplace where I'm finally happy.

My eyes open and close, blinking rapidly, forcing the tears out for good. I need to get through this and the crying isn't helping. "I came here to tell you I forgive you. I know I told you this already, but I lied then. I said what I thought you needed to hear at the time, but it wasn't how I felt. It took me almost a year to come to terms with your death, and even after I accepted it, I couldn't bring myself to move on. You have to understand how hard it's been. Just try to put yourself in my shoes, for a quick minute, just try to see my side of things. I was left here. It was just me and our unborn son, left to pick up our lives after you left. Try to imagine it being you. What if I was the one who was dead and you were right here, right now, standing over my grave? Would you forgive me? Could you move on and start a new life? Because I can't. I don't think I could ever love anyone the way I love you. But that's okay. Maybe I'm not supposed to fall for anyone else. Maybe this is how things were meant to go."

I close my eyes. My brain playing back the day we spent in my hotel in Paris. The day I fell in love with him.

"William, I know you can hear me, and I need for you to hear this. Please ignore my tears. I'm not hurt, nor am I broken. Not anymore. I want you to know that even though you're gone, I still have my life planned around us. We never were given a chance to do some of the things we wanted, but we did make it halfway. We have our son. We have our homes. We're engaged. And you have no idea how lucky I feel to even have those things. You gave me all of this just by choosing me. Thank you. I mean that. No one will ever be able to take your place, and I don't want anyone else."

A smile sweeps across my face, my tears a thing of the past. He chose me. Day after day after day, night after night after night. He chose me, and I chose him. And I still do. I always will.

"I want you to know that I am yours today, tomorrow, and forever. I never knew what true love was until that unforgettable day in Paris. Thank you, William. Thank you for our infinity. I love you baby."

My eyes stay close as I focus in on his smile. I see it every day in the photographs that hang all around our home. I thought over the years, and trying to fight off the urge to hate him, or to lash out whenever I felt like it, that maybe I'd forget his smile. That maybe after a few weeks, or maybe years, I'd get so pissed off, I'd snatch every picture of him off the walls and the tables and just hurl them all into the garbage.

I didn't know what my reaction was going to be. I was still pregnant and in so much pain. Physically, mentally, emotionally. Who knows what I would've been capable of. But I didn't do it. I didn't lash out. I hurt, for a long time I hurt, but I remembered. I remembered every last thing about him that made my heart smile and I couldn't help but forgive him. There was no way I could ever be able to hate him. It's just impossible. He has that effect on me.

Before I stand, I lean in to his tombstone once more and leave a long kiss on his name. My lips linger, not ready to stop. I know it's not him, but in a way, it is. The kiss still feels right, like somehow it will make its way to him, wherever he may be.

I raise up, my eyes on the trees that rest before me. I wave my hand without looking back, my free hand wipes away the last tears left on my face.

Footsteps grow nearer, my eyes now positioned back on the tombstone. A smile on my face. "I think it's about damn time you met your son. What about you?"

I turn, William Jr. has his eyes on me, his fingers rest in his mouth. I give him a reassuring smile, my hand stretched out to hold his. "It's okay love. You're safe here. Come on now."

He takes my hand; his tiny pale fingers wrap around mine. Taking a few more steps forward, his feet rest only inches away from the dead flowers left here by Emma.

His eyes drift from me to his father. I squeeze his hand, nodding, telling him everything is going to be alright.

"Do you remember what I told you William? About daddy?" He nods his head, never taking his attention off his father. "You know, he's here with us now, we just can't see him. He's been with us every day these past two years. You remember when I brought your shiny new bike home? Remember how strong the wind was that day, it almost pushed you right off. Yeah?" He nods, his tearful eyes on me. "Well that was daddy. He was there the whole time, running alongside you as you paddled down the block. He was also right next to you when you fell, holding you while I kissed your wound. He has always been here. Always. And as long as we both shall live, he'll still be here. Watching over us. You will never, ever be alone William."

His eyes fill up, his sobs muffled behind his hand. He only knows the things I told him about his father. He knows his voice from the home videos and the one tape he made especially for him. I wish he could've met him. I wish they both could've met each other, but sometimes we don't always get the things we want.

If we did, William and I would be long married, with another baby on the way.

"It's okay honey, you don't have to talk if you don't want to. I just thought it was a lovely day to come and visit daddy."

I look away, my concentration back on William's grave. I blow one last kiss to him, his blue eyes the first thing to pop in my head. "I love you baby. And I miss you." And I always will. "Infinity and always."

I turn back, pulling William with me, but he yanks his hand from mine. I circle back around to see him throw his arms around his father's tombstone.

"Thank you, daddy, for the videos. Mummy and I watch them every day." He pulls away from the stone to look down, his hands tracing his father's name. "I love you. And so does mummy. She still kisses your picture every night. I like to kiss the one where you are kissing me, when I was still in mummy's tummy. I miss you, daddy. I hope you miss me."

He mirrors me, blowing his dad a kiss before turning back to me, his beautiful blue eyes soaked. He grabs onto my hand, using his other one to wave at his father one last time.

"Ready to go mummy?" I nod, tears streaming down my face. Only one and a half years, and he already has the manners and features of his father. It's good to know he still takes after him, even though he's never known him.

He pulls me with him, as we make our way back over to Jade, who rests against the car. She waves to us, a smile letting us know she's proud. I wave back, my heart so happy, yet so sad. I didn't think William would say a word. He still to this day struggles with coming to terms with his father's death, but seeing him hug his grave, hug his father, something stirs deep inside me, but it's not pain. It's joy. And I'm so glad we made the choice to come today.

"Mummy?"

I wipe my face on my sleeve. "Yes love?"

"Are you going to love daddy forever?"

I smile, my head tilted back, with my eyes watching the sky. "Infinity and always.

My darling Olivia,

There are so many ways I wished I didn't have to do this, and writing a letter was number one on the list. My hopes are to never have to send this to you. I hope it never comes to that, but if it does, I have a few things I desperately need to get off my chest.

First things first, I never meant to hurt you. Those weren't my intentions, please believe me, but also try to see my side in this. Yes, I kept a very important and huge secret from you. And yes, you have every reason to be angry with me. But know this Olivia, I did what I thought was right at the time. I never wanted to be the reason you cried, every time I saw tears in your eyes, a little piece of me died inside. Seeing you in pain hurt me more than it hurt you, and I wasn't okay with that. So I kept my illness to myself, it was easier. I didn't care that I suffered, I just couldn't handle watching you suffer.

I know I don't have very much time left, and I need to say everything that's on my mind before it's too late. I love you Olivia, I do, and no matter where I may be, or what happens next, know that every time the wind blows, that's me walking beside you. Every time you feel a chill, that's just me greeting you with a kiss. Or anytime you feel alone, or just feel like crying, remember what I told you the night you came back to me- 'I may not have long on this earth, but I will always live on in your heart. Infinity and always.

Try to remember me as the man you fell in love with, and not as the one you watched slowly fade away. I know in time you'll be fine. You have your entire life ahead of you. You have decades to live. You'll travel all around this beautiful world of ours, seeing things that will take your breath away. Someday maybe you'll even meet someone new, someone who will make you forget me, someone who will make an excellent father to our boy. God I wish I

could've met him. I wish I could've held his hand, or kissed

his pinkish cheek as soon as he was brought into this world.

I wonder what he'll look like. I sometimes picture it, my

own little image of my little boy. He'll have brown hair,

just like his parents, with his mother's eyes. He'll definitely

have my nose and your lips. I picture him with his mother's

smile, the same one that stole his father's heart. He'll have

both our hearts and grow up knowing right from wrong,

because you'll teach him. He couldn't possibly ask for a

better mother. You're going to be amazing, so please stop

stressing about it, and like I said, I'll be there with the both

of you, always. Neither of you will ever be alone, I promise.

Can you do me one last favor Liv, and please forgive

me. Please hear me, this isn't how I envisioned my life.

Growing up, I thought I'd walk this world alone. Afraid of

letting someone in, for it to only end up like my parents. I

didn't want to have a loveless marriage, or relationships. I thought I'd leave this world never knowing love and now

that I do, I hate myself. I don't want to leave you; I don't

want to leave my son. I want to marry you; I want to have

three more kids with you. All girls. I want us to plan family

holidays together. I want us to fight over how to raise our

children. I wanted a family with you. I want forty more

years with you. I want to hold your hand as we watch them

go off to college. As they walk down the aisle, ready to start

their own lives. I want us to retire in Paris, in the city we

fell in love. I want so much that I will never have and I hate

the world for it. Why can't I just die an old man? An old

man who was granted his infinity with you.

Please tell our son his daddy loves him. Tell him I'm

sorry and I wish I could've held him. I wish I was there for

his first steps. For his first words. I wish I could teach him

to tie his first bowtie, or play fútbol.

Tell him whenever he has a bad dream, I'm lying right next to him, protecting him from the monsters. He'll always be safe.

I hope you can find it in your heart to forgive me, and even if you don't, I'll still be here like I promised. I could never leave the two of you. Ever.

One last thing before I go- I love you Olivia Grace Fitzgerald-Edwards, and I'm waiting for you.

Infinity and always,

William.